THE MIGHTY SWORD OF SKELOS!

The Iranistabi had a foot on the second stair when the sword came alive in his hand.

The dragon twisted, twisted again; it pulled free of his grip, for his fingers had loosened in surprise.

The sword whipped about. It lunged at him as though wielded, driven by a mighty, invisible arm. The prisoner threw up an arm in automatic defence – and the blade chopped nearly through his wrist. The hand dangled on a scrap of skin, a morsel of muscle and a stick of splintered bone. At once the sword redirected its aim and plunged into the man's breast – just left of centre. The sword stood above his body. It quivered as if the silver dragon surmounting it were alive, and angry . . .

Also in the CONAN series from Sphere Books:

Conan
The Sword of Skelos

ANDREW OFFUTT

Illustrated by Tim Kirk

SPHERE BOOKS LIMITED

First published in Great Britain by Sphere Books Ltd 1980
27 Wright's Lane, London W8 5SW
Copyright © 1979 by Conan Properties Inc.
Reprinted 1982, 1983, 1984, 1986

Printed and bound in Great Britain by
Collins, Glasgow

CONTENTS

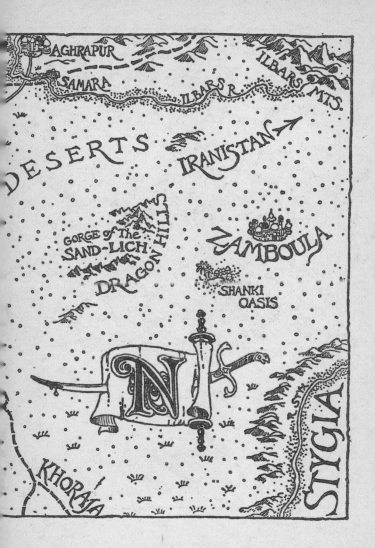

"... he growled deeply like a tiger in whom the strength of the animal is combined with a demon's intelligence."

—BALZAC

PROLOGUE:

THE SWORD

Naked, bearing marks of hunger and the torturer's skills, the two men stood in the stone-walled pit and glared upward. On the landing just within the door at the top of the dungeon steps, four men stared back. Three were bearded; two were mailed and helmeted. Two were robed and one wore an odd cap. Swords were sheathed at the hips of three while the fourth held a sword in his unwrinkled hand.

The young man in the strange Ferygian hat and long mauve robe took his gaze from the prisoners below, and addressed him in the multicolored robe. "You have all you require of these two prisoners, my lord Khan? You would have them slain, now?"

Greasy of ringleted black hair, protruberant of belly and yet not an ill-featured man at all, the man in the silver-girt, gold-trimmed robe of diverse hues raised his brows.

"Aye," he said; "surely though, *you* do not intend to go down there and act as executioner?"

One of the two soldiers grinned beneath his peaked helm of bronze on leather over sponge. He made a sound, and the robed man with the sword cast him a dark look. His squared face took on a thin smile, however, and he returned his gaze to the khan.

"No, my lord. I ask only that you wait a time, and observe. Just a little time, my lord."

Nearby a low, bandy-legged iron brazier squatted like a black demon whose head was flame that cast eerie flickers of light over the walls of the dungeon. On either side of the robed man rested a pail; one held sandy earth, the other water. Squatting, that square-faced and cleanshaven man laid the sword on the landing, so that its blade pointed directly from him. The blade was well made, a long deadly leaf of shining steel whose tang disappeared into a silver hilt: the neck and rearing head of a dragon. The *quillons* or guard formed its wings, and the topaz pommel crowned its head as with gleaming yellow gold.

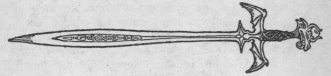

Magic Sword

Muttering, the squatting man sprinkled dirt from the pail of earth over the sword. He soiled thus its blade, hilt, guard and pommel, and he had care to cover the entire weapon, minutely. The older soldier, obviously disapproving, stared down and his face was grim. To treat thus a weapon so well made and so laboriously, the end result of the genius of a master artisan!

Turning the sword, the mage—for so he manifestly was—repeated his action. All the while he continued his sorcerous, murmured invultuations.

Heedless of the wine-dark robes stretched so taut over his upturned rump, the mage went onto hands

2

and knees as though in worship of the blade. Hardly; he continued to mutter while he blew gustily, all over the weapon. Again he was at pains to cover it completely, this time invisibly with his breath.

Dirt stirred, then was flung free when he lifted the sword and slashed it thrice through the air of the silent, close chamber. The very air moaned, sliced by that keen blade.

Below, naked and weal-marked prisoners gazed up at these rites. They exchanged looks of puzzlement and apprehension, and returned their gazes upward. Both knew sorcery when they saw it, for their native Iranistan farther still to the east was hardly free of mages and visitors from the plain between the dimensions.

Likewise stared khan and soldierly pair, and they too felt a stirring at napes and a certain breathlessness. They knew that they watched sorcery. They could only wonder at its purpose and ultimate result, in this chill and murky dungeon.

The mage dipped his hand into the pail of water. Again and again he sprinkled and dipped and sprinkled the sword—whilst he muttered. All this to the obvious scandalizing of that same older of the two guards; this man had seen action and had great respect for a good weapon. Anyone could own an ax, but a sword was a thing of art and great craft. The veteran had saved and saved to purchase the one at his side. He treated it with more respect and care than he gave his wife, who had after all not come so dear. Lips tight, he watched the crouching mage cover the blade with the worst enemy of a good blade or steel armor: water.

And all the while the mage muttered, murmured so that his watchers knew he bespoke words though they understood none of them.

Now that soldier was perhaps somewhat mollified: taking up the dripping sword, the mage continued his throaty inçanting. His lips barely amove, he passed the blade through the flame dancing above the brazier.

The metal hissed as if in preternatural anger. Turning it over, the mage repeated the action and, presumably, the words of his curse or ensorceling invocation.

At last, still murmuring his incomprehensible cantrip, the mage rose. With no warning whatever and almost without taking aim, he launched the sword in spear fashion at the naked pair below. And now the caster of spells spoke aloud, and all understood the words.

"Slay him."

The sword was still in air, a streak of silver, when the mage spoke those words in a deadly dull voice full of menace and malice like deadly spores crowding the pod of a Black Lotus from Khitai's doom-shadowed jungles. Soldiers and khan stared—as did the two Iranistani prisoners below. The one, scarred and sunken of cheek and belly, made to dodge from the blade that rushed at him, point foremost. Voices rose then, murmurs from lips other then the mage's; did the flying blade swerve, just before it plunged into the breast of the dodging man . . . just a fraction left of center?

Taken in that fictional wise beloved of the more careless tellers and scriveners of tales—precisely through the heart—the Iranistani jerked violently. He voiced a sepulchral sigh, and fell. He did not lie still at once, but twitched in his dying. The sword had plunged deep. It quivered above him.

"An *excellent* throw, Zafra," the khan said in surprise, once he'd broken the bonds of petrific shock. "I had not dreamed that you—"

Below, the second prisoner had grasped the dragon-hilt of the sword standing like a slender silver-and-steel grave marker above his comrade's body. He drew it forth, releasing a freshet of blood. He stared upward

4

at the watching quartet of enemy captors. His thoughts and emotions could be read in his sunken, hunger-bright eyes: the khan! The very khan, only a few ells away, and the Iranistani with sword in hand . . .

With deliberate steps, the naked foreigner paced along the dungeon's floor to the base of the stair. His gaze was fastened on the khan. Blood dripped from the sword in his fist.

Behind the mage, swords scraped from wood-mouthed sheaths as two men of weapons prepared to defend their ruler. The Iranistani, weakened by torture and lack of food, would be the work of but seconds. Surely the guards would survive little longer were their khan to be murdered, for he was a Turanian satrap and the Empire of Turan was powerful and jealous as a killer stallion just past its youth.

The young mage lifted a hand, staying them. Quietly he said, "Slay him."

The Iranistani had a foot on the second stair when the sword came alive in his hand.

The dragon twisted, twisted again; it pulled free of his grip, for his fingers had loosened in surprise.

The sword whipped about. It lunged at him as though wielded, driven by a mighty, invisible arm. The prisoner threw up an arm in automatic defense—and the blade chopped nearly through his wrist. The hand dangled on a scrap of skin, a morsel of muscle and a stick of splintered bone. At once the sword redirected its aim and plunged into the man's breast—just left of center.

Driven a pace back by the force of the blade's driving into him, the Iranistani tottered and fell backward. He lay thus, one bare heel on the bottom-most stair. His legs twitched. The sword stood above his body. It quivered as if the silver dragon surmounting it were alive, and angry.

The mage turned to look at his khan with brown

5

garnets of eyes cold as chastity. His squared, beardless face showed precisely nothing beneath the high cap; neither triumph nor expectancy lighted his features. Now he completely ignored the two guards, whose hearts were as invaded by a dreadful chill that was cold as steel—ensorceled steel.

"Impressive, wizard!"

The mage bowed at his khan's words. And he smiled when his face passed thus momentarily from the others' sight, for he was a young man recently apprentice, and not often praised, and his future and fortune had been in doubt. Now he knew that both were assured, more firmly than the khan's. He was apprentice no more, but valued wizard to Akter Khan.

"Enchant a thousand swords so," the ruler went on as his mage straightened, "and I shall have an army requiring no upkeep whatever and the smallest of quarters—and invincible!"

"Ah, my lord," the young mage dared say. "I have shown you something horrifically impressive, and instantly you think only of more, more!"

From one of the soldiers came a gasp. Yet when his ruler spoke he knew that henceforth this shuddersome demon in human guise must be treated with care and respect, Ferygian cap, snake's eyes and all.

"Think me not grateful, wizard . . . though I will not be chastised by you."

The khan's eyes shifted in their sockets, toward the two guards. It was a silent reminder that the prisoners were now corpses.

"I regret that only two blades can be so enchanted at any one time, my lord," the mage said. Perhaps it was noted that he did not apologize; no comment was made.

"Why?"

The eyes of the mage shifted a glance at the soldiers; gazed again upon the khan.

"There is nothing here we need guarding from, now," the khan said. "Await us beyond the door."

After a moment's hesitation and the opening of a mouth—which closed, words unspoken—the two soldiers departed. Their ruler did not glance after them; he continued to look into the face of the mage who had proven himself lacking only in years.

"Why?" the khan repeated.

"It is a Law of Skelos, whence comes the enchantment I laid on the blade, my lord Khan. One must employ the proper ancient words in *just* the right manner and tone, and the four elements in *just* the right order and while certain specific of the words of the invultuations are being uttered: the elements that comprise all things: earth and air, and water and fire."

"Most unfortunate. However . . . a great feat, and I remain impressed and most pleased, wizard. You will wear this."

A ring set with a huge sundane transferred itself from finger to palm, from palm to waiting fingertips and thus onto a finger of the mage. His bow was not low, nor did he speak.

"I will have that sword."

"So I thought my khan might desire. And I had another thought, which is why I wanted us shut of the guards. Might I not instead lay the enchantment on my generous lord's own blade?"

The khan laid his hand on the jewel-set hilt of the curved sword that thrust up past his left hip. "Aye! By Erlik's entrails—aye!"

"The sword must be blooded immediately the spell is laid, my lord."

"Aye; methinks we shall be able to find someone to give up worthless life that his khan may be protected by such a blade, wizard! Proceed."

And the satrap of Zamboula drew his jewel-hilted sword, and presented it to Zafra his mage.

7

I

CONAN OF CIMMERIA

The big youth gave the girl's tawny arm a squeeze and swatted her backside. She danced a step from the slap, tossing long hair the color of a roan horse; and gave him a look that combined taunt and caress. He'd done with her, this night. With a jingle of her belt of coins, she went her way while he went his.

She hurried to reach a better lighted area, for this was the very worst section of the City of the Wicked. Throats were swiftly slit in these dim narrow streets of the area called The Desert, and even more swiftly in the darkness of alleys slippery with refuse and vomit.

The big youth walked no more than four swinging strides before he turned to enter just such a narrow alley. Visibility might have been a bit less at the bottom of a well. The best light was at the corner of the street behind him, from a pair of lion-lamps outside a noisy tavern. Their light attempted to follow him, and soon gave it up.

Odor assaulted and tried to overwhelm his nostrils with the miasma of decaying garbage and old wine, sour from stomachs; and damp earth over against the buildings, even as the darkness sought to whelm his smoldering blue eyes. The lack of lines in this one's face proclaimed him youth. Something akin to sword-steel hardness in those eyes gave that the lie. The more careful observer would know that this near-giant of less than twenty years had seen much, had experienced and endured . . . and prevailed. None could be so stupid as to believe that his dagger and the sword in its worn old shagreen sheath had not been blooded.

All that, and his size, lent him confidence; he swung his big frame into the alley almost without slowing.

His was the swaggery confidence of youth, of a wolf among dogs. He had laid two ghastly liches, this wight born on a battlefied; he had thieved while the victim lay sleeping mere feet away; he had slain two several wizards bent on his death and aye, a highborn lord of Koth as well, and he had broken sorceries, and had sent ahead into another life so many arms-wielding men that he had lost count, despite his lack of years. They were but dogs yapping at the wolf, and the wolf was larger, and swifter, and more feral and vicious, and radiated the confidence of competence as a candle sends its nimbus all about it.

Into the alley swung the wolf, and the dogs awaited.

One step the rangy cat-sinuous man took from the black shadows against one wall, and his swordpoint creased the tunic over the youth's muscular stomach.

"Be still and do not reach for your hilt, Conan, or I lean on this blade and give you a second navel."

Cold blue eyes glared fiercely at the man behind the sword. He was of medium height, meaning his prey was a foot taller. The man wore a long dark cloak with its hood up; in the darkness of the alley not even the young Cimmerian's keen eyes could see the face of his accoster. Conan stood still, his brain sending messages of looseness throughout his big frame. Very slowly, he eased one foot back. And then the other, and as the pressure left his tunic's front, he pushed out his muscular midsection to hold the point and make the man think he was an inch or two closer then he was.

"By Bel, god of all thieves," he said, "what sort of treacherous idiocy is this? What of the Code of Bel, fellow; thieves do not rob thieves!"

"Just . . . be quite still, Conan, if you value your belly."

"I never move when a sword is trying to open my tunic," Conan said, and just as he ended the lie he heard the rustle of cloth behind him.

It was not the time for further playing. Conan was not the sort to let himself be skewered or hooked from behind because of menace in front. At least he could see the cloaked man's blade; the one behind would end his life without his ever seeing it. If luck were with him this night, he thought, his accoster would lunge automatically and stick the treacherous wight behind him! Darkness, the sages of the east said, baffled rogues as well as honest men. Nor did Conan pause to reflect that all here were rogues.

Already he was dropping into a squat, and he did not stop moving to wait for that possible stab over his head; just before his buttocks came down onto his knotty calves, he lunged sidewise. At the same time his arm swept across his midsection to the pommel of his sword.

He heard the wheeping whine in the air and knew by the sound that it was not sword the man behind him had swung at his head; the wind resistance was too strong. His sword scraping out, he saw that it was a cudgel. The man wielded a five-foot staff thick as a woman's wrist. Conan saw, too, that the hooded man had not lunged with his sword.

Cudgel

Odd, Conan thought, never having ceased moving. *When one had me at sword's point, why sought the other to club me from behind—and why didn't the swordsman lunge to spit or at least wound me when I moved?*

As he came up into a combative crouch he sent his own blade sweeping out. The hooded man elected to spring back rather than try to block such a stroke with his sword. Moving, ever moving, Conan continued that swing—and his tip angled unerringly up to slash open the cudgel-wielder's throat. The man staggered back and for the first time Conan noted the coil of rope in his left hand.

The man fell back against a wall, still standing while his life ran out of his neck in a scarlet tide. Conan held his ready crouch, showing his teeth in a feral grin, facing the other man . . . who fell to his knees. The sword clanked to the filth of the alley.

"Do not kill me Conan. Please. I did not try to slay you . . . I would not have. See? I am unarmed. See? You would not slay an unarmed man?"

"I might," Conan said, concealing his surprise. "Stand up."

The man in the long dark cloak obeyed.

"Turn. Put back that cowl and walk before me, out into some light."

The man stood, and was most hesitant about turning his back.

12

A wolf snarled: *"Move."*

"I—I . . . please . . ."

"Move, damn you. I do not stab backs. If I meant to kill you, I'd do it face to face. I'd take pleasure in the look in your eyes and the blood burbling out of your mouth like vomited wine."

The man seemed to reel at the Cimmerian's deliberately horrendous words. He'd put back his hood, and Conan was able to see the brightness of his eyes, staring in horror and fear. He saw too that a scar ran down the fellow's face and parted his beard. With a sound like a sob, he turned shakily. Conan squatted briefly to wipe his blade on the other, now fallen and still, unbreathing. And he picked up the dropped sword.

Conan rose and took a step. The cloaked man heard and hurried, without running, down the alley ahead of the Cimmerian.

In The Desert of Shadizar where no men of the Watch came, people melted off the street the moment a frightened man appeared, followed by a huge other carrying not one but two bared swords. The man in the cloak stepped under the glim of an oily torch that flared in a cresset mounted over a red-painted door.

"Stand right there," Conan said. "A whorehouse door is a good place for you. What's your name?"

"Yavuz," the fellow said, watching the giant examine the sword whose tip had so recently disturbed the hand of his open-front tunic, though not his mental equilibrium.

"We never intended to kill you," Yavuz added, in a pleading voice.

"No," Conan said. "And you knew me. You were waiting for me, not just any passerby. You were sent for me. The man who hired you loaned you this blade, didn't he? He wanted me alive, didn't he? I was to be struck from behind while you held me nice and still

13

like a steer stupidly facing the butcher's hammer. The rope your comrade carried was for binding me."

Conan looked up. Yavuz's eyes were even larger. "By Bel . . . how know you all this? Was I duped?"

"Only in thinking a wight like you could take me, hireling. A man from Iranistan hired you to fetch me to him, alive but trussed like an unbroken stallion . . . so that he could ply me with a few questions."

The man's eyes told Conan he was right. "Mitra's name—that Iranistani dog sent us for a sorcerer, didn't he?"

"Of course," Conan said smiling. He hefted Yavuz's sword. "This knife comes from the Ilbars Mountains. I've seen one aforenow, in the fist of a man of Iranistan. Now where were you to take me? Speak, or . . ."

"You are not going to kill me?"

"I see no reason for it. Do you?"

"No! None!"

"Take off your left buskin."

"My . . . left buskin?"

"Aye. Hurry! We haven't all night. I have no patience, and your employer will be growing impatient ere we reach him."

"Ah! You want me to lead you to him. Aye!"

Seeing that his life was to be continued for the time required to lead his intended quarry to the foreigner who had hired him—and affording opportunity to dodge into an alley and run for all he was worth—Yavuz squatted. Hurriedly he loosened the laces of one short, soft boot. This would not slow him down, he thought, almost smiling; he would show the big tough giant some running, one foot bare or no!

"Into the doorway," Conan said, sheathing his sword and transferring the Ilbarsi knife into his right fist. It looked big enough to bludgeon an ox.

Yavuz obeyed. Squatting, never taking his menacing gaze off the man, Conan felt about the hard-packed earth of the street until his fingers encountered a piece of bone. "Ah." It was the thighbone of a chicken he found there on the street in that low and lawless area of Shadizar, and he picked it up. Grinning wolfishly and totally without humor at the staring Yavuz, he dropped the bone into the buskin. Conan rose and kicked the short boot over to its owner.

"Put it on. Tie the lace."

Yavuz's scar-split beard quivered as he chewed his lip. He was visibly trembling. "Is this . . . sorcery?"

"Aye. Try to run as you and I walk to meet your employer, and the bone will kill you."

Trembling, Yavuz pulled on the buskin. He tied its rawhide lace. When he straightened and put his weight on that foot, he winced. And he understood. He would not be running.

"You see? As I said. Try to flee and the bone will slow you by making you limp—and I shall kill you. Sorcery. Now give me that cloak, so that as I walk beside you with this blade in my hand, no one will see it under the cloak. You walk *beside* me, Yavuz, not ahead like a captive. And do not fall behind."

"But . . . my tunic is torn in back."

Conan showed the man his teeth, and a look of evil from cold blue eyes beneath black brows. "Fine. It is not a cool night, and you seem to be sweating in all that cloak. Off with it!"

Moments later Conan, having violently shaken the long dark brown cloak in hopes of ridding it of any small six-legged inhabitants, made the garment look short by wearing it. It fluttered about his upper calves as he walked beside the smaller man, who was of perfectly normal size. No casual observer would take note that the cloak never belled away from the big youth's right side; there he held it with two fingers to cover the long weapon he also held.

15

"We are heading toward the bazaar," Conan observed.

"Aye," Yavuz said, limping. "The Iranistani dog is in a good inn, out of The Desert."

"Do not call him dog, dog; you worked for him! Let's see your wallet."

Automatically Yavuz's hand clapped protectively to the square pouch he wore slung from his belt, on a double thong; Yavuz was thief-wary.

Yavuz's Purse

A hand closed on his arm. His eyes widened as the fingers tightened. Pain began, very quickly. The hireling of a far eastern foreigner knew that considerable additional strength remained in that big hand. One-handed, Yavuz loosed his pouch. He handed it across him to the other man. The clamping grip left his arm and Yavuz looked down to see four distinct white marks; while he looked, they reddened with the rushing of blood back into that area of his arm. A hand big enough to bludgeon an ox, he thought. Why, the overgrown lad could *strangle* one!

"Mitra," Yavuz muttered.

16

"No, Crom," Conan said.

"What?"

"I swear by Crom."

Gods were plentiful in Shadizar, and some were weird and others obscene and their rites worse. "Crom then," Yavuz said, and thought: *Who's Crom?*

"Junk," Conan muttered, going through the other man's pouch. "Junk . . . nice ring. Stolen so recently you've not had time to fence it, eh? And some coppers . . . what's this? Two gold pieces! Hoho, still warm from an Iranistani hand, I'll wager! I'll soon return them. You did not earn them, did you. Here; I do not want the rest of this junk."

"Junk!"

"Aye. The emerald in that brass ring is so tiny it won't bring enough to feed you for two days."

"Brass!"

"Take it out again and fondle it as we walk. See if your fingers are not green when we reach our destination. How much farther?"

Yavuz doubly fastened his purse to his belt again, and did not open it to "fondle" the ring. "Not . . . too much farther," he said. "You who hand back coppers and a ring you know is stolen . . . it is good walking with one your size. No one challenges. All step aside."

Conan grinned.

"You do not happen to need a bravo, do you? Swift-fingered, quiet; discreet?"

"Hardly. Besides, you're a cripple."

"I walk this way because of that bone you put in my buskin! I am sound as a Turanian gold piece!"

"Well, you're in Zamora, now. Walk, Yavuz. I want to talk with an Iranistani, not a limpy scarface from Shadizar's cesspools!"

"You are not going to kill me, are you, Conan?"

"Probably not. But I am growing impatient."

Despite his limp, Yavuz speeded his gait. They

turned onto a street a block beyond the bazaar, which marked the beginning of better Shadizar. A pair of uniformed men of the city's Watch ambled along toward them, glanced at the pair without interrupting their quiet conversation. To say that Conan did not like such men was an understatement. Yet this night he was most definitely not looking for trouble with the

Lion Sign

18

enforcers of the laws of Shadizar. He made a great concession, gritting his teeth; he stepped streetward, to let the men of the Watch pass on the inside. They did, and went on.

A sign swung on creaky old chains; on it was depicted the head of a snarling lion. Head and mane were painted scarlet.

"Here," Yavuz said.

"Peer within. See if you see our man."

Yavuz did, briefly, and back-paced hurriedly. Coming thus down on his bone-lined buskin, he winced.

"Aye. He is there. In the back to the left near the keg, wearing a green kaffia."

Conan's hand again clamped Yavuz's arm while the Cimmerian looked within. "Um." He turned. "Your cloak will be hanging on a peg just inside the door on the morrow, Yavuz. You will need only give the taverner your name."

"But—"

"It is not cold, and I need it just now while I walk back to that jackal's table—to conceal his blade in my hand."

"Mitra!" Yavuz said, and amended: "Crom! You are not just going to go in and stick him!"

"Whether I do or not does not concern you, little Yavuz, *very* little Yavuz. You are free, and alive. I bid you fly, and burrow deep."

Released and so bidden, Yavuz wasted no time staring or expressing gratitude for his life. He scuttled —limping.

Conan entered the inn of the sign of the Red Lion.

II

KHASSEK OF IRANISTAN

The man seated alone in the rear corner of the Red Lion was middling handsome. His mustache and short, pointed beard were black, as his eyes very nearly were. He wore a headcloth in the eastern manner; the green fabric covered his crown and three sides of his head to the shoulders. A fillet of cloth, yellow and black woven in spirals, held it in place. His long-sleeved shirt was yellow and his full, loose pants red; so was the sash at his waist. Wideset eyes peered at Conan from a long face with a large thin nose and prominent jaw.

The Cimmerian went directly to that table. From beneath Yavuz's dark brown cloak came his hands, to lay before the seated man two coins of gold and the three-foot "knife" from up in the Ilbars Mountains.

"These gold pieces I took from a man with a beard parted by a scar. They are not enough to pay the kind of man who could take me."

The other man's left hand remained wrapped around his henna-hued mug of earthenware; the fingers of his right remained visible on the table's edge nearest

21

him. He stared up at the very young man looming over him. Young or no, the fellow was dangerous; anyone could see that, anyone who knew what to look for.

He was unusually tall and built massively. His mop of black hair was square-cut above blue eyes. He wore a short tunic of good green over nothing, and the garment's unusual deeply v-cut front displayed the molded muscular plates of his great chest. Sword and dagger swung from a belt of worn old leather, which

Tribal Amulet

was slung low on lean hips. A tribal amulet of pitiful "jewelry" lay on his chest, slung on a leathern cord: a longish blob of red-brown clay set with a bit of yellowish glass that was definitely not a gemstone. Probably something to do with his religion, whatever that might be, or a ward against disease or evil eye. His only other decor was a nice little gold ring on the smallest finger of his left hand. Set with an emerald of no great size, it did not appear to be a man's ring.

About this youth there was a look, almost an aura of savagery barely contained, of constant readiness for violence. He spoke again.

"Once I knew another man of Iranistan. We met in the home of a certain man of certain powers. Only coincidence brought us there at the same time, of an evening. Together, we fought off guardians who were not . . . natural men. Then two serpents emerged from a panel in a certain door: vipers. Both bit the man of Iranistan. He died while I watched, powerless to aid him."

Standing over the table, Conan removed Yavuz's cloak while he watched the other man decide that Conan knew who he was, and choose whether to dissemble or no. When he decided to speak, his words were relatively straightforward, assuming that each knew who the other was and why both were here. At the same time he maintained some caution: "Was his name Yusuphar?"

"You are interested in talking? —With me *not* trussed up?"

"I may be."

"Do you wait, then, while I give this cloak to the taverner. It belongs to Yavuz, whom I did not kill."

The seated Iranistani showed a little frown. "The other—"

"He sought to strike me from behind. I dodged,

23

and struck second. He did not dodge. Had I known he wanted only to take me alive, I might not have opened his throat with my sword."

The other man nodded. "Deep?"

"He is dead," Conan said, and walked among the tables to the taverner.

"This cloak was loaned me tonight," he told that large-eyed man, "by a good friend. His name is Yavuz and he wears a scar that splits his beard, here." Conan touched his own cleanshaven face. "I told him I would leave the cloak on that peg nearest the door."

"It might disappear if you do that now. I know Yavuz. Best give me the cloak; I will hang it there when I open on the morrow."

"Good. I would hate for it to disappear. Once a man tried to cheat my friend Yavuz, and now he is called Three-finger. I am joining the Iranistani. Do bring him another, and me a cup of your best wine. There's gold on the table."

The taverner looked. "Hmp. Also a sword. That will have to be put out of sight. You would do best to let me hold yours, too, until you are ready to go."

"I shall get the other one out of sight. I am body-guard to that wealthy Iranistani, and must keep my arms." Without yielding time for a reply, Conan turned and walked back to the table. Standing, he said, "Lean your oversized knife against the wall there on your left."

The Iranistani's smile was tiny as he did so; the youth had swiftly noted that he was left-handed and could not quickly whip up a wall-leaned sword on that side. Conan sat down facing him.

"Was his name Yusuphar, this other man of Iran-istan you met by accident in the home of a certain man of certain powers?"

"We both know that it was not," Conan said. "His name was Ajhindar. He told me that another of his land was about: a spy on him. He bore a blade such

24

as that one I took from two hired men—kidnapers, not
killers. One is dead and the other probably still running. You have your weapon and your gold, and I am
here. Why did you want me brought to you?"

The Iranistani's left hand left his goblet, and the
table. "Leave the dagger alone," Conan said. "I'll have
mine through you before you have a good grasp on the
hilt."

A hip-swinging young woman in two beaded strips
of scarlet cloth sewn with green thread appeared beside
Conan, with wine for both of them. The two men did
not look at her. She went off tight-lipped, noting how
interested the pair seemed in each other. She saw all
kinds.

"You are Conan, a Cimmerian."

"I am. You are of Iranistan, far and far from
here. You have traced me up here from Arenjun. Your
name?"

"You Cimmerians are called barbarians. How is
it then that you come to me and ask my name, rather
than wait outside to kill me when I leave this place?"

"We Cimmerians are also curious, and known to
give way to whims. Too, had we heard of Iranistan up
in Cimmeria, we'd have called you barbarians, because
you are not Cimmerians."

The man smiled and leaned back. "My name is
Khassek. Did Ajhindar in truth die as you say?"

Staring directly into Khassek's eyes, Conan said,
"He did."

"You know . . . Crom take me if I don't believe
you!"

"Crom! You swear by the grim Lord of the
Mound?"

Khassek smiled. "I have been learning all I could
of Cimmeria."

"And of me. Looking for me. Preparing to question me."

"Aye, Conan. I would even bargain with you. You and Ajhindar both sought a particular . . . prize. I believe you have it."

"Naturally I don't know what you are talking about." Conan sipped his wine. "You are paying, by the way. Is this thing you seek of some value, back in Iranistan?"

"You know that it is, Conan."

"Why?"

A group of people across the inn erupted into loud laughter. Khassek gazed at Conan for a long while. At last he came forward, with both elbows thumping onto the table. "I believe," he said, "that I shall tell you."

"Name this prize you mention," Conan said blandly. "A jewel?"

"Several," Khassek said. "They form an amulet of far, far more value than your ring and that bit of earth and glass about your neck, Conan. Were the amulet called the Eye of Erlik placed in the hands of my khan, you could wear a gold one there, set with rubies . . . unless you prefer emeralds."

"A *god's eye?*"

"That is only the amulet's name."

"A yellow stone or two, perhaps."

Knowing that Conan was hazarding no idle guess, Khassek only nodded.

Conan toyed with his wine mug. "A valuable amulet indeed. And he would give me one as valuable, your Khan."

"More valuable, to you. Give listen Conan, Cimmerian. That amulet is important to the Khan of Zamboula. You probably know that. Zamboula lies between here and Iranistan. You have been there?"

Conan shook his head. "I am only a hill-country youth," he said disengagingly.

"Who wears a tunic made in Khauran, I believe."

"You have been astudying, Khassek! No, I have not been to Zamboula, and a month or so ago I had never heard of Iranistan. It lies beyond Zamboula, you say? That is very far."

"I believe you know that it does. Iranistan plans no war on Zamboula, and no harm to its ruler, who is a satrap of mighty Turan. With the Eye of Erlik in his possession, though, my khan could negotiate a far better trade arrangement with Zamboula. That is our goal."

"Perhaps," Conan said. "As you thought the amulet was in the hands of a mage, and as Ajhindar sought it there . . . perhaps it is a sorcerous thing, a thing that will enable your ruler to torture or slay Zamboula's worthy khan, from a distance."

"Conan, it is not—as Zamboula's khan is not worthy. Yet, even if it were so . . . does that concern you? I tell you that there is a rich reward for you if you aid me in placing the Eye of Erlik into my khan's hands."

"Two months away!"

"You have pressing business in Shadizar, Conan?"

"You are right," the Cimmerian said. He shrugged. "The health of the satrap of Zamboula is of no more concern to me than Iranistan's trade arrangements. Or—who owns a particular amulet. An eye!" He shook his head. "Is Erlik missing an eye, then?"

Khassek nodded. "Now let us suppose that you have it, or know where it might be found. If both of us returned to Iranistan with it, both of us would be rewarded. Do you have another thought in mind?"

"Iranistan is so far," Conan said, continuing to tease—and to think.

"That is true. I have not journeyed so far to return without the amulet, and I won't. What holds you here? I know that in Arenjun you are . . . still sought."

"Ride so far with a man who paid two others to have me clubbed and captured, only to talk with me?

27

Surely you meant to torture me to learn of this Eye, if necessary. An *Eye!*"

"I'll not deny it. How could I know you might be a reasonable man? I thought you had killed Ajhindar."

"And now you do not?"

"I have the feeling that you have told me the truth—about that," the Iranistani added significantly.

Conan chuckled. "I have. And so once you were sure that I knew nothing of this thing you seek, you would have slain me."

"That I deny. Once I learned where you had hidden the Eye of Erlik, I'd have taken it and departed posthaste for Iranistan. I'd have seen no need to murder you—unless forced, of course. Such is not our way, Conan, or my way. Come with me now and I still feel the same. My only concern is putting that amulet into the hands of my employer."

Though he did indeed have the amulet, for which he had gone to a great, great deal of trouble, Conan reflected now that there was surely still that which he did not know about it. Would a man call his ruler "my employer," for instance?

"The amulet is more important to my ruler than my life, Conan," Khassek said, speaking directly to Conan's eyes. "If I knew you were taking it to him, I'd be happy. If I know you will not, I must fight you."

"Best I slay you here and now, then."

"Killing me now would be very unwise. Four men of the City Watch just entered the inn. Departing this place might be wise."

Only the men of the Watch of Arenjun had reason to want him, Conan mused—dead or alive. Up here in Shadizar . . . well, better he had never left the comparative safety of The Desert, which was Shadizar's equivalent of Arenjun's Maul. He said, "Why?" with a perfectly open face. "You are the foreigner. I need have no fear of the local Watch-men."

28

"A Royal Dragoner is with them, and they are looking for someone."

"Certainly I have no quarrel with the King of Zamora!"

"Umm. Unless he has had a complaint from Arenjun. I had heard that down there you wounded two and disgraced another, *uptown*—a certain former Watch-sergeant. I am glad that you have no fear of any friends he might have in Shadizar, or of Arenjun's governor making complaint to the king, because the five are coming over here now."

"One was killed, too, in Arenjun," Conan said. "I did the wounding—it was Ajhindar who accounted for the dead one."

"One of these has a crossbow. Hm . . . Conan . . . it may be true that I am the foreigner and you of course, nine feet tall and with your blue eyes, are a native of Zamora . . . . but the crossbow quarrel is aimed at you."

"Damn."

Khassek stared. "You—that's just the way Ajhindar said it!"

"I know. What else is there to be said? I came in here all swaggery and smug, to brace you. I forgot an important Zamoran saying: 'When thou wouldst enter, think first how thou wilt find a way out again.' A rule I must remember to hold to is 'Never sit with your back to the door'! What's all that scuffling?"

"Most of the other patrons are departing with haste. Here they come, king's men first. By the way, in Iranistan the sages say 'Wherever thou wouldst enter, ascertain if there is another door.' "

"Sensible." Conan started to rise.

"Do not move, Cimmerian! You can not dodge the crossbow quarrel aimed at your back, and three swords are drawn!"

The speaker stepped past Conan to face him,

smiling, from Khassek's side of the table. The man was not tall, and he was slim, though his face showed some signs of high living. His glossy brown-black hair was neatly banged, curling slightly under all across his forehead. The large gold pendant on the breast of his gold-broidered blue tunic—which Conan saw was of silk—bore the arms of the King of Zamora, lately a drunk dominated by a sorcerer of Arenjun. *The bastard should be grateful to me for getting rid of Yara,* Conan thought morosely. This man's perfectly trimmed, thin mustache twitched as he smiled. Conan saw a flash of gold in his mouth. Dental work, by Crom— and the fellow no more than thirty!

"Conan of Cimmeria, lately of Arenjun, you are my prisoner in the king's name. You will come quietly?"

Conan stared at him. Nice pretty blue leggings; polished black boots, tight-fitting. A lovely fancily tooled belt supporting sheaths; from them thrust up the jeweled hilt of a dagger and a sword whose pommel was a lion head—and surely was of silver.

Conan glanced at Khassek, who sat below the king's man, just beside him; looking shocked, he was staring at Conan. The Cimmerian glanced around. He saw an inn nearly emptied—and uniforms. Swords, naked. Aye, and the crossbowman, moving slowly in, the tip of his nasty little shaft trained on Conan.

"You mean—you mean this man is a *criminal!*" Khassek exclaimed. "Oh!"

The king's Dragoner looked down at him with a contemptuous lifting of his brows. "You are not his friend?"

"Hardly! I am here on the queen's business of Koth."

"Koth! You look like one of those . . . you look as if you came from well to the east, not the *west!*"

Khassek heaved a great sigh. "It is true. My mother was a slave, from Aghrapur."

"Aghrapur!" The king's dandified agent was astonished anew.

"Aye," Khassek sighed sadly. "She was kidnaped in her youth by an armor pedlar of Koth. Carried her back with him, he did. As the gods would have it, he found by the time of their arrival that he loved her. I was born. He had me educated. Now—well now I am here representing the queen herself! As for *this* fellow —he seems clean, and when he walked so boldly into this good inn—this is a good inn, isn't it, my lord?"

The Zamoran smiled, flattered. "Aye. There are better, in Shadizar—but there are many worse! Agent for the queen, you say?"

"Uh—my lord Ferhad—" One of the men of the Watch began.

The Dragoner jerked his head to give the man a blazing stare. "In time! Do not disturb a man on the King's Business!"

"Well, he offered me the ring he wears, saying it was his mother's," Khassek said, while Conan wondered at all this elaborate tale, and where it was taking them. "And dropped these gold coins on the table to show that he was not penurious. He gave me this strange sword as good faith, and said he needed two more gold pieces to get to Nemedia—"

Predictably, Lord Ferhad said, "Nemedia!"

"So he said. Now . . . now oh my lord . . . is't possible this fellow sought to peddle stolen goods to me, me, the queen's own buyer of jewels and cosmetics?"

"Entirely possible," Ferhad said. "This one is a desperate and lawless man. He is responsible for a great deal of mischief down in Arenjun—and dares fly here, to the very capital, to take refuge!" Ferhad fixed his lionish gaze on Conan again, standing tall with his chin high, looking down his considerable nose and being considerably more officious now, with such a distinguished audience of one; the queen's own buyer of jewels and cosmetics, of Koth!

"It is a royal offense to interfere with men of the City Watch anywhere in our kingdom, barbarian! Now rise, slowly, and let us be off with you—to some accommodations I fear you will not like so well as this fine inn wherein you have tried to mislead a distinguished foreign visitor!"

"Aye," Khassek petulantly said, "and take this awful sword with you!" Half-turning, he brought up the great Ilbarsi knife. An instant later, he was standing behind Ferhad, the sword-arm across the man's chest and his other tawny hand holding a dagger at his throat.

"None of you move! Lord Ferhad: Give order that all swords and that crossbow are to be placed on that table to your right!"

"Wha—wha—you can't—let me g—ah! Careful with that dagger, man!"

"Aye, it is honed to razor-sharpness, as I have tender skin and use it to shave, daily. The order, Ferhad!"

Ferhad gave the order. The crossbowman raised the point that his weapon was cocked and dangerous. Khassek advised the man to shoot the quarrel into the wall just below the ceiling, and Ferhad confirmed. Soon the quarrel thunked home and remained there, high above the floor, quivering only a little; a souvenir for the Red Lion's owner.

"Conan," Khassek said, "do persuade our host to show us his cellar."

"Cellar!" Ferhad echoed in a yelp, and his adam's apple bobbed against the chill blade of Khassek's knife. Trying not to swallow, Ferhad stood as tall and stiff as a military recruit, and said no more.

III

FAREWELL TO SHADIZAR

Imraz, the large-eyed proprietor of the Red Lion, lifted a squared trap in the floor of his pantry. One by one, the four men of Shadizar's City Watch grumblingly descended into darkness. Each shot a last dark look at the huge barbarian who stood above, grinning just a bit as he leaned on a sword—their sergeant's.

"My dear lord Ferhad," Khassek said, "I am grievously sorry, but see no way out of this other than to beg you to join those men below."

"Below!"

"Try to look on the good side," Conan said. "Maybe our host Imraz keeps his best vintages down there."

"Morelike rotting turnips, spiderwebs and mushrooms," Ferhad said tightly, which was the only way he could speak with his head tilted back. "Why not tie me and leave me up here? Pent in the dark with those common soldiers—"

"—who doubtless know many fine stories for your entertainment, my good lord." Khassek released the man, easing out his handsome sword as he did. "Below, and I wish you a good good evening."

33

Sergeant's Sword

"Me too," Conan said as the fancily dressed fellow gingerly set foot on the top of the seven old wooden steps that led down into earth-smelly darkness. Conan neatly plucked Ferhad's gem-winking dagger from its sheath.

"You will both be very, very sorry for this," the descending Ferhad promised.

"Well, just you come up to Brythunia and talk with us about that," Khassek said affably.

"Brythunia!"

Khassek kicked the trap down. "Doesn't lock, does

34

it," he muttered, and looked up to see the Red Lion's owner backing slowly.

Conan took four quick steps. "No no Imraz, no running off now. Here, help us to move that big full keg over atop the trap, there's a good man."

With a bit of grunting, the three men accomplished the barrel's moving and placement. Conan glanced through the pantry doorway to see several faces gazing interestedly in at the front door.

"Ho!" he cried. "Hand me that crossbow!"

The faces vanished and Khassek trotted lightly through the inn to slam and bar the door. When he turned back, he was frowning. "Just realized . . . Imraz! Where is that serving wench of yours?"

His host blinked. "Why—I know not—"

"Damn! Gone by a rear door to fetch even more brave soldiery—the King's Own this time, I have little doubt. Conan—"

"We take all these swords and daggers, and the crossbow," Conan said. "We take him with us." He nodded at the taverner. "We go out the back, and we run!"

"I doubt Imraz can roll this huge keg off the trap all by himself," Khassek said, scooping up the crossbow.

"No, but he can open the front door and let others in to help him!"

"Ah, too true. I think I have quit thinking clearly. If only you had brought back the length of cord I gave those two fellows, along with the gold and my little sticker! Come Imraz—you must accompany us for a little way."

While the taverner looked profoundly reluctant and even larger of large mournful eyes, Khassek opened his pouch and brought forth five more pieces of gold. "Two still lie on the table, and we have drunk no more than a few coppers' worth of wine. Here, take these. Think what fun to see such a pompous fop as that Ferhad dealt with—and think of all the business the telling of this wonderful story of the comeuppance of the king's Dragoner will bring in! Why, customers will flock in like flies. *Come*."

In silence Imraz accompanied them. Conan dropped five swords and four daggers into a smallish empty keg, while the owner of that little barrel made five pieces of gold vanish even more efficiently. He led them through a doorway into an alley that was very different from those of The Desert, and they hurried along like three friends.

"Right, here," Conan grunted, carrying his keg with both arms enwrapping it, and they turned right; at the next intersection he muttered "left."

"You look a bit loutish lugging that armory-in-a-keg," Khassek pointed out. "Do you think we really need them?"

"One can never have too many weapons," Conan assured him, and walked on, his back arched and his belly thrust out under the keg he bear-hugged. Its contents rattled and clinked.

After another turn, they bade good evening to their former host, and hurried on whilst Imraz turned back.

"What's this about Brythunia?" Conan asked.

"I gave him the names of several places—"

"I noticed!"

"—none of them our destination," Khassek patiently finished. "Let him wonder. Who knows an Iranistani on sight? We do share a destination, Conan, do we not?"

"We're an unlikely pair," Conan said.

"Trio; forget not your barrel of blades. But not so, not so. We are both very clever fellows who'd have tried to slay all five of those wights had I not been even cleverer and Ferhad so easy, and we both know it. Conan . . . does it also occur to you that all the while

36

you've been carrying that keg I could have stuck a knife or two into you?"

"We are walking deeper into The Desert, Khassek. Assume that we are being watched, though you see no one. I have friends down here. They don't look upon *me* as a foreigner."

"Hmm. You don't happen to own a few camels, do you?"

"I hate the beasts. I own no less than four horses. No camels. Why don't you carry this keg a while?"

"No, thanks."

Reluctantly Conan set the thing down, then turned it over. He separated Ferhad's jeweled dagger, which he stuck into his belt. Three good raps with a Watch-man's sword on the pommel of Ferhad's ruined a good blade and placed into the Cimmerian's hand a nice lion's head of silver. He tossed and caught it, smiling.

"This look like a camel to you?"

"Probably only silver plate," Khassek said.

Conan frowned. "That bastard! Just my luck if the jewels in this dagger aren't real! What about you, by the way—have you no horse, no camels? You came a long way."

"I have some nice clothing," Khassek said with a mournful sigh, "several changes; and a handsome ring, and two horses—I came up here with a caravan, most of the way. And, also in my room at the inn—*the Red Lion,* remember—twenty gold coins of Zamboula."

"Twenty!" The Cimmerian stared, and his mouth and eyes vied with each other for achieving wideness. "Mitra, Crom and Bel, man—why didn't you whip up and fetch them ere we left?"

Khassek looked even sadder. "I seem to have forgot. I fear they are now forfeit to the crown of Zamora."

"Ishtar's eyeballs," Conan mourned, "twenty pieces of gold!"

"Look at it this way, Conan: I saved you from durance vile and doubtless a lot worse."

"Both of which still loom," Conan said in a low growl, "if we don't get ourselves out of this city—and this kingdom!"

The two men stood alone on a darkened street, at their feet an overturned keg and a jumbled assortment of weaponry. The dark eyes of Khassek gazed into the sullen blue ones of the barbarian. Khassek said, "We?"

Conan turned and began walking; Khassek swung along at his side.

"Damn," Conan said quietly, thoughtfully. "Ajhindar was a good man, one I liked at once. He was devoted to his khan and his mission, to the point of risking his life: he tried to slay me even after he had seen my skill and strength! Also after I had just saved his skin. A bit treacherous, but all for his ruler. Now you too have risked your life to aid me, Khassek of Iranistan . . . because, of course, you don't know where that amulet is. All for your khan! I think that I would meet a khan who has such loyalty from two such good men."

"He will be interested in meeting you too, my friend with hands the size of hams! Good, then. Two such men as we can get out of Shadizar, surely, even though all three gates will be watched. Let us to it."

They walked deeper into Shadizar's Desert.

"Oh—Conan. Do you have the amulet?"

Conan chuckled. "I know where it is. I buried it between here and Zamboula, on the desert."

"Damn," Khassek said, and took his hand off his dagger.

Hours later, the three men in charge of Shadizar's Gate of the Black Throne watched the approach of a mounted pair. Astride two handsome horses, the woman and her young son led two others, well laden. She reined in to stare down at the uniformed man beside the wheel; it turned the cable and heavy chain that raised the enormous bar across the two gates.

"Well, open up. No use guarding on this side; I want out, not in."

"My dear," a voice said, and she looked up at another uniform. Its owner peered down at her from the arched, narrow doorway of the watchtower. "I am a man of feeling and sensibilities, and would not sleep well did I not warn you against leaving the city at this hour."

"Thank you. You are a good man. We are going. It is a holy mission."

"A pilgrimage?"

"Aye. My son and I serve the temple of Holy Khosatra Khel Rehabilitated and Twice Established, Lord of All, the Father of Mitra, Ishtar, and Bel."

"A busy and doubtless venerable god, my dear, but . . . surely the sensible person waits until dawn, at least. Mayhap then you could join other such dedicated pilgrims, peradventure even a caravan, the ultimate protection. Here you are in the bosom of the capital of mighty Zamora. *Out there* . . ." He trailed off with a gesture to indicate that naught but peril and travail lay outside the Gate of the Black Throne of Erlik, in Shadizar.

The cloaked woman, who was hardly ill-formed, spoke up stoutly. "I fear the world outside, even the desert, far less than I do this city of thieves and woman-beaters and wicked wicked cults dedicated to gods no one ever heard of or wants to! Let us through, please. We depart."

"Would that I had the power to prevent your taking so peril-fraught a step," the gate commander said.

"Well, I appreciate it. But you have not, and I am going and my son with me, and my neck is getting stiff looking up at you. If you are not going to open the gate, would you please tell me where I go to complain?"

"It lacks only a bit more than two glasses until dawn . . ."

The woman burst out, "What do I have to do or say to get *out of here?*"

The man in the tower sighed. "Open the gate."

A man grunted, chain rattled, and the bar rose. The gate creaked. A strong-willed woman, her silent son, and four horses passed out of Shadizar. She never kicked her mount or so much as jiggled the reins. The horses only plodded, steadily away into the dark. The gate commander leaned on the narrow sill of his tower's watch-window and watched until she had become one with the dark night at moonset. At last he straightened, gave his head a shake, and turned. He called down.

"They are not coming back. Close the gate."

Neither he nor his men had any notion that well away from their gate, meanwhile, two men dropped outside the city's eastern wall, which they had scaled. They hurried into the night.

A few hours later, just after dawn, the same woman and her son returned to Shadizar. Though they were unscathed, they were forlornly bereft of horses and packs; even the woman's cloak was gone. The name she gave turned out to be false, and later no one was interested in scouring The Desert for her. Nor did the head-shaking gatemen who passed her within know that she was the fast friend of a certain huge northern hillman now assiduously sought throughout the city, and that she was considerably wealthier today than she had been on yester day.

40

Away from Shadizar, riding and leading those same four horses, wended Conan the Cimmerian and Khassek of Iranistan.

"A nicely worked out ruse and tryst, Conan," Khassek said.

"Ah, Hafiza is a good woman and a good friend, Khassek. Once you added that nice little bag of pearls to Ferhad's silver pommel, she was doubly glad to help."

"Trebly," Khassek said. "She emerged well ahead."

"Aye, and took a risk to earn her profit. Your employer sent you well supplied with wherewithal, Khassek. All that coin you've been spending, and twenty of *gold* you left in the Red Lion, and those pearls . . . are we still wealthy?"

"*We* are not, my friend. I have been up here well over a month, seeking you in both Arenjun and Shadizar, and we will be poor men or worse by the time we reach Iranistan. But, once there—"

"Umm. Once there," Conan grunted. "Aye."

And what am I doing, he mused, *heading off this way on a trip of months? Ah well . . , why not? It's a big world, and as I told Khashtris in Khauran . . . I've a lot of it to see before I think about settling!*

IV

THE MONSTERS

"Your sword is ready, my lord."

The khan smiled at his wizard, but only after bending his gaze on the sword rather in the manner of a merchant into whose stall has just wended a bumpkin with a fat purse, or of a peasant child looking at the banquet-laden board of a king.

"Ready," he murmured, that satrap of the Empire of Turan who ruled Zamboula in the name of mighty Yildiz upon his carven throne. He feared for his life, this khan of Zamboula, and for his succession through his son Jungir, and he had reason. That men plotted, he was sure. That somewhere was the Eye of Erlik, he had no doubt.

"Aye," Zafra said. "Save only that as I have said, it must be blooded to complete the spell."

He glanced downward, for neither man had given thought to the fact that ruler and mage were alone on the gloomy half-gallery that brooded over the doubly gloomy dungeon. "One regrets that we did not . . . *save* one of the Iranistani spies."

With his head slightly to one side, the khan looked at the slimmer, younger man around the great bony ridge of his accipital nose. The corners of his mouth twitched; it was a sensuous mouth. Abruptly he gave his head a swift downward jerk of decision.

"Aye," he muttered, to himself only, and his red-purfled, gold-broidered house cloak of gossamery silk swirled and fluttered susurrantly as he turned quickly to the door.

On this side, the prisoner's side, the door was a massive sheet of iron thick as a maiden's finger and heavy enough to stagger an elephant from the nighted Southern lands. Nor was its dark surface relieved by a sign of handle or lock. Folding his left hand into a mallet, Zamboula's ruler struck the slab, and stepped aside. The door had given out a dull boom and yielded not at all and Akter Khan flexed his left hand several times.

The door swung inward. The older of his two guards looked questioningly at him.

"The girl those Shanki gave me a fortnight ago, Farouz: fetch her here."

"My lord." Yet Farouz hesitated.

"You know the maid I mean, Farouz?"

"Aye, my lord. Am . . . am I to fetch her as a prisoner, my lord?"

"Oh *no,* Farouz! Tell her that her lord and master has a gift for her. But fetch her here, *now."*

"My lord!" The soldier gave his head the military jerk of acknowledgment, backed the minimal requirement of two steps, and whirled to hurry off along the brightly tiled, well-lit corridor that disguised the entrance to the second ugliest area of the khan's accursed domain; the squalid Squatter's Alley being the ugliest —a disgrace even to accursed Zamboula, built by Stygians and peopled by varicolored hybrids ruled by Hyrkanians.

Akter Khan turned back to Zafra, and almost he smiled; at least he looked pleased with himself.

"Little bitch! That bustling dog Akhimen 'Khan' of those grease-headed desert nomads brought me her as a gift and tribute, a lovely child of twelve, all virginal and formed like Stygia's sensual Derketo Herself!"

Zafra nodded. He had seen the maiden whose name his khan had instantly disregarded, to call her instead Derketari, after the pleasure-loving goddess of old Stygia. Her form and great dark eyes were enough to arouse lust in a statue, by Hanuman . . . by Derketo!

"And she acted as if she feared and hated all men, the dissemblingly formed, accursed little viper! Cower she did, and shriek when brought to my privy chamber—that very night! What an honor for a stupid uncompleted little daughter of the dunes whose mother doubtless had a mustache by the time she was eighteen! She . . ."

The khan went no further.

He would not tell Zafra the young mage or anyone else how, in the face of her cowering, her whimpering and pleading and crying out, he who was used to willing women, even actively participating ones proud and honored to be called by the khan himself, had disgraced himself and failed his manhood. Akter Khan had wanted to beat her, to put his two hands on her lovely throat and strangle her!

Instead, he had but sent her weeping from him and her too stupid to be disgraced. He called for his Argossean, Chia. Her he called Tigress, and with her he had proven himself man and khan. On the morrow he had bade his Tigress prepare and train the maiden of the Shanki—stupid child! And for a week of days she had seemed happy and was beautiful, beautiful. Lithe as a boneless serpent, she excelled at the dances those doubly damned nomads commenced teaching their girl-children when they were but three years in age. She was temptation itself, and wore the man-

45

pleasing clothing provided her as though born to it, as if in love with it, flaunting her hips; all as if pleasing a man was her only desire. Yet Akter Khan had forced himself to wait for a full week, and then a day longer the more to sharpen his appetite. He treated her then to the honor of sharing a most private supper with him, and was kind and gentle. Solicitous even, he remembered now with embarrassment. And then . . . once he rose, his eyes told her of his emotions and wholly normal intent—she was again the cowering, whining, pleading, even screaming child.

Even so he had not sent her back to her father, in disgrace. But by Tarim and the very Lord of the Black Throne . . . how much could a man bear?

A man? A khan, by Hanuman's stones!

Khan and mage waited in silence, each occupied with his thoughts and only one wondering at the thoughts of the other. Between them lay the sword; Akter Khan's sword of the jeweled hilt and, though invisible, rune-scribed tang. Below sprawled the two Iranistani, stiffening in death. Zafra's sword stood from the one, nor did it quiver but stood above him like a sentinel of death.

With both hands Akter Khan drew over his head the silver chain that held the large pearl-bordered wheel on his chest; it was set with a sizable ruby of many facets, which was surrounded, in a six-pointed star, by twelve bright yellow topazes.

"Take you this below, and my sword," he bade the mage so recently an apprentice, and him not yet thirty years of age. "Thrust the sword into the floor. That will not affect the spell?"

"No, my lord."

"Hang this then," Akter said with a brief nod, "from its guard, and fetch up the other sword."

Without question Zafra took sword and pendant. Hitching up the left hem of his robe while he descended, stepping across the corpse of the second Iranistani slain, he paced to within a step of the other dead man. His first thrust failed to anchor the satrap's blade in the floor of hard-packed black earth, so long cemented by human blood. He used both hands on his second attempt, and the sword was fixed. He hung his ruler's chain and pendant over the guard, prettily draped and glinting as it swung in air, tinging gently against the blade, yellow gold on silvery steel.

Both his hands and some exertion were required to force the other sword from the body of its victim, so deeply had the fell weapon imbedded itself. Zafra paused to stoop and wipe the blade, with care, in the dead man's long black hair. It was dirty, but removed blood and incidentally oiled the blade. A servant would give it proper attention, later.

The young mage mounted the steps. As he approached the landing that broadened rightward into the semi-gallery, he saw the girl appear in the door. The entirety of Farouz's unhandsome, helmet-surmounted face was visible behind her, even from Zafra's lack of vantage; so short was this beautiful maiden of twelve.

Akter Khan turned at the sound of her gasp.

"Ah," he said, "my lovely desert flower! Come you in, pretty Derketari, and see what I have for you." He reached for her hand.

Beauties at twelve and raging beauties at thirteen, it was said of the daughters of the sands; and mothers at fifteen and raging hags at five-and-twenty. And this girl was twelve.

Zafra was unable not to stare at her. He took in her mass of shining black hair, laced with pearls so that it was as the night sky besprent with stars; her sweet oval face with its cavalry archer's bow of a mouth, stained crimson and shining; the great round beauty of her eyes that were like staring down into a well by night a moment after moonrise. And at least they had got those voluminous Shanki garments of scarlet off her!

Her breastplates were of gold, and from each cup the tiniest golden chains dangled so that pendent gems danced before her and gently thumped her tiny belly with her slightest movement. Well below her navel, her girdle consisted only of three strands of cloth-of-gold braided into a cord no thicker than her smallest finger. From it shimmered down an arm's length of snowy gauze sewn to white silk with pale blue thread; this pretense of a skirt was in width but the length of her hand. The strip of cloth was hemmed between her ankles, and the strip behind was only a little shorter. Cloth-of-gold straps climbed her lovely legs, criss-crossing, from soft little ankle boots of red felt sewn with pearls. The gaiters were tied off just at the lovely child's knees.

She might, Zafra mused, have been one of those tender young virgins with whose blood incantations had been writ on a sort of parchment made of serpents' skin; incantations Zafra had read, and committed to memory without his mentor's knowledge.

The twelve-year-old gift of the Shanki wore only two decorations: a garnet-set tribal rite-ring of camel's hair braided with one strand of her own tresses, and the little silver-and-opal pendant with which she had come to the satrap. On a silver chain of passing delicacy, the pendant hung in the center of the slight swell of her breast.

She stared, huge-eyed, past Zafra at the two bodies below. She seemed unaware that her lord had taken her hand in his hairy one.

Reaching the landing, Zafra pressed his own sword into the hand of Farouz, that it might be outside the dungeon. Zafra stood back and seemed to blend into the wall at the head of the stair.

"M . . . my lord! To such a place—? Those *men!*" The Shanki maiden's voice quavered with her trembling.

"Rejoice!" the khan bade her. "They are Iranistani, spies sent against us by a king whose mind is set on conquest! Yet one was a seer, and he made the happy prophecy that of you anon shall be born a beautiful boy who will grow up to rule not only Zamboula, but all the magnificent empire of Turan!"

She looked at him from black eyes surrounded by black cosmetic. Her hand remained in his, and she wondered, seeming enchanted by his words, in their thrall. Behind her, Farouz quietly closed the great door, paneled with wood on its outside.

"Below stood my very own sword, symbol of my rule. So overjoyed was I that I removed my own medallion of gold and pearl and topaz and the pigeon's egg from my mother's bosom, and hung it there. It was then that the spies made at me, and had to be slain by my loyal guards who fetched you here. For I set my hand on the pommel and made vow: She who retrieves this Gem of Zamboula shall by first among the women of Zamboula and all the land round about, that the way may be prepared for the ascension of the fruit of her loins."

The stare of those great dark maiden's eyes had left the khan's face while he broidered thus, and was now fixed on the winking pendant that swung like a victor's waiting prize from the gem-hilted sword below.

"M-mer . . . my lord . . . I . . . I cannot go down *there!*"

"Why Derketari . . . Lotus of the sun-kissed desert . . . you must! Shall the prophecy of a dead man come to naught? Shall the proud tent-dwelling Shanki not then be elevated above all others and receive the favors of a great ruler-to-be—of Shanki blood?"

The child stared down at the dangling medallion. She looked again at the hawk-nosed man beside her. Now he held his honeyed tongue. She looked again upon the two corpses, and again at the pendant. It dangled, beckoned silently in flashes of gemmy fire through the flicker of smoky dungeon torches. Her tongue appeared to trace over her full lower lip.

She heard; she heard every word. Khan and mage knew she had thought of her poor desert-bound people, sun-wrinkled of face and hand ere they were twoscore years in age; of her father's pride and hopes—and doubtless his shame unto rage, did he learn she had robbed him and his people and incidentally herself of great glory and high honor because of a childish trepidation; merely a dungeon. Merely two dead men, and new-dead at that. None among the people of the desert but saw corpses long ere they were twelve. Most saw them at least once at their most hideous; sun-bloated, fly-bedecked and vulture-pecked.

"Hmp," the child whose name was not Derketari muttered to herself, "I have seen corpses afore. Hmp!"

And Akter, smiling, looked down at her over the bridge of his vulture's nose. He released her hand at the moment he felt the beginning of a tug. He wiped the hand on his multi-hued robe, for her palm was sweating.

In a gesture almost queenly, she bent her knees just a little to gather in one hand both ends of her "skirt," drawing the strip of white behind in between her legs. She descended, slowly. Her steeling herself was visible every step of her way downward.

Across the head of the steps, khan's eyes met those of mage. The khan spoke, quietly.

"You have a spell that wants completing, have you not?"

The maiden continued her descent without glanc-

ing back. The stair numbered five-and-twenty slabs
of stone; she set her felt-shod foot on the nineteenth.

"Aye, my lord."

Akter glanced down at the gift of the Shanki. She
set her left foot on the twenty-first step.

"Complete it, then, wizard, and doubly happier
will by my life, whilst for you . . . would you entertain
a very tigress this night, Zafra? A Tigress, of Argos,
whose claws are sheathed in silk?"

Below: the twenty-fourth step bore both the girl's
feet, for she hesitated there, seeking a way around,
rather than across, the naked corpse of a man she did
not know had been one of nigh incredible bravery and
daring.

"Aye, my good lord," Zafra said, and his eyes
seemed to glitter when he looked down at the girl's
back, and then at the pendant-strung sword standing
from the dungeon floor like a monument to two violent
deaths.

Three, Zafra thought, and he said very quietly, his
lips hardly moving, *"Slay him."*

Earth and water, fire and air had anointed the
sword while the ancient words were said over it. Gold
rang off steel as the sword of Akter Khan drew itself
from the earthen floor. Without hesitation, it turned
itself in air and rushed, like an arrow loosed by a strong-
thewed archer of great skill, at the little daughter of the
desert.

She had naturally glanced at it when she heard the
ting of metal on metal—as Akter Khan had glanced
at Zafra when he heard the pronoun the mage used.
Her throat was frozen in awe and terror; the khan's
was not.

"Him?" he demanded.

"Even a sword of sorcery knows no gender, my
lord. Too, any against whom my lord presently em-
ploys it are almost sure to be men."

51

Below, the girl's nascent cry broke off in a horrid indrawn gasp as the ensorcled blade proved it had no knowledge of gender or pronouns. Between and just beneath her golden breastplates it plunged, and just left of center.

The khan drew a deep long breath through his nostrils. He expelled it from his mouth in a windy sigh.

"Ah, and to think she died a virgin," he said, as though making paean at graveside, "and to such a great cause! Nor will her people know this, for not for a month will we sadly send word that she died of a fever that also nigh took the life of her beloved lord—" the khan coughed— "and was buried with honor and mourning in the Cemetery of Kings, doubtless bearing within her a royal son and taking him with her . . . *to Hell!*"

Even Zafra swallowed.

So recently wizard's apprentice; votary of abominable sorceries gained from the ancient Book of Skelos and the evil-reeking tomes of Sabatea of the golden peacock and envenomed ink; caller upon Set and dark Erlik and even those Pictish Children of Jhil of which those savages knew less than he . . . and recent slayer of his late master; all and each of these was Zafra, and yet more, for he dreamed of rule, and broad sway in future with kahns subject to him while he said "my lord" to no man . . . and yet he swallowed at the sheer evil and toxin-laden words of his employer, if not at the murder of innocent beauty.

Villain! Zafra thought. *So men will call me in times to come—and none will know that once I served the greatest villain since Thugra Khotan died in Khorshemish three thousand years agone!*

Akter Khan, having vindicated his manhood, droned on in the same deadly voice. "That sword will hang in new brackets of gold on the wall behind my throne, Zafra, and I shall steel myself not to test it now and again. And you, O genius, are henceforth Wizard of Zamboula, advisor to the Khan, quartered in the second apartment of the palace, served by him of your choice from among mine own and a girl chosen by my very self. And . . . this night . . . visited by a Tigress!"

"My lord," Zafra said with sudden oleaginousness, "is exceeding generous."

The khan looked at him, and above his eagle's beak his eyes were eagle-bright.

"Not passing generous, Zafra, Wizard of Zamboula. Not so long as you serve me."

Zafra executed one of his abbreviated bows. "I am your liege-man, Khan of Zamboula!"

"Good. Now fetch me my magnificent new sword! Next, go out into the city, and employ two ruffians for a piece of gold and the promise of three more—each—for an hour's work. That baggage below is to be stripped, mutilated, and carried from here in leathern bags—several. The bags are to be left in Squatter's Alley. That done, the two are to return to you, here, for their additional three pieces of gold." A moment the khan stared at him, and added, "Your new apartment will adjoin the throneroom, Zafra."

Stripped, mutilated so as to be unrecognizable—and then butchered like so much meat! Zafra was only just able to avoid another sickened swallow, for now the khan gazed upon him. "My lord: I understand. And their reward is to be steel, rather than gold?"

"Perhaps a celebratory cup of wine, well spiced."

"I understand, my lord. I possess such spices."

"None but I and you will know what has happed here, Wizard of Zamboula, for as I leave now I take my two guards with me. Do you follow after an interval; they will be let know that you are escorting back to her quarters that bitch I insulted with the name of thrice-sensuous Derketo! Then, mage, get you to your old apartment whilst the new is being prepared

53

for you, and see you bring me word of the Eye of Erlik ere I sup!"

Zafra nodded, and descended to wrest the sorcery-laden blade from the maiden's heart.

V

TALE OF TWO WIZARDS

Conan and Khassek had ridden due east, to cross the Zamoran border as swiftly as possible. They had discussed continuing in that direction, thus crossing the steppes and the narrow strip of land that was Turan proper; that way they could reach the coast and take ship down the Vilayet. They decided, wisely or no, against that. The overland journey south would be long and not easy. Even so it was a bit more certain than a voyage asea.

Once they were out of Zamora, then, they sunsighted and made their way south. They avoided the eastern border of Zamora's little southern neighbor, Khauran, and paced their mounts southward, through the steppes. Their gazes roved, for this land held nomads, and among those were raiders who felt most territorial about their rolling steppes.

"Conan . . ." Khassek began, rocking a little in the saddle of the big roan horse he had named Ironhead. "One night Ajhindar went to rob the home of Hisarr Zul, and you must unfortunately have chosen that same night. Ajhindar never emerged. Not alive, I mean; his corpse was found a few days later in a wadi

outside Arenjun. He had indeed died of snakebite. Only
I assumed that he had not been bitten so while wander-
ing in that wadi. At about the same time one Conan, a
Cimmerian, disappeared from Arenjun. Now, nearly
two months later, I have found you in Shadizar. And as
for Hisarr Zul . . . a few weeks ago his home burned.
Was that your work?"

"I will tell you the story," Conan said. "I was a
thief in Arenjun. I knew nothing of Hisarr Zul. I had
had a couple of successes, thieving, and was in an inn
uptown—where I did not belong. How long ago that
seems! So much has happened, since that night it began; how young *that* Conan seems! The girl I was
plying in that inn of Arenjun turned out to have a lover
who was a Watch prefect—a sub-prefect really, and he
was the jealous type. He entered the inn with his men,
and I assure you that he worked hard to provoke me.
One Kagul. At last I heard the scrape of his sword—I
was ignoring him—and I moved. There were four of
them. Kagul got himself hurt a little, and so did a couple
of others. It was then another man I didn't know slew
one, and helped me escape, for he heard more men
of the Watch coming. That was Ajhindar. I went out
the window and onto the roofs; we Cimmerians are
climbers."

"Were you wounded?"

"Not scratched."

"You Cimmerians are more than climbers!"

"Umm. It was thus, by accident, that I heard two
agents talking in an upstairs inn room; agents of Zamboula's khan. Karamek and Isparana—a woman; what
a woman!—were planning to rob a certain wizard.
Hisarr Zul. Hearing them speak of the great value of
something called the Eye of Erlik to Zamboula's Akter
Khan, and that this Hisarr Zul had it, I tarried to listen.
Once I heard them say that they would break into the
mage's house two nights thence, I departed that roof—

vowing to gain entry on the following night and beat them to the prize!

"Next day I reconnoitered, and made my plan. That night without too much difficulty I entered Zul's keep. There I found Ajhindar attacked by the awful creatures of Hisarr Zul; he had stolen their very *souls* from them, enclosing them in mirrors and breaking the mirrors. They were dull, vacant-eyed creatures of the wizard's will; stupid watchdogs with swords. I recognized Ajhindar; he had helped me the previous night. Though it were wiser to leave him to keep those 'men' busy whilst I went for the amulet, I . . . rescued him. We carved several of those creatures nicely, and my judgment is that we did them a great service!

"When Ajhindar and I exchanged names and he discovered that I too was after the Eye, he shocked me by attacking without warning. Only his slipping in the blood of one of those dead soulless horrors saved me from succumbing to the first stroke of his surprise attack! We had been conversing; we had saved each other's life, and we were friends, blood-brothers!" Conan shook his head and rode for a time in a brooding silence, grim-faced.

"He slipped, as I said. He fell against a door. A hidden chamber sprang open in that door, and two vipers came slithering out on the instant. They bit him again and again, all in seconds—in the face."

Khassek asked, "This is all?"

"No, it isn't all. He had tried to kill me yet again. Now, though he knew he must die in seconds, he tried again; he hurled those damned vipers at me! My sword was out by then, and a stroke of my blade sundered them both in air. Then I could only watch Ajhindar swell, and blacken, and die. He told me a little of the Eye, trying to recruit me to complete his mission: to fetch the amulet to Iranistan. And he died. Khassek, I was doubly saddened. I *liked* that man, respected his ability and his honor. And he had tried to slay me without warning, at a stroke. Now he had died in no decent way, but stupidly and hideously."

"Ajhindar deserved better," Khassek said.

"I went for the Eye. The two Zamboulans were in that chamber afore me. She had it: Isparana. Quite a woman, Isparana! Karamek her partner engaged me while she fled, and by the time I had disposed of him she was through a door and had closed and barred it against me."

"By now," Khassek said thoughtfully, "several of Hisarr's soulless minions were dead, and Ajhindar, and Karamek. All, one way or another, by your hand or because of you."

"Aye," Conan said without concern. "I whirled from that door and made for a window—and fell into the trap Hisarr had set for anyone coming *in* by that window! I was locked there, in iron jaws. I broke my sword and several nails trying to get free. I could not. I could only wait for him to come. He did, all gloating, and told me I must fetch back the Eye from Isparana, for him. Huh! I'd have agreed to dance all week or fly to Khitai and bring him a dragon and the emperor's beard, to get out of his keep and avoid going to prison! But he was too smart for that. By means of some powder he made me unconscious. When I awoke, he had . . . taken my *soul!* He showed it me, a little me in a mirror. If it was broken, he said, I'd be soulless forever—like that once-men that served him.

"After that I agreed, and went after Isparana—for Hisarr Zul."

Khassek heard the sound and glanced over to see Conan grinding his teeth until his jawline showed white.

"You have you . . . your soul back, Conan?"

"Aye. It was returned to me less than a fortnight ago, by the queen of Khauran."

"Khauran! Is that where you have been whilst I

searched Shadizar! But why did you come back, with such a friend in Khauran?"

"She's dead," Conan said, and rode again in silence for a time. "I saved her and Khauran from a sorcerous plot to deliver it up to Koth," he muttered at last, "and in the doing of it I . . . condemned her."

Khassek said nothing, but only rode. What adventures this northish youth had had! Into what plots he fell or thrust himself—and from them bloodily extricated himself! Ajhindar was dead. Karamek was dead. And Khauran's queen . . . and doubtless some other participants in that "sorcerous plot" the Cimmerian had alluded to so briefly. Khassek also knew that Hisarr Zul was dead. He wondered about this Isparana . . .

"Tell on, Conan. So you set off after Isparana."

"Aye. Alone, on the desert, with a single horse. I was a fool, and I was lucky. At the first oasis where I stopped, two men attacked me."

"That was lucky?"

"Aye . . . that way I gained their horses and supplies. Else the desert would have killed a foolish boy of Cimmeria, surely."

"Oh," Khassek said quietly. "And those two . . ."

"Dead."

"Of course." And let someone else try calling you "boy"! He glanced over to see that his companion was giving him a look. "Don't stare at me, Conan. You do tend to leave a bloody trail, you know."

"Crom, god of Cimmeria," Conan said while staring ahead, "breathes power to strive and slay into the soul of a Cimmerian, at birth. He takes no note of us after that. We are men."

"You . . . strive, and slay."

"Yes." After a time of silence while the horses plodded on, Conan said, "I seldom seek trouble, Khassek. It stalks me, haunts me, seeks me out." He sat up straighter and Khassek, looking across the few feet separating their horses, was treated to the sight of the swell of that mighty chest. "I do not flee it!" Conan said, to the universe.

"Sages in my land bid a man 'Take the road that waits,'" Khassek said. "It is good advice. There is little else a brave man who is also sensible can do. You caught up to Isparana?"

"Aye, eventually," Conan said dully, and did not say anything thereafter, for miles.

Khassek let his younger companion brood. The grass of the steppes was growing more and more sparse. They approached the great desert. Due south on it, Zamboula reared its walls and towers and domed palace just beyond the sand's edge. South and east of Zamboula, Iranistan sprawled at the base of a great mountain range. It was very, very far. Khassek wondered, now they had taken the road that waited, where it would lead them. He thought perhaps that Conan was reflecting similarly.

"Far down on the desert," Conan began abruptly, and Khassek physically jerked at sound of that voice from his left, "I came upon some soldiers from Samara. They were nice fellows, dully tracking a couple of thieves northward. The thieves were the two men who had also tried to rob me. I had most of their booty, with their horses—I hadn't been able to deal with their camels."

"Who can?" Khassek said, with a smile.

"Oh, I can now! At any rate, those good men also left me a few things of the booty of those they followed. And went on, warning me to stay out of a certain pass."

"The Gorge of the Sand-lich!"

"Just so. Unfortunately, I saw Isparana, miles ahead, and knew that the pass would put me much closer to her than riding up one of those damned Dragon Hills and down and then up the next and the next. I took the Gorge of the Sand-lich."

"And lived!"

"And lived, Khassek. It attacked. There was no fighting it, and my horses fled back the way we'd come. The very sands rose up. They formed a sort of figure, vaguely human, constantly amove with swirling sands —and it seized me. I was helpless as a child, and smothering. I heard a voice—its voice—it demanded to know if I were Hisarr Zul! Somehow that voice was speaking within my mind, and somehow I made reply: No, I told the monster, I was seeking to slay Hisarr Zul, as only I could." Conan glanced at his companion. "A slight exaggeration, perfume procurer for the Queen of Koth."

Khassek nodded without smiling. *So we both know how to lie,* he mused, and wondered if he might have had the presence of mind to lie when some sort of sand-demon was assiduously smothering him to death!

The sand-lich had released him then, Conan said, and told him its story: it was the eyeless ghost of Hisarr Zul's brother, and it had died here ten years before, and over those years it had gained control of the very sands. Thus it had slain any who sought to follow the pass. Blindly seeking its killer, Hisarr, it attacked and slew every traveler. The ravine-like pass was strewn with bones and clothing and weapons. For years that long shortcut through the maddening Dragon Hills had been taken only by fools or those who had no knowledge of the moaning sand-horror that haunted it.

"Hisarr and his brother—he had been Tosya Zul, the Sand-lich—had for years studied the ancient learning; the arcane knowledge of long-dead wizards. They had learned secrets known to no others who abide among men; the demonic lore of formless horrors that abide lurking about the hills of the world and in the very blackness between the worlds, in dark caverns where men go not and even in the ever-shifting deserts baked by the sun to eternity. They sought power. As they brewed abominations in their house in Zamboula, the khan learned, and sent men to take them. They fled with sacks of wealth, but left their lore—so Tosya Zul thought. He had actually risked his life to hurry back and save Hisarr. They fled, leaving behind priceless treasures of awful knowledge. They fled into the night, like dogs—rich dogs!

"Hisarr had lied to his brother. In the Dragon Hills, Tosya discovered that Hisarr had brought some of the old writings with him. They quarreled. In the night, Hisarr slew him and burned out his eyes with white-hot coins, that he might not be able to see his way to the next world. And Hisarr went on up to Arenjun. There he perfected his means of stealing men's souls, as I learned to my dismay—worse than dismay! He would use that to gain control of certain officials, you see, thereby soon controlling a city. And then a country, all through the blackmail of the souls in his possession. After that . . ." Conan shrugged. "Another country, I suppose, and then another, perhaps. For ten years the Sand-lich that had been Tosya Zul knew agony, and slew all who sought to pass him by. Jackals had eaten his flesh, and though he was dead he knew, and felt! The lich lamented his decade of anguish, dead and yet not dead, and even stated itself that I must realize it could no longer be sane. Oh I realized it, all right!"

"You stood and talked thus with . . . sand? You saw this dead wizard?"

"I saw an ever-shifting pillar of sand. The voice spoke inside my head. It told me the means of regaining my own soul: I must prevent the mirror's being broken, for that condemned me forever. Yet I must cause it to be broken—by the wearer of a crown. It said that there is power in all those who rule, power that not even they themselves know. First, though, I had to regain the mirror. For you see I had little doubt but that Hisarr Zul would prove treacherous, once I had returned the amulet to him. I did not believe that he would return my soul to me, and let me go. The Sand-lich told me how I might free those soulless creatures of his brother."

Khassek looked at the Cimmerian, and saw that his profile had become the stern-visaged statue of a grim stone god while he laid out that horrid means of giving those un-men rest, and on the instant Khassek knew that Conan had done it: the head of the wizard must be severed, and the skull stuffed up with earth, and its ears and nostrils, and that head must then be consumed, utterly, by flame.

"Ah. And the keep of Hisarr Zul burned, and all in it. That was your work, Conan?"

"It was," the narrow-eyed statue said. "The flame spred from his head, once the very bone was reduced to calc and ash."

"How did you best him?"

"The lich of Tosya told me several means of accomplishing that, and all but one were too horrible to contemplate. I——"

"Tell me," the Iranistani said, with gooseflesh on his arms, "those several means that were too horrible even for you to use against one so horrible as Hisarr Zul!"

"I remember them," Conan said, dull-voiced. "I will never forget. Upon the death of his brother, the lich told me, he would at last be freed of his life-in-death, able to depart the gorge and go to . . . wherever such evil souls go, at death. He told me what I must do, and I asked for another way, and another. Though he flew into rage after rage, I reminded him that I was his means of gaining freedom; of destroying Hisarr Zul." And Conan quietly, dully recounted those means:

Hisarr Zul could be slain by strangulation with the

hair of a virgin slain with bronze, and made woman in death after the hair was removed. Upon hearing that, Conan said, he felt his stomach lurch—as Khassek's did now. What an abomination! Or the waters of the Zarkheba River would slay Hisarr, for they flowed with venom; the problem was that the Zarkheba was far, far away in southwestern Kush. Or he could be slain by iron forged in Stygia over a fire of bones, for from that dark and sorcery-haunted land of leering demons and mages had come most of the spells learned by the two wizards.

"Gods and blood of the gods!" Khassek said, with a shudder he did not seek to conceal.

"Aye. Finally he told me also that Hisarr might be bested by turning his own magicks back on him. That I saw as impossible—but that is what I did, in the end."

"How?"

"I will not tell you," Conan said calmly, and Khassek did not ask again.

Conan was bereft of steeds and supplies. Tosya Zul solved that problem—to him; he had no care for the Cimmerian save as his weapon against his brother. A sandstorm rose. It lifted Conan up; he was blown and carried by it many miles south, to an oasis. For that oasis the lich thought Hisarr Zul was making; Conan knew that it was Isparana who approached, for now he was ahead of her, in the path of her and her camels.

"The wizard had given me a harmless copy of the amulet. I was able to make the exchange without her knowledge. Then . . . well, due to this and that—she is some woman indeed, Khassek, and good with a sword too, treacherous as . . . as Hisarr! Due to this and that as I was saying, we were overtaken by a caravan. It was from Khawarizm, and they were slavers. Soon Isparana and I were heading north again as traveling companions—in coffle."

"You have been enslaved, amid all else?"

"Aye," Conan said calmly. "Not without slaying several of their caravan guards, I assure you!"

More corpses in his wake, Khassek thought, and said nothing.

"It was that damned Isparana who laid me low! She tried to escape, then. They caught her. They put us both in coffle. And northward we both marched, chained. Each of us had an amulet—she did not see mine, and did not know that hers was not real, valueless to the Khan of Zamboula."

"How in the name of Erlik and Drood did you escape a Khawarizmi slave caravan, on the open desert . . . chained?"

"Drood is a god I am unfamiliar with," Conan said, and his seeming calm was maddening to his companion.

"A most ancient god still worshiped in Iranistan," Khassek said shortly.

"I will admit it," Conan said. "I did not escape. I mentioned the five soldiers of Samara I had met previously. We met them again; they were on their way back. I shouted and shouted, and Captain Arsil of Samara got us freed. Because I am too kind for my own good, I caused Isparana to be freed, too." He smiled. "The last I saw of her, she was headed south, being 'escorted' to Zamboula by Arsil and his men—who knew nothing of our real purpose, Isparana's and mine—whilst I rode north with her camels and horses."

Khassek laughed aloud. "And so she took the false Eye back to Akter Khan, who doubtless wears it even now, believing it is his own sorcery-wrought protection! For it is peculiarly and particularly attuned only to him, Conan, by sorcery."

Conan shook his head. "No," he said, and Khassek stared. There was *more?* "To ascertain that the one I brought him was indeed the real one, Hisarr wrought a spell that caused the copy to melt into formless slag.

I regret that. Even for Isparana, I would not wish such pain or, if she survived it, such a burn-scar between her breasts. They were good ones."

Like his fellow Iranistani before him, from whom Conan had picked up the habit, Khassek responded to that disappointment by uttering a single word: "Damn!"

Conan glanced at him, and for once those volcanic blue eyes were almost placid. "Aye," he said.

They rode on, and they were entering the desert. Even the sun seemed hotter. Scraggly plants erupted here and there from yellow-white soil, tenaciously clinging to earth and life. Sun and sky brightened, seemingly reflecting the increasing paleness of the terrain beneath their horse's hooves.

"Conan," Khassek said. "You . . . wouldn't also happen to know about the destruction of a certain mighty tower of one Yara, priest of Arenjun, would you?"

Though a little shiver took him at memory of that sorcerous encounter of but a quarter-year ago, Conan chuckled. "Perhaps Yara angered the god he served and his gemmy tower was struck by a lightning bolt, Khassek."

"Perhaps. And mayhap I am in the company of a truly great thief—and bane of wizards!"

Conan only chuckled, but as they rode on, he wondered. Bane of wizards? It was true that he had several interesting experiences with several wizards, and products of wizardry . . . and survived, while they did not. He pondered that, while they rode southward into the shining sand.

VI

THE WIZARD OF
ZAMBOULA

Far, far south of Conan and the Iranistani, on that same desert and indeed but a few days north of Zamboula, four soldiers of Samara awoke to find that one of their number was missing. So was the "guest" they had been escorting. The Samaratan captain pounded fist into palm.

"Blast and drought! I'd have staked my sword arm on Sarid! Tarim's beard—that damned witch . . ."

"Aye, Captain," one of his men said. "Sarid was eyeing her from the first, when we took her and the Cimmerian from the Khawarizmi coffle. In truth Sarid appointed himself her guard. None of us thought to note them or listen to the words they exchanged while we rode, and camped, and rode again."

"And now the slut has persuaded him to ride off with her! Sarid! He has deserted us . . . deserted duty and king . . . for that treacherous Zamboulan woman! Tarim damn the day we let that Cimmerian foist her on us!"

"Peradventure she will die of that burn . . ."

"Which we salved and bandaged for her with such tender care! Hmp! No such luck, Salik. Her kind lives forever."

"Captain Arsil . . . she did continue to swear that she was an agent of the Khan of Zamboula. And that the beasts and supplies the Cimmerian took were hers. Too, she never left off claiming that he had an amulet that belongs to her khan. And the one she had . . ." the Samaratan soldier broke off with a quaver in his voice. He made a ward-sign and muttered the name of a god.

Captain Arsil's head jerked. "And the Cimm— Conan said otherwise. Now I wonder . . . have she and Sarid ridden north, Kambur?"

"It appears so," the third soldier said.

"So. She turns her back on Zamboula, and with us nearly there. To try to track down Conan the Cimmerian, no doubt! Mayhap that rogue with the weird eyes lied to us, at that. I admit I liked the man . . . all for an amulet, eh? Kambur, I'd hazard that poor foolish Sarid will never see the new moon. That Cimmerian is big enough to eat him up. Ah, poor lad! By Tarim, I hope Conan cuts that accursed witch into dog food!"

"Arsil . . . Captain . . . shall we . . . follow them?"

"No! By Tarim, no! I have no mind to spend the rest of my life on this desert, or keep you here. We have the stolen goods we were sent after . . . most of them . . . and I do not look forward to telling that girl of Sarid's what happened to him." Captain Arsil groaned. "Or his mother . . . or the Commander!"

"Uh . . . mayhap they were all better off—and we too—did we claim that Sarid was slain. Heroically. Then . . ."

"And have him somehow turn up in Samara next day or next month or next year? Oh no, Kambur, and you will never make sergeant with that kind of muddy thinking. No! And—Kambur." Arsil's good-looking dark face took on an expression of thoughtfulness. "Best we make absolutely no mention of either Conan of Cimmeria or the accursed Isparana whilst we are passing through Zamboulan territory."

Kambur, an Iranistani in the employ of Samara, nodded. Arsil was right, thinking wisely—though Kambur would bet his boots that big straight-nosed man with the sky-colored eyes had tricked them all. Kambur would not miss Sarid all that much . . . though he was sorry that Isparana was gone. He had been happy to leave her in Sarid's care, knowing that Sarid had a girl at home, and their betrothal announced and registered. Kambur had cherished a few notions and hopes himself, about the Zamboulan witch they had found with Conan in the Khawarizmi slave caravan.

So Arsil fears for Sarid, does he? Kambur gave his helmeted head a jerk. Sarid be damned! Let that big barbarian look out! Isparana was woman enough, temptress enough, to bring even him to his knees! And how she hated the Cimmerian!

The paraphernalia cluttering the spacious room ranged from the commonplace to strange, through exotic to weird and truly horrid. The young mage in the room was strange only in that he was young. He was scrying, and he smiled as he studied his glass. His brown cap was of a strange tall design; otherwise he wore a plain white tunic, long, over tan leggings. A pendant swung on his chest with his movements. The pendant was a large wheel bordered with pearls; in its center flashed a many-faceted ruby surrounded by twelve sunny topazes forming a six-pointed star. The pendant was a gift of his khan. So was one of the two rings he wore.

Smiling without showing his teeth or softening his eyes, he turned from his scrying glass. On shoes of soft red felt he crossed the chamber to a tall paneled door. He thumped on it twice with a single knuckle, and returned, whistling, to his glass.

Within minutes the door was opened and another man appeared. He was balding, and though hair ran down his cheeks and jawline on both sides, it was shaved down the center to bare his cleft chin. A design of tangled vines, wrought in scarlet stitchery, decorated his dark brown robe at hem, cuffs and neck. A silver chain rustled on his breast and he too was shod in red felt. His wrist was encircled by a bracelet of copper.

Neither he nor the mage spoke. While he held the door, the mage paced past without glancing at him from those cold, hard brown stones of eyes.

The youthful wizard entered a sprawling, lofty hall under a sky-painted ceiling supported by columns carved to represent acacia trees. The hall was dominated by the dais at its rear wall; the dais by the great fruitwood chair there, etched with silver. The man seated in the chair was neither handsome nor ugly, neither fat nor thin, though he had a paunch. His long yellow robe was topped by one of figured blue silk obviously imported at expense from far Khitai. It was interestingly cut and slashed to display the saffron-hued garment beneath.

As he approached the throne, the young mage made a tight gesture.

The enthroned man responded instantly to the signal: "Leave us, Hafar."

Leaving open the door to the chamber of the mage, the older man crossed, brown robe whispering, the sprawling throneroom. He passed through a small door in the wall opposite, and closed it behind him.

The enthroned man gazed with dark, dark eyes at the mage.

"My lord Khan, the Eye of Erlik is once again on its way south from Arenjun."

"What? Good!"

"I escry that it is in the possession of an Iranistani

70

and that same one who has it of Hisarr Zul . . . and Isparana."

Akter Khan's face lost a bit of ruddiness. "An Iranistani! Erlik protect! Zafra: *Which of them has the Eye?*"

The wizard stood before the throne now, at the base of the dais whose steps were carpeted in blue the color of the khan's over-robe or surcoat. His gaze slewed to the wall behind and to the left of the throne. A sword hung there, sheathed, alone on the wall. Gems flashed on the sword's hilt. The sheath was supported by two braces that were of gold, or gilded. The mage's cold snake's eyes met his khan's gaze.

"Alas my lord, my powers are not unlimited. The two travel close together and I can be certain only that the amulet travels with them. Only were they to separate would I know which bears the Eye."

"You are well kept, Zafra," Akter Khan said. "Your chamber adjoins the very throneroom. At your signal I emptied this room and at your gesture I dismissed my vizir! You want for nothing here. I want more information."

Zafra felt it wise to bow—however briefly and shallowly. "No man in the world could tell you so much as I already have, lord Khan of Zamboula. This I swear by my beard and my power! The Eye of Erlik gives off an aura, because it is an object created in sorcery. Were it among three persons, though, or even ten, not even the most adept of those famed sorcerers of demon-shadowed Stygia could say which of them held it, until he parted from the others. I have the amulet located, lord Khan. I can keep watch as it approaches. I shall. It is far from us, now. Whichever of those two men has it, we can take it easily once they are near enough. Meanwhile Akter Khan: *they* approach *us,* and we need take no action. I shall watch."

71

"Unless they should swerve to eastward, to avoid Zamboula on their way to Iranistan!"

"I shall maintain watch, my lord. I believe that they are south of the Road of Kings. Yet should they turn eastward, toward the sea, there is no way we can get men there before them."

Akter Khan's fingers drummed the silver-threaded arm of his chair of state; his nails clicked. "Watch those two, Zafra, and report to me thrice daily, no less. Sooner, if they change direction or you ascertain which of them carries the Eye."

"Yes, Khan of Zamboula. Of course. At least we now know that the amulet is again wending its way toward us."

"Or toward Iranistan. That must not happen!"

"They are weeks away, my lord Akter. We will know. My lord need not worry. I will keep you apprised."

"Ummm. And still we know naught of Karamek and Isparana! Plague take—Hafar! *Hafar!* Best I make another contribution to the temples of Erlik and of Yog, for surely some god is angry with me and I cannot believe it is Hanuman! Hafar!"

When Hafar entered Zafra the mage was departing, and the Khan of Zamboula had twisted about to stare at the sword on the wall. He did so several times daily, and Hafar wondered at its meaning for his lord, and at Zafra's influence.

Zafra, meanwhile, closed his door behind him and leaned against the panels to stare at the woman who waited. Even as he secured the door, she smiled and let her single garment drop from her in an amethystine puddle at her feet.

"Chia," he breathed. "You should *not* come here. Must I take to locking the corridor door?"

She smiled lazily and flaunted a hip. On it lay a delicate gold chain, which was slung across the lower

72

curve of her deep-naveled belly. It was all she wore now save for her rings, and it, like Zafra's pendant, was a gift of her lord the khan.

"But who can stay away?" she asked softly. "Come, and make your Tigress purr."

The man most favored by the Khan of Zamboula went to the woman most favored by that same khan.

VII

ISPARANA OF ZAMBOULA

"Easy, Ironhead; we are out now, boys. Even as you said, Conan! All the way through that haunted pass and no sign of ghost or sand-lich. I apologize for doubting. Why man, you are a hero! This is a full day and more off the journey from Zamboula up into Zamora!"

Conan nodded, rocking with the movements of his horse. He felt heroic, conveniently forgetting that sheer rashness and illogical stubbornness had sent him riding through that pass of death two months before. He had put out of mind the fact that only luck or some other whimsical god had kept him from being merely another victim of the ghost that had so long haunted the gorge slicing through the Dragon Hills.

"First," he said, "travelers will have to be assured that the pass is safe. I believe it best that we just keep the knowledge to ourselves, Khassek. Zamboulans might ask too many questions."

Riding just ahead and left of him, the Iranistani nodded. "I understand. The amulet. I would feel much more comforted if you showed it me, Conan."

Conan's throat spat up a short laugh that reminded

the other man of a lion's cough. "And I'd feel more comfortable if I could believe that you are content for both of us to fetch it to your . . . employer, Khass! You saw me go off into the sands to dig it up. We have it."

"Conan, I like you. You are a fighter, and you have some sense, and I think you are an honest lad. In—"

"If I had more sense I'd doubtless be less honest," Conan said, his face darkening at the word "lad."

"I do not believe it. In any case, I know my lord. I know that he will reward us both. I have no reason to wish you ill, or try to gain the amulet from you. Even were we enemies, I should prefer to cross the desert with you than alone!"

Abruptly Conan laughed. "I can think of one who wishes me ill *and* has reason to try to gain the amulet of me . . . preferably off my corpse!"

"That Zamboulan woman."

"Aye!"

"You believe that she was wearing the amulet when Hisarr Zul made it melt into a blob of yellow metal."

"With three gems imbedded in it. I'd not have expected her to take it off. Poor Isparana! A good thief, and so clever—and so good to look upon too, Khass."

"A nice reward for her thievery, I'm thinking," Khassek said, ignoring the fact that he, sent to steal the amulet for one other than its owner, rode in the company of a thief. "And you did not have her."

"No."

"Tsk. And now that pretty bosom of hers may be burn-scarred."

"It may."

"You do not, ah, sound too . . . sorrowful, my friend."

The horses paced south, leaving the Gorge of the Sand-lich and the Dragon Hills behind them. Their two pack horses plodded along in their wake, surely insulted to be turned from riding beasts into sumpter animals, every second day. Only Conan's fine mount seemed to recognize its unimaginative name; Khassek called "Ironhead" whichever horse he rode at the time. At least that was what he told Conan was the meaning of the Iranistani word by which he called the animal.

"She tried to kill me, Khass. Twice. And then again, come to think: three times! And left me for dead or to be slain by those Khawarizmi slavers. After I had saved her from them, mind! It was only because she so treacherously struck me down that we both put in years trudging along in their slave coffle."

"Years!"

"So it seemed," the Cimmerian growled. "A day without freedom is a year, to a Cimmerian."

"Conan . . . about the Eye. Since Hisarr combined its components to destroy the copy—he must have seen the original." Khassek adjusted the crotch of his baggy trousers. "At the time, I mean."

"That was my mission for him," Conan said. "He had placed a time limit on me; I had to take the Eye back to him. Of course he saw it. He just did not get it."

"I weep for him. But in that case . . . Conan . . . it seems strange to me that after you had returned to Arenjun with it, and shown it to Hisarr, and slain him . . . it seems strange that you would then leave Arenjun again, to ride out into the desert to bury the Eye."

"Questioning my word, are you Khass?"

Khassek twitched his horse's rein a little more leftward and looked back over his shoulder at the other man, who was adjusting his sweatband. Khassek was not all that far ahead; Ironhead's right flank practically rubbed the nose of Conan's mount. The Cimmerian had given the chestnut-brown animal the name Chestnut. It served. The other one he called Horse.

"With great care, you son of a Cimmerian, since you are behind me!"

Conan smiled, then chuckled. "All right. If my story were a bucket it wouldn't hold two drops. I did not bury the Eye of Erlik in the desert."

"You had it hidden in Arenjun?" Khassek slapped his head. "With the horses!"

Conan shook his head. "It has been on my person all the time, Khassek."

Khassek swore, in two languages and by four several gods. Conan grinned and nodded appreciatively. Swearing was good for a person, and some ability at variety in languages helped.

"But why—"

"It seemed a good idea to be sure that we remained both fugitives, and out of Shadizar—and past Arenjun too—before I let you know I had the thing, Khass. With only the two of us, together, I think I can handle you."

"Crafty hillborn barbarian!" The Iranistani was grinning.

"Tricky kidnaping mountaineer!" Conan, too, grinned, and wagged his head. And the horses plodded on, ever southward. Behind the pack-animals, the line of razorbacked hills called Dragons seemed to shrink, to clump together, to diminish.

"Ha! Hold my horse!"

Hurling his mount's reins forward over its head to trail the ground, Khassek swung a leg up and over and sprang from his saddle. His dagger flashed into his hand as he ran; Conan watched him throw it. The abandoned horse stood staring. The dagger flew as aimed, and Conan nodded, pursing his lips. Best he remembered Khassek's ability at knife-throwing!

Grinning, the Iranistani returned, boots crunching in the sand. He carried his prize: a hideous little lizard.

"Fresh meat for dinner," he announced.

"Ugh," Conan said.

"Feast on that accursed salt-meat then," Khassek said, and forced the lizard through the loop on the side of his boot before he flung himself up and settled into the high-cantled saddle.

Conan said nothing; he knew the lizard would smell as good as the finest beef when they roasted it over a couple of the camel droppings they had picked up, and that he would love it. They rode on. The sun stared down at them, and its great eye burned. Conan's nose had peeled days ago. And again yesterday.

"Conan: about this Isparana. After all you told me she did—treacherous bitch!—you still had her released from slavery to your . . . Samaratan friends."

"I wish slavery on no one, Khass. She served her lord, and I was her rival, her enemy. *Am* her enemy, I mean! She tried to serve him well. I had the power to free her or to condemn her to slavery. I do not hate her so much as that, and did what I had to do."

"What you felt you had to do."

Conan pulled off his headband, squeezed sweat from it. "It is the same, to a Cimmerian." He restored the headband, blinking.

"I would not have had her freed," the Iranistani admitted reflectively. "It is not the same, to an Iranistani."

"I will remember, Khassek of Iranistan."

"Conan!" Khassek's tone was accusing; mock-petulant.

"Just stay a little ahead where I can see you, Khassek my friend."

Days and shimmering, sun-baked days later Conan had not responded to Khassek's queries concerning the whereabouts of the amulet; Khassek thought he had guessed; and he still rode a little ahead when they emerged from the long "ravine" formed by two dunes. Water was low, and both men had at last admitted nervousness.

It was the Iranistani who first met the couple riding from the opposite direction. All three were much surprised and disconcerted, and two of their horses. Harness jingled and leather creaked as hands tightened to jerk at reins.

From behind the Iranistani, Conan saw beyond him a twin-bearded soldier in a peaked helmet and, beside and just behind him, a smaller rider muffled in a jallaba whose sand hood covered the face. It was from that invisible face that the first words issued.

"Sarid! It's he—Conan!"

"What the—" Khassek was reaching across himself to draw steel even as he spoke. His horse pranced nervously. The Iranistani's full-cut trousers, yellow and filthy, fluttered a little in a slight breeze—warm.

Sarid drew first, catalyzed by his companion's words.

The Iranistani's Ilbarsi knife had not quite cleared its sheath when Sarid's swordblade struck, drawing, across his face. Khassek spluttered through a spray of blood and the wind of the words he could not form turned the blood to red froth. Tatters of tongue and lip fell down the front of his surcoat.

He reeled back; Sarid's backstroke slammed his edge into the side of the other man's face with a *chok* sound.

Sarid had to twist his blade free hurriedly, as the Iranistani fell back and sidewise out of his saddle. His face was a hideous ruin, the mouth destroyed by the first stroke and the whole side of his head by the second. He struck the sandy ground with a sound like that of a bag of grain dropped by a careless dock-worker—dropped wetly into a puddle. Khassek flopped, twitched, made hideous wet sounds.

Only seconds had passed. The dry warm wind whipped garments. Conan was sure that Khassek would not suffer long and knew too that he would never let the man live with such a face.

Khassek's horse, in the mouth of the narrow passage betwixt the dunes, reared when Sarid tried to spur forward. He had struck at his companion's shouted words, and struck without a thought; now the trained

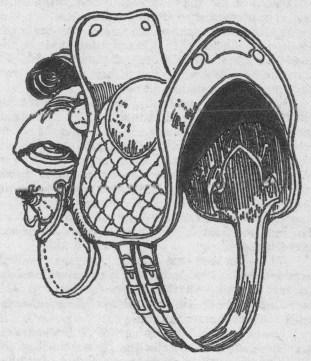

Saddle

soldier recognized the real quarry. Isparana had told him all about the big dogson Cimmerian. Sarid tried to spur past the rearing riderless horse. It backed into Conan's mount. The Cimmerian cursed and clung to rein and swiftly drawn sword. Remembering the lead-rein of the sumpter horses, he reached back to force it up off his saddle's high back. The leathern strap dropped; the animals stood where they were, though restlessly.

"Accursed dumb . . . beast—get . . . AWAY!" Sarid stormed, striving to spur past the riderless Iron-head. The horse neighed and half-reared again.

Behind Sarid, Isparana had thrown back her hood. She, too, now held sword in fisted hand on which the knuckles showed pale and bony. On the ground Khas-sek twitched. His horse remained between Conan and Sarid, at the very mouth of the ravine.

More seconds rushed by. Leaning out from his saddle only a little, Conan struck Khassek's beast; he twitched his wrist at the last instant so that the flat of his sword loudly slapped Ironhead's rump.

With a cry almost human, the animal lurched blindly forward. Thus its shoulder struck Sarid's mount just back of the arching, long-maned neck—and Iron-head kept moving. He forced his way on, and his shoulder and then saddle nearly tore Sarid's leg off. The man screamed in a voice as high and un-human as the animal's.

Then Ironhead was bolting past Isparana, and Sarid was no longer in control of horse or self, reeling, his face twisted, and Conan kicked his mount with both heels—which he then clamped. The muscles bulged in the Cimmerian's legs.

His horse jerked forward to follow the animal it knew and had followed all the way down from Shadizar. And Conan struck from the right, across Chestnut's neck, across his own chest, and into Sarid's left arm.

The blade went deep. Both horses were amove, in opposite directions. The swordblade held, imbedded in muscle and bone. Conan's arm was twisted across himself and pressed back against his chest. His horse kept moving. Conan grunted and his body twisted. The horse strove on. Conan, already unbalanced, at last let go his hold in desperation—too late. Conan fell.

The left rear hoof of Sarid's big bay horse missed the Cimmerian's head by the breadth of two fingers.

The bay lurched into a trot, free of restraint, for Sarid's left arm was half severed and fountaining blood in a glistening wash around the blade that stood out from it. The horse galloped past Conan's pack-animals, which were still within the little pass betwixt the dunes. There was not enough room; the bay did not care. Sarid was wiped from the saddle by a protruding pack. He fell heavily. The sword standing from his arm seemed to shorten.

Sarid, out of desire for Isparana and spurred into a reasonless fever by lust, blandishments and promises of reward beyond even her enticing self, had abandoned his oath as a soldier of Turan. He had attacked mindlessly, had slain Khassek, a complete stranger . . . and had lost his left arm and the use of his left leg.

Now a prancing, panicky sumpter horse stepped on his chest, and into it.

Conan, meanwhile, plopped heavily to the sand. Twisting even as he struck, he was up in two seconds. He had lost both horse and sword and narrowly missed being stepped on. He was angered to an extent that approached madness. Facing back the way he had come, he gazed at the rump of Isparana's horse. Its long black tail fluttered behind like a banner, a taunting pennon.

The big Cimmerian snarled and did the insane. He grasped that long flowing tail in both hands, and he set himself.

83

In an instant his heels were deep in sand and horsehair was cutting into his fingers.

With a squeal and a jerk that rocked the woman in its saddle, the animal came to a halt. It strained, snorting—and Conan held!

Its rider, twisting in a high-backed saddle of leather over wood, leaned back to cut at Conan with her sword, which was curved in the eastern manner; a drawing blade. Her mount's tail was beautifully long and the straining man was well back. He was just out of reach of her swordtip. She tried again.

The reshifting of her weight rearward on her mount, along with her violent movements and Conan's dragging at its tail, brought the horse up into an air-pawing rear.

Grinning like a wolf, Conan released his grip just as Isparana tumbled onto him.

They rolled, man and robed woman. Both cursed. The offended horse looked back with large, rolling eyes that showed considerable white and seemed to mirror shocked sensibilities. Then it turned away, to exchange stares with the pack animals. One of them—the one with blood on its right forehoof—whickered. So did Isparana's horse. Several yards beyond it, Conan's chestnut looked back. Harness jingled as it bobbed its head. It too made that low, gentle whickering sound, then lifted its muzzle and whinnied. A quarter mile away, Ironhead heard and slowed to a stop. It turned to gaze back the way it had come. It bobbed its head. The horse neighed loudy.

Isparana and Conan floundered and rolled in the sand. When they came to pause, she was atop him. She rose up, kneeling-sitting astride him in a flash of yellow-trousered knees, and her sword rushed up. Hate and kill-rage made her eyes ugly and the sun flashed fire from them as well as from her crescent blade.

Conan saw the glitter of those hating, mad eyes,

though the flash of her sword was of far more immediate interest. His arms shot up, just as she struck.

Her wrist slammed down into his right hand like an oar into its groove. Her whole arm shivered with the impact, and was arrested as if she'd struck stone. Conan's arm held, staying hers, and his hand closed. It tightened.

His other hand drew her dagger.

Isparana groaned and her scimitar fell away as her wristbones grated and her fingers flexed involuntarily open. She cried "NO!" on seeing her own dagger come flashing at her, and then he struck—to slash open her jallaba, all down the front.

Under the desert robe she wore naught but a cotton bandeau and the slashed, lowslung drawstring trousers. Both were of a bright yellow that contrasted beautifully with her tawny skin. Conan saw no scar on her bilobate chest. He tossed away the dagger, and pulled. She fell onto him and he rolled over once. He was atop her now, staring into her eyes. When she bit at his hand, he let go with the other long enough to slap her.

"NO, damn you!" she cried and she writhed wildly.

Khassek of Iranistan lay still, and Sarid, Turanian soldier of Samara lay still; and Isparana of Zamboula writhed and panted and soon Conan saw the ugly burn-scar on her hip. The uncaring desert sun smiled brightly down on them and soon sweat strained the sands and after a time Isparana's curses became moans and little cries, and after another while they took on a different note, for she was no girl.

VIII

STRANGE RELATIONSHIPS

Southward on the desert rode a man and a woman. All about them rolled low dunes forming shallow ravines, and above the sun was an enemy that turned the sky into a brass cauldron. The horses they bestrode paced slowly, heads down. To the back of the woman's saddle was attached the long lead-line of four more horses. Two were saddled in addition to being laden with packs; the other pair bore even larger packs.

The man was most definitely a man, though quite young. Tall and burly with massive shoulders straining the white burnoose he wore, he could have been a wrestler. None would have called him handsome—nor could he have been called ugly, with his face in repose. A sweatband of yellow cotton circled his head above his brows and confined his mane of black hair. His face was dark, as were his hands, though the long wedge of chest displayed by his robe's slashed front was of a lighter hue. He had been riding with the legs of his loose desertman's leggings drawn high up on his thighs; now, deciding he had taken enough sun on his muscular legs, he drew the dun-hued leggings down over his boots. The eyes that stared out of that sun-darkened face beneath the jet mop and garish sweat-band were strange, on this southern desert of Turan's expanding empire; they glowed with a smoldering blue that imitated the sun-hot sky.

The day was hot, as every day was hot. Pale sand reflected the light of the snarling sun in a billion diamond-like flashes so that the world of the desert was both hotter and bright with glare. The horses plodded. Man and woman rode slumped, their lips compressed and their eyes fixed ahead. Clothing clung to sweat-filmed bodies.

The woman was most definitely a woman, and older than the man. Her face was longish, with molded cheekbones and staring dark eyes and a slightly curved nose above pronounced lips and a chin that was center-holed by a round dimple. None could call her truly beautiful; only another woman might call her less than pretty, and that not in truth. Her ballooning leggings or *sirwal*, a dirt- and sand-soiled yellow that was sweat-dark in patches, were both side-slit and torn. Sliced from her jallaba, her sand-hood lay across her thighs, for the dirty white robe had been raggedly slashed and torn across so that it ended well above her knees. The full-blousing sirwal vanished into red boots that rose above the considerable swell of her calves. A superb mass of waving black hair glinted blue and purplescent in the angry sunlight; it crowded her face with curls and toppled over the dirty old sweatband she wore; it had been the man's. The unfettered halves of her bosom were as restless animals beneath her jallaba's slashed front that displayed much of their curves; her confining bandeau had become a man's sweat-band.

Her tawny skin, he had ruthlessly pointed out, was well adapted to the sun and would not burn. He had infuriated her with that and surprised her by aiding her in the renewal of the bandage on her hip. There, the saffron sirwal was sadly burned in a ragged, black-edged hole.

"The skin of my breasts stings, dog!"

"It won't burn," he said, riding placidly at her right. "Not much, anyhow," he added, and she compressed her full lips.

"Why take me along at all? Why not leave me to die on the desert, used and ill-clothed and helpless, *barbarian?*"

"After all we've been through together? Isparana, Isparana! I feel responsible for you, woman! Beside . . . your outlook is to get the Eye of Erlik to Zamboula, isn't it?"

She stared at him bright-eyed, and her sweat-sheened, partially bared chest heaved. She almost whispered, "Ye-esss . . ."

"Right." Conan shrugged. "Khassek—whom I liked, damn you—is gone. Zamboula is a lot closer than Iranistan, and I owe nothing to that far land. You will have accomplished your task, 'sparana. You and the amulet return to Zamboula together. It is just that I will be carrying the Eye, not you. Do you comport yourself in manner friendly and I shall be glad to tell your employer that you persuaded me to bring it home to him, in your company."

Blinking, staring, Isparana said nothing. Her tonguetip emerged to wet her lips while she considered, reflected, surely puzzled over his words and his accursed hillman's unpredictability. Wisely, Isparana said nothing. The big dog of a barbarian was obviously a survivor, and a worthy fighter as well as fair companion—and, damn him, a worthy lover at that.

Besides, they *were* headed for Zamboula, and he had assured her that he had the amulet, though all he seemed to be wearing was that ugly, cheap clay thing hanging from its thong around his neck.

That afternoon she essayed a few complaints

about the scant attire allowed her. She received a friendly slap on the thigh and assurance that this way she was less dangerous. Again he repeated that as she was hardly white to begin with, she was in no danger of suffering sunburn.

"If we are attacked," she said, "I don't even have a weapon!"

Conan gave her a dark and very serious look. "If we are attacked," he said "you will not need a weapon."

Warmth rose in her, and she did not welcome the reaction. Isparana maintained her wise silence, compressing her lips and facing front. They rode south toward Zamboula.

"I do not like your presence here when I am at my work," Zafra said. "Also I do not care for that decadent incense you insist on burning, or the scented candles. This is my place of work. It also adjoins the throneroom. I do not like your presence here at all! Should he find out—"

"*Him!*" the woman spewed forth the word as if it were an epithet. "How can he find out? Balad has our poor little Akter *frightened!* Balad wants the throne and I think he will have it, Zafra! Akter nervously keeps his son under constant close guard—the closest. Meanwhile our lord khan is afraid to order troops openly against the challenger Balad—least the people favor Balad!"

She walked from the couch to Zafra's scrying table, slinking in her few ounces of silk and a pound of gems and pearls. She was sinuous as a lithe slinking cat, this woman of Argos whom Akter Khan called Tigress. Well he might. Chia was a magnificently if economically constructed woman with a catlike speed and grace and an aura of sensuality to arouse an octagenarian. Wild tawny hair sprayed out over broad shoulders the color of amber and her eyes, large and surrounded by kohl with blued eyelids, were a disconcerting gray. A slave from far Aquilonia brushed that mane daily for many minutes, measured by the time required to move the sundial's shadow half the distance between two-hour points. Once she had done, her mistress deliberately disarranged it to maintain her careless, sensuously tousled appearance.

For all that he knew her well, for all their hours together, Zafra still watched her movements in fascination and appreciation and was aroused merely by the sight of her, walking.

She was born to tempt, he mused; a woman worthy of an emperor—or a mage who would in years to come *rule,* and rule a broader domain than little Zamboula of the desert. Trustworthy as her predatory jungle namesake was Chia of Argos, and her morals were those of a cat in heat. She was effete and she was estheticism and decadence personified, and it pleased Zafra that he had made her his, who had been Akter Khan's. Not that the khan knew she was no longer his!

Only last night Akter had called for her and of course she had gone, while Zafra ground his teeth and plotted darkly a future dominated by sorcery; dominated by Zafra who would be Zafra Khan.

Lounging, her eyes on Zafra scintillant as with flashes of mica in their deeps, she spoke on, scornfully. "Through that young priest, Totrasmek, hardly more than an acolyte, Akter believes that he keeps watch on Balad who would be Balad Khan . . . and Balad pays Totrasmek the boy-priest and tells him what to report to our noble khan!"

Her scornful laughter was not pretty. Nor was her face when she made the throaty sounds that emerged from a full-lipped, wide and sensuous mouth that contrived to wear a little lift of contemptuous superiority even when she smiled—one-sidedly, for she was not perfect; she had a bad tooth on the left.

Zafra turned for another look into his scrying glass, and he smiled a smile as imperfect as hers; in his, the eyes never entered. Aye, the two still came on, ever closer to Zamboula though still far out on the desert.

"As for Akter," Chia said on; "well you know of *him,* Zafra! He is sleepy with wine ere he has finished his dinner each night, and drunk within an hour of his finishing. Every night. His pot belly grows visibly by the day! He is no khan! He is a fearful sot, Akter the Sot . . . or the Gored Ox, as more and more of the soldiers call him."

Bending over his table of paraphernalia, Zafra twisted his neck to fix her with a look across his shoulder. "Chia . . . you have contact with Totrasmek?"

She gave him a look. "I? Am I the sort to have do with those who give their manhoods to *gods?*"

Almost, Zafra smiled. "Well . . . find a way to let him wonder whether that girl of the Shanki, that gift to our lord Khan . . . to let him and thus Balad wonder whether she *really* died of illness, or . . . otherwise?"

"Oh! Did she?"

"How should a mere mage know, Chia, and him so young? Just see that the concept is imparted to those who will carry it to Balad."

"Oh, well, it is simpler than having to deal with that ambitious little priest, my love. My own dear Mitralia is a spy for Balad!"

"Your slave? That pretty blond Aquilonian? Why have you not told me this before?"

Chia tilted her head on one side and gave him a look from beneath heavy lashes. "I just have. Do you tell me everything you know, my sorcerous and ambitious love?"

Smiling, deliberately she yawned and stretched,

lengthening and tautening her coppery form for the vision of the man she knew loved that body. She was fascinated with this strange anomaly of a man in his strange hat. The khan's favorite and most trusted man in the sprawling city; a mage, and him neither aged nor bald; a young man with knowledge of the Book of Skelos, and more knowledge than the Picts possessed of their own abominable Children of Jhil, and knowledge too of the evil-reeking tomes of Sabatea of the golden peacock; as much knowledge, surely, as was possessed by the sorcerous Stygians in their nighted vaults.

In a year or less, did Akter retain his throne, Zafra might well rule hero, Chia knew. And did Balad succeed—well, she had her own little plans going along that line.

He was fascinated with her, she knew, as if it were she who was the mage, not he. Yet she was fascinated with him as well, for his differentness and his daring . . . and his power and the prospect of more. And of course Chia of Argos knew that eventually she must tire of him—unless perhaps he retained and consolidated his power, and gained more!

"Balad is hardly without support," she said, arching her brows while lowering her lashes heavy with kohl applied to perfumed salve. "And his . . . talkative supporters, up in Aghrapur, the capital."

She always referred to that city not only by its name, but as "Aghrapur, the capital," and Zafra knew that she lusted for it; the seat of Empire. "Add 'of Turan, of which our Zamboula is a satrapy,' " he said, "and I shall wring your lovely neck."

Smiling lazily, deliberately disarranging what clothing she wore, she said it.

"Ah witch," Zafra said, "witch!" And on the instant he decided to raise a wart on her cheek. Just a little one, to give her something to think about.

"What better consort for a mage," she said, smiling lazily, "mage; intimate of demons!"

"Hardly. Now look you, Chia—"

She stretched, lithely postured for him with a rippling of magnificent tigerine musculature beneath amber skin taut as the head of drum. "Call me Tigress, Zafra, Tiger!"

"*He* calls you that, Chia. Listen, or I shall show you some of my powers! Do you know that I have but to do this and that, and you will drop to your knees, to your belly, to grovel and crawl like a snake?"

Sorceror's Table

She gripped the edge of a table lined with aludels and athanors, and jars and phials of strange content. She arched her back, thrust out her backside, and wagged her hips while she stared cat-eyed at him.

"Oh? Would you like that? Would you like me so, mage? I will do it, if you but ask, my sorcerous love! No need to waste your spells!"

He clenched his fists, wondering if she mocked him, or feared him and was covering—or was serious. "Ah!" he burst out exasperatedly. "And pain . . . suppose I give you pain so that you beg for surcease and to hear my commands?"

She bared her bosom and ran her tongue over her lips, slowly. "Would you like to give me pain and see me writhe, my sorcerous lover? Beat me!"

"Chia."

Zafra's eyes had gone flat and serpentish; his voice was as flat, and laden now with warning behind which there was menace. She knew he'd had enough of her teasing. She spoke softly and sweetly.

"My love?"

"I must go and tell the Khan that his agent Isparana wends toward Zamboula, in company with him who has the Eye that our besotted lord so desperately wants. I shall suggest that he consider despatching a . . . honor guard, to meet and escort them to us."

"How fortunate he is to have you, ever looking out for him! Why do you not remove Balad for him?"

"I have told him that I am at work on it, and that Balad is protected by great spells. Now—you must be still, Chia, and quiet, Chia, while I pass through that door. For if you do not, you ruin us both."

"I shall be as quiet as a little naked mouse," she said, and stripped with only a few swift movements, and lay on the floor in a pose of wanton abandon. Strung on a tiny chain of gold, a tiger-eye winked on her belly.

Grinding his teeth, Zafra went to the tall paneled door, to report to his khan. *What a magnificent animal,* the mage thought, his face composed and his eyes flat and hard. *How long, I wonder, before I have to rid this world of her?*

IX

DEATH AMID THE DUNES

There were six of the green-robed men with the darker scarves across their lower faces, and their leader fastened the gaze of burning eyes on Conan's and told him that all they wanted was Isparana.

"I do not understand," Conan said, while he decided what to do. "My sister is not for sale."

"We do not want to *buy* her, mule-brain!" the man in the green robe said, and two of his comrades laughed.

"Oh," Conan said. "Isparana, these men want to use you a bit. You do not mind, do you? Also, you had best slip the lead of the pack-horses off your saddle." He hoped that she would assume the unspoken words: *and be ready to ride fast and unencumbered.*

The eyes above the dark green scarf shifted their glance to the woman. Conan's right arm whipped across his middle. His fingers closed on the hilt of his sword and, reversing the same motion so that it became all one flowing act, he whipped his arm back to the right. His point destroyed the staring fiery eyes.

At the same time he kicked his horse with both heels, and held them clamped.

The accoster screamed, lifting both hands uselessly to his bloody sockets. Two of his companions loosed shouts while another cursed. A third, just bringing his sword up, was struck so hard by the shoulder of Conan's horse that he was knocked from his saddle. His scimitar went flying. Others scraped from their sheaths while Isparana freed herself of the pack horses.

Whirling his sword high to gain force, Conan drove for the green-robed man who was a little apart from the others. That would-be rapist proved to be strong of thews within his loose desert robes; with a frightful scraping clangor his blade met and stayed Conan's.

Behind the Cimmerian, a fourth of the *jazikhim* or nomadic raiders reined in close, and his sword swept up above Conan's broad back. Conan was blocking a cut, kicking his opponent's horse hard enough to hurt his own booted toes, and slashing the man's sword arm just at the wrist. At a strange gurgling sound behind him, Conan clapped heels and bent low. Chestnut leaped forward and his rider, hanging on with both legs, looked back.

It was easy to understand that a man had been about to strike him from behind, and would have succeeded but for interference; the interference took the form of a little seven-inch dagger. Isparana had hurled it strongly enough to pierce his left upper arm. With the light hilt and half the blade standing from the flesh between tricep and bicep, the man forgot Conan and kicked his horse around to make for the woman.

"THANKS, 'sparana," Conan shouted; "RIDE, 'sparana!"

Three men came at him from two directions, though one had a wounded sword arm. Conan bullied his horse into driving between them, dodging the slash of the nearest while being unable to strike back. He saw that Isparana had eluded the man she had wounded and was riding south, at speed.

As none of the desert men bore a bow and thus could only pursue, Conan yanked Chestnut about and raced after her.

Behind him, no less than six men screamed their rage and frustration. Two were wounded; three were not. Howling their rage, those five gave chase. The sixth, their blinded leader, floundered about, calling after them. His horse whickered, and hurried after the others.

Eight horses galloped southward on the desert, in a long line.

The four pack horses stared after the others. One whickered and pawed the sand. The second lunged forward. The first allowed himself to be led from behind. The four broke into a trot along the wake of the other eight.

The blinded man, staggering and stumbling, crying out, blundered into their path. The first pack horse swung around him. The second and third trampled him. The four sumpter beasts of Conan and Isparana trotted after them, and twelve horses hurried south on the desert, strung out in a line nearly a league long. The blinded man had ceased crying out.

Ironhead and Chestnut ran well. Both horses had spent much time on the desert, and were accustomed to such strange terrain that yielded beneath every hooffall. Conan glanced back to see the howling *jazikhi* pursuers. They sped with green robes flapping and their whirling swords flashing in the sunlight. Leaning over his mount's neck to distribute his weight and lessen the wind resistance of his massive frame, the Cimmerian called after the Zamboulan, again and again.

Stupid to expect her to slow and let him catch up, Conan thought, since her horse had a lead and bore less weight. Yet he wished she were armed. He wished he could pass her the long blade slung behind his saddle; the mountain-man's knife that had been Khassek's.

Still, she had contrived to cling to a dagger and conceal it—and with it, to save his life when she could have fled, armed. Perhaps she had another, Conan mused. He realized that he had never checked her boots for concealed sheaths. No other part of her clothing or body was unknown to him.

"Here, stop that!" he objected, when Chestnut lightly leaped a long ridge of blown sand, to come down with a jolt that made his rider's teeth clack.

The horses's tail streamed behind like a tawny banner and his blowing mane snapped at Conan's face, stinging. His garments blew and fluttered. He did not glance back. There was no reason to believe the pursuers could catch up. All he had to do was keep galloping . . .

Forever?

Hardly. Perhaps for hours, perhaps not so long. Eventually Ironhead and Chestnut must slow. They were surely less fresh than the mounts of the greenrobes, who must dwell or have their tents pitched nearby. Then Conan and Isparana must face their enemies, or be carved from behind. It would be nice to come upon a jumble of rocks or one huge, scalable one, from which he could fight off more even than five attackers.

Biting his lip, Conan lifted his head enough to send his squinting gaze this way and that. He saw only rolling sand, and the long, tall acclivities were only sand, or perhaps sand drifted against stone hills worn smooth beneath.

Chestnut floundered up one such long slope now. Conan glanced back as Chestnut topped the slope. The pursuing quintet had not quite reached its base. Conan saw that one was unsteady in his saddle. The wight whose right arm he had chopped, the Cimmerian assumed, was weakening from loss of blood.

Over the sandy slope Chestnut kicked and dragged himself. Below and ahead, Isparana was galloping to a far higher dune or hill, not yet worn down by gritty, ever-shifting sand. She was guiding Ironhead so as to make the descent at a slant, to save the horse. Conan made a barbarian's decision, just as he had when he had attacked the leader of six men who had every reason to believe him easy prey.

His chestnut mount grunted when his master's left fist tightened and pulled the gathered reins. Descending, the horse was not happy to swerve leftward. It did, hooves slipping. Conan hung on, trying to lean leftward, uphill, while he continued to drag the rein in that direction. More than reluctant, fighting, Chestnut was now re-ascending the hill. Conan nearly lost his seat and his calves bunched to cling to the horse. They would quiver for an hour, later.

Now—

Now Chestnut again topped the summit and without a sound Conan loosed his two-legged grip, kicked with both heels, and clung again.

After emitting a grunt of outrage, Chestnut plunged down the incline a few ells to the left of the tracks of his assent.

Flee and be overtaken, Conan had thought. Turn while his pursuers couldn't see, and plunge down upon them while they were put at disadvantage by their assent, and he could surely reduce the odds with a totally unexpected attack. Once he had plunged past them it was up to the *jazikhim* whether to pursue, or be pursued, or give it up.

One man plunged down the slope to attack five.

"Haragh!" one of them bawled, or something like; perhaps it was "by Yog!" He had seen their quarry plunging down at them with the momentum of an avalanche. There could be no mistaking his grim purpose, however lunatic. His fellows looked up. Eyes and mouths went agape.

About all they were able to do was halt their mounts. One turned aside at an angle; though the down-rushing attacker was but one, the green-robed wight instinctively sought escape.

Leaping, slipping, sliding and lunging again, Chestnut kept his feet only by rushing with his own increasing momentum. The horse hurtled down like a diving eagle that had spotted its prey. Conan manhandled him into the narrow gap between the bunched quartet and the single *jazikh* who was turning from them. That man was to Conan's right.

The Cimmerian felt a sword's tip rake his cheek while he chopped across his body, into the leg of the man on his left. At the same time, he yanked Chestnut's rein—to the left, again.

As he had expected, the horse's hindquarters slewed and slammed rightward. The impact of his right flank with the other man's horse was as if the *jazikh*'s mount had been struck by a boulder. The beast slid several feet on his hind legs, sought his balance, failed to find it, and fell. Its rider, wearing a dagger in his shoulder, fell with the beast. That his leg was doubtless broken in more than one place was of little import, for the horse rolled completely over him.

Chestnut somehow maintained his footing while maintaining his mad downhill rush. Conan's left arm continued tense, dragging the beast ever leftward in a long hillside turn. He felt no sympathy for an animal that was by now surely developing a sore in one side of his mouth. His slobber streamed back over Conan's leg.

Only when the grunting, panting animal was again ascending did Conan glance over to see what his mad surprise attack had wrought.

Squealing, a riderless horse was slipping and sliding, on its haunches, down the slope. Another was lunging up the incline. Two men were down; one moved. And three, shocked into silence, stared at the Cimmerian. Their leader had been slashed blind in an instant; another had taken a hurled dagger in the shoulder and had now been crushed beneath his own rolling horse; a third lay downslope, clutching with both hands at his deeply chopped thigh. Six had sought to rob and rape a woman with one man; three survived on their horses, and one of them was wounded in the sword arm. Indeed he was reeling in his saddle and his robe's skirt was covered with blood.

"Come, jackals!" Conan bellowed. "Meet me atop this rise, and I'll lay you low as the curs you are! Already your number is halved, and I'm not scratched!"

Blood trickled down his cheek and dripped on his jallaba even as he challenged so loudly, but Conan did not consider that scratch to be a scratch. And his chestnut horse, blowing, its sides heaving, pawed itself upward.

The three *jazikhim* exchanged looks, glanced over at their dead comrade and the wounded one, and at Conan, and back at each other.

"Vengeance!" one bawled, and waving his sword he booted his mount up the slope. His green robes flapped and fluttered about him and his curved blade flashed sunfire.

Damn, Conan thought, *they might have given it up but for that bigmouth.*

Now Isparana had gained a good lead while he reduced the number of their pursuers—while considerably reducing his mount's strength. And three enemies rode up the slope on a course parallel to his, seemingly undaunted. He decided to take the horse down, start up the second hill, and then wheel for another attack from above.

103

Just as he started to turn Chestnut's head, loud shouts attracted his and his pursuers' attention. All looked back the way they'd come—to see a clot of seven horsemen coming along their trail at the gallop . . . and all wore dark green scarves and lighter robes of the same color.

I should have kept running, Conan thought.

That is it then, he told himself mentally. *It is death. Well, I'll flee and then fight. They will have to kill me fighting—I'm damned if I give them opportunity to take me and amuse themselves by torturing me to death! No, I will flee as long as I can, and see how many of these motherless desert jackals I can take with me to Hell!*

Chestnut pawed his way to the ridge and kicked over. He went slip-sliding down the other side. Conan hung on and let the horse have his own way; he did not lunge this time, but slid-floundered, in a wallowing sort of gait. Perhaps this was granting the animal a few moments of rest.

"Get me out of this," Conan muttered, "and I'll give you a better name!"

He had no need of glancing leftward to check the enemy; twenty feet away and angling toward him as they descended, they paralleled his course. The right arm of the rearmost was tucked into his robe, and he bent, clinging to his saddle with his left hand.

Ahead, Conan saw that Isparana was just topping the other, taller hill that cut off their view further south.

Why was she reining in?

Chestnut reached the base of the incline. He stumbled, and indicated he would be very happy to gallop rightward, along level terrain. Conan indicated otherwise. The horse stumbled, tried to shake his head, broke wind, and with faltering strength and obvious reluctance, started up the long, steeper hill. Conan set the animal to climb at an angle to make it easier for him. He chose a direction opposite the angling line of Isparana's tracks.

His pursuers were closer, and coming, yelling. They too had seen their reinforcements, and obviously now hoped to save face by destroying this lone rider before their fellows arrived.

Conan decided to saw Chestnut's reins the other way. Isparana could see to herself while he turned his right side to the enemy. Yet to do so, he realized, would put him instantly in danger of running combat or worse, for the green-robed riders were now that close.

It was then that the discordant chorus of yells and battle screams rose from above, and Conan looked up.

Isparana sat her nervous mount on the very ridge, while on either side of her swept camel after camel, in two files. Atop each, a man in fluttering white kaffia and white burnoos shouted, screamed, and waved his sword. Their ungainly mounts came pounding down the declivity on big feet designed for the desert. Sand flew in pale yellow clouds. High saddles creaked atop those ridiculous single humps.

Cries of consternation rose from Conan's pursuers. They forgot him to turn their horses' heads back down the slope. Down the opposite one, with Conan's pack animals among them, came their seven fellows. Conan's grin was grim and ugly as he watched one of the three fall off his mount. The man whose sword arm he had chopped was finally succumbing to loss of blood, exacerbated by pursuing his wounder and being forced to manhandle his horse on several hillsides.

Camels plunged past Conan and their riders hardly glanced at him.

The last two of his original accosters were hacked to the ground ere they reached the brief stretch of level terrain between the two slopes. Up the other incline lunged over a half-score camel riders, still yelling. All these desert people, Conan reflected, were a noisy lot when they attacked one another! And he remembered the shrieking Cimmerians he had accompanied at Venarium, and he put the thought from his mind.

The green-robed horsemen also yelled—and fled. Six sat their mounts on a downhill slide-run to the west; the seventh, greed making him think he was clever, snatched the lead-rein that connected Conan's four sumpter animals and urged his mount eastward.

With an owner's snarl, Conan kicked Chestnut to bolt after him. Four of the camel-riders, too, pursued him; the others swerved westward, ten camels after six horses. These white-burnoosed men, Conan mused, must be mean fighters! With odds of ten to six who were *men*, the six stood and fought.

The green-robed *jazikh* with Conan's supply-laden animals glanced back, saw the pursuit, and dropped the lead rein. The four beasts slowed to a halt. They tried to prance and kick as four camels tore past them. Again Conan changed Chestnut's course. As he reached his pack animals, swerving across their new course to herd and stop them, he heard their would-be owner shriek and die.

Conan nearly lost his saddle in stopping Chestnut and regaining the lead of his supply horses. He sat his mount on the slope, waiting. Chestnut heaved and blew; Conan patted his sweat-running neck. Now they were still, Conan felt very very hot indeed—and nevertheless vowed not again to ride thus without wearing that excellent vest of linked mail he'd bought in Shadizar with a Khaurani gem!

Four men on camels came up the slope to him, and separated. Running sweat, Conan spoke quickly.

"You are most welcome, hawks of the desert!" he hailed them, in the Turanian he hopefully assumed they spoke.

They said nothing; their leader nodded without

showing his teeth. All four wore thick, short beards of black or brown and were made to look weirdly ferocious by their black-encircled eyes.

"These belong to me and my woman," he said, briefly pointing to Isparana, who waited atop the larger hill. "The green-robed dogs beset us in their numbers, and we struck down four ere we flew. Their leader is a few leagues back; I blinded him."

A big-nosed, curly-bearded man only a few years older than Conan stared at him from atop his dromedary. "Who are you? Where go you? Why is the woman unarmed?"

"See his eyes!" one of the others said in barely hushed excitement.

"I am Conan, a Cimmerian," said the owner of those blue eyes, unknown to many so far south. "We go to Zamboula, which is her home. Over there lies a man I bowled over. He was crushed by his horse," he said, not wishing them to take all credit or think he was ineffectual. "He lies near another whose leg I chopped. Her dagger is in the first one's shoulder. As for her sword . . ." He shook his head and lied easily. "A few leagues back. She lost it, in the onset of these brigands. They are your enemies?"

"They are everyone's enemies—ah!"

The camel-riders stared westward, toward the source of shrieks and metallic clashes. Their fellows had overtaken the green-robes, and would presumably make short work of thieving wights who fled rather than fought.

The man with the curly beard and unusually deep-set eyes framed in black returned his gaze to Conan. Conan noticed a scar on his forehead, a small v, neatly etched.

"You two are alone? I know of no . . . Cimmeria?"

"Cimmeria is a nation far north, beyond the kingdom of Zamora," Conan said, wondering if these desert tribesmen knew of Zamora. "Aye, we are alone. We were four, and two were slain far, far back. Two of these are their horses, bearing their weapons. She is most anxious to reach Zamboula. Are you men of Zamboula?"

"No. Do those packs also contain the ears of those who slew your companions?"

Conan shook his head. "We, uh, do not take ears."

The four white kaffias turned each toward the other, and their wearers grinned. One of them held out his dark-skinned palm to show Conan a bloody trophy: ears, freshly sliced off.

"We do."

"Oh. Well, you are welcome to the ears of those I slew—unless that is not honorable," he rather hurriedly added, when he saw their frowns. He also noted then that two others had the same v-shaped scars just above the inner corner of the right eye. He could not be sure of the fourth, whose kaffia was pulled a bit lower in front.

"It would not be honorable. They are yours."

"Umm. Well, as my people do not take ears, perhaps your leader will accept them as gift." Conan felt that they did not look overly happy about that, either. "You are not of Zamboula, then."

"No."

"Citizens of the Turanian Empire?"

"No."

"These, uh . . . this is within the area it claims, is it not?"

The curly-bearded man shrugged. "We do not acknowledge the suzerainty of Turan."

Conan thought, *I think we're in trouble.*

X

TENTS OF THE SHANKI

The tall Eagle Gates of Zamboula swung wide. A file of horsemen came cantering importantly forth, by twos. Ten such pairs emerged while the gate sentries looked down upon onion-shaped helms the peaks of which trailed three yellow streamers each. From each helmet depended a shoulder-length arras of linked chain that gleamed and rippled like snakeskin in the morning sunlight. Each fall of steel mesh was bordered by three rows of bronze links, for color and decor. Twenty strong, horse-soldiers of the Empire rode forth. They expected no trouble and wore no other mail.

The blousy white leggings of each were tucked into crimson-topped boots of brown leather. Over that each man wore knee-length, back-split tunic of crimson, and over that a sleeveless white surcoat split front and back and blazoned with the golden griffin of Turan. Two yellow sashes, around hips and from left hip in front over shoulder to right hip behind, gleamed boldly against the white. Ten men wore swords and from ten high-cantled saddles swung axes shaped like pregnant half-moons. All the men were mustached; sixteen wore beards. Six horses bore crossbows and each man led a change of horse bearing food and water.

From the horn of every saddle swung a short wide-mouth trumpet.

They rode north and north, and on the fifth day they spread out in a long, long line. Each disposed himself so as to be just within sight of another. Somehow Akter Khan knew that a foreign male and a woman of Zamboula approached, having come down the steppes and the desert from the far north. He had sent forth twenty men to meet them. None knew why the pilgrims were so important to their khan. They were soldiers whose business was not to know, but to do. They were escort. The pilgrims were to be aided, guided, politely escorted—unless they evinced desire to go somewhere other than to Zamboula. In that case every effort was to be made to persuade them to continue to the city.

If they persisted in recalcitrance to visit the khan, they—with all their possessions, that was most important—were to be conveyed to the khan at any cost, dead or alive.

The sun blazed and the desert shimmered and twenty men rode north and behind them in Zamboula a young mage looked into his mirror to watch the progress of the two who approached, and reported thrice daily to his khan. And he plotted, and so did the rebel Balad and his followers, while Zamboula shimmered and festered like a boil on the southern desert.

Conan and Isparana were not in trouble.

They were guests of the little desert community of the Shanki, whose ancient religion dictated that they ride camels, not horses, and that each child be marked with the little v-shaped scar on the forehead—above the leftmost corner of the right eye, among boys, and the rightmost corner of the left eye, on girls.

Even so, as they returned to their oasis community, they were accompanied by eighteen horses. Two were bestridden by Conan and Isparana. Two had been the mounts of Sarid and Khassek. Two had been Conan's and Khassek's sumpter beasts. The remaining twelve were the erstwhile mounts of the green-robed raiders the Shanki called Yoggites, after their god; one beast had been wounded in the encounter. It had been slain and left for scavengers on wings or legs. The Shanki would not ride horses, or wear their hides, or eat their meat.

The sun was low and the sky streaked with blood and topaz and nacarat when the camel warriors and their guests reached the nameless community; it was the home of the Shanki. Here palms reared tall and hung their topknots like dangling arms over tents and little rounded storehouses. Here men wore long-sleeved white tunics over loose leggings or trousers of yellow or orange or red or a rich brown the making of which involved camel urine; their women wore scarlet, and only skirts sheathed their bodies and legs. Married women showed no portion of their heads.

Though the visitors were told that the Shanki had occupied this oasis for "hundreds of years," the only buildings were storehouses; granaries of mud and dung. The Shanki lived in tents, as had their nomadic ancestors, and they preserved the trappings and customs of a warrior people. Here dwelt less than five hundred persons—the oasis was home, and population was strictly controlled—under a man called khan.

He was Akhimen Khan's son Hajimen who led the attack on the old Shanki enemy, the *jazikhim* called Yoggites. Akhimen was not yet twoscore years of age; his son and heir was four-and-twenty, and his older sister was in the harem of the Great Khan in Aghrapur; Akhimen's gift. The Shanki lived within the bounds of the Empire of Turan, but were not of it. As they patrolled the desert hereabouts and would occasionally act as caravan guard, the King-Emperor in Aghrapur of Turan suffered them to remain, without Turanian soldiery or taxation.

Both Akhimen and his son, Conan noted when they removed the white outer robes they donned only when riding out of their community, wore loose yellow tabards over scarlet shirts and very long, loose white leggings. To the breast of each man's tabard was pinned a black star of five points.

Shanki Tabard

Hajimen's wife, faceless and all in scarlet hung and encrusted with opals and garnets and silver, took Isparana away to see to her toilet. Akhimen welcomed Conan to his tent. The Shanki leader wore an extraordinary mustache; greased and oiled to glisten, it was curled up in a thick coil that arced on his cheeks nearly to his lower eyelids. Above his eye, the Shanki mark was oddly bent by two of the vertical furrows etched by sand and wind. Forty years on the desert created the face of a man of sixty. His single ring was set with a large garnet, and a hemispherical opal swung on his breast from a thong of twisted camel hair.

"Conan of Cimmeria is welcome among the Shanki. We will pen your horses."

"What do the Shanki do with captured horses, Akhimen Khan?"

"The Shanki trade them in Zamboula," that most courtly man said, "for good camels and a few things they need. The Zamboulans are happy to receive them, along with the opals my people carve into the likeness of camels, and stars, and split and smooth into perfect hemispheres."

"I have noted many opals among the Shanki," Conan said, "and all are beautiful. You are artists. The Shanki have this day captured eight horses, and I five."

Akhimen inclined his head. People stepped respectfully from their path as they approached his tent, and stared at the strange-eyed man who towered over their khan, for the Cimmerian was nigh a giant and the Shanki were not a tall people. Conan never learned whence they came.

"We respected the right of Conan to lay claim to all those horses. However, I have heard my son, and agree that eight horses fall to us and five are Conan's, by right of combat and capture. One of ours we slew. Here: fill this man's mug!" For Conan had been handed a large Shanki-made cup of earth and fired sand within a minute of his dismounting.

While a young warrior was honored to fill the cup, Conan said, "I beg the khan of the Shanki to choose three of the five for his own, for without his people my woman and I had died this day."

They entered the tent, which was in the community's center and was no larger than any other. The warrior of the Shanki—he looked about twelve, Conan

113

thought—did not enter with them. Inside were low tables that were surely not of Shanki manufacture, and mats that surely were; they were of the hide or woolly hair of camels, and some were dyed red and the brown that was a Shanki secret.

At his guest's words, Akhimen again inclined his head. "Conan is generous to a fault, both with horses and words. However a mighty warrior who was attacked by six and slew five appears not to have needed our aid!"

Conan bowed his head, which he felt would be proper among these ferocious camel-warriors of the desert who were so courtly within their community and who used no direct form of address. He made no denial. The Shanki chieftain knew as well as the Cimmerian that Akhimen exaggerated.

"They were only Yoggites," Conan said, knowing that would please a man he respected; the Cimmerian had known few such men. He noted that Akhimen affected to spit.

"I shall accept one horse as Conan's kind gift," Akhimen said.

Encouraged by such reverse bargaining, Conan nervously made bold to be expansive and to affect a ridiculous generosity. "Akhimen will displeasure me by not accepting five."

"Perhaps my guest will not be displeased if I accept three," Akhimen said, returning to the original offer, "of his choice."

"It shall be three of the khan's choice," Conan said. While it was his life's hope to become wealthy, he could not conceive of doing so by the steady acquisition of animals or real estate.

"I shall be honored to choose two from among my guest's five horses."

"I trust that the khan will choose well, though they are only horses, not camels."

"I am pleased," Akhimen Khan said.

"I am pleased," Conan said.

"Fill our guest's mug!" Akhimen said.

As there was no one else in the tent, he lifted an ewer and filled the mug himself. Conan bowed. The khan, whose tent was the color of sand and hung with a string of human ears on either side of its entry, turned to a partition formed by a thick curtain of opaque scarlet. He snapped his fingers, twice.

From behind the partition came two just-nubile girls who looked enough alike to be slim sisters. Each wore enormous heavy earrings of bronze that would surely in time lengthen their lobes past their jawlines; each wore a tallish, thick anklet of bronze; each wore a

Brazen Earrings and Anklet

115

strip of braided camel hide wrapped and bound about her left upper arm, dangerously tightly. Each wore nothing else whatever, and Conan essayed not to stare as they dropped to their knees and bowed deeply. Despite their age, Conan of a sudden wished himself behind them.

From behind them, between them walked a young woman. She was shapeless in several overlapping garments of red strung with silver and opals. An opal stood from her left nostril, which Conan thus knew was pierced, and the left sleeve of her garments was tightly wrapped with dark leather. Pinned to her bosom was a black star of five points. Her lips were stained black, her eyes completely circled—with obvious care in the application—by kohl so that her pupils looked huge, and the ivory decoration that hung below her waist in front was obscene.

"My daughter Zulfi," Akhimen Khan said.

While Conan sought within his mind for words courtly enough for the Shanki, Zulfi covered her face with her hands and bowed very low. Conan came of a warrior people and was among such, and felt that it behooved him to stand perfectly still. If he offended, he would apologize and remind his host that he was from afar. If that were not enough, the Cimmerian thought, his ever-effective solution hung at his hip.

"The khan's daughter Zulfi is a beauty and a credit to his tent and loins," Conan said, and the uncharacteristic words obviously pleased both the weird-lipped young woman and her father.

Another now emerged; she was faceless and indeed headless beneath a long gold-arabesqued scarlet veil that dangled to her waist's cincture, which was of silver disks and fell below her deep belly. The disks were coins, Conan saw, and knew that the woman bore much weight of them.

"My wife Aqbi," Akhimen said.

Her bow was not quite so deep, Conan saw, as her daughter's.

"I am honored, and . . . pleased to be spared the doubtless blinding beauty of the mother of the beautiful Zulfi and so handsome a son as Hajimen." *And a few more such speeches,* the Cimmerian thought sourly, *and I may throw up my beer!*

Again Aqbi bowed. She and Zulfi retreated to a dim corner to seat themselves, in flowing movements that scarcely disturbed their all-covering scarlet garments. Akhimen snapped his fingers. The two naked girls crawled awkwardly backward to flank the two women.

"Daughters of the Yoggites," Akhimen said, and affected to spit.

Conan said, "Of course," and wondered how long captives were kept naked . . . and how long it might be before their left arms withered and died.

The khan turned to his wife and daughter. "Zulfi, you will serve me and this guest in our tent. Woman: take your animals and cook for us."

Conan noted that the two "animals," limping slightly because of their large metal anklets, preceded their mistress from the tent. Zulfi came to the men and inspected their mugs. Both still held plenty of the thick Shanki beer. Even on the desert with grain at a premium, Conan reflected, men managed to make beer! Or perhaps the Shanki purchased it in Zamboula, with carven opals from some area of soft clay stone, and with the horses of slain men.

The Cimmerian hoped that Akhimen expected no return gesture. Isparana had seen the wisdom of being referred to among these warrior primitives as "Conan's woman." However, Conan could not imagine so proud and competent a thief and agent of her khan acting as

117

servant, even to this mighty chieftain of all of five hundred peoples. At the same time, he wondered about her.

"I would ask where my woman Isparana is."

"She receives clothing suitable to a woman," Akhimen Khan told him, "and will supervise the placing of the pegs of Conan's tent, as befits a woman who rides with her man."

Conan said, "Oh."

"Fill this man's cup!"

Zulfi did; Aqbi was outside with her "animals," where Conan had seen two mud-walled stoves and now smelled garlic heating in grease.

"My guest is not accustomed to the desert," Akhimen said, slipping sinuously down to his knees and then seating himself on a camel-hair mat spread on a camel hide laid on the ground. He indicated that Conan should join him.

Conan did. "No," he said. "My homeland, which I have left, has no desert, and during part of the year grows very cold."

Akhimen nodded. "I have heard of cold," he said solemnly, though Conan well knew the desert could grow grievously chill at night. "Nor have Conan's strange sky-hued eyes suffered from the glare-sickness."

"No."

"Conan is blessed. It is a plague, the glare-sickness. We wear a stone to ward against it. And kohl beneath the eyes, of course. Zulfi: you will fetch our guest a glarestone."

Zulfi rustled and jingled away behind the partition, and Conan heard his stomach rumble; outside, Aqbi was preparing something most savory. Bread with garlic, he was sure, and, he hoped, more. He knew better than to refuse any gift . . . and then, as Zulfi

118

returned carrying a garnet the size of a plum, he remembered Akhimen's reverse bargaining.

Accept that immense stone, the Cimmerian thought, *and I am as one with the—spit!—Yoggites!*

"I will accept a gift of glarestone no larger than the fiftieth part of that treasure."

"Ah! Theba shows displeasure," Akhimen said as if lamenting and naming, Conan assumed, a god; the name was unfamiliar to him. "A guest will not accept my proffered gift! Zulfi, protect our honor; fetch in a glarestone half the size of that one!"

"I shall accept a gift of the khan," Conan said, with the concept of Shanki bargaining and honor battling natural avarice within him, "of no more than a twentieth the size of that one."

Akhimen sighed as if exasperated. "Our guest will accept of us naught but a gift of a third that which we wish him to take. Fetch such, Zulfi."

"Too much honor is done me," Conan said, trying not to show his sadness at swallowing a choking lump of greed. "My own honor will not allow me to accept so rich a gift! I can accept no more than the tenth part of the stone in the beautiful hands of the khan's daughter."

"Our guest honors himself by his modesty," Akhimen Khan said, striking his forehead.

He shocked Conan then by producing a curved knife from the broad scarlet sash that encircled his waist under his tabard. Even as the Cimmerian's arm started to move to seize and crush the man's wrist, Akhimen touched his own chest with the point of his blade.

"Does my guest, who gives me many horses, not accept two gifts of glarestones the tenth part of this one which is in truth too large for the wearing so that such an offer shames me, I shall slay myself on the instant."

"Let the khan's hand be stayed," Conan said, wanting to laugh. "Rather would I spill my own blood even to the death, than bring doom upon the Shanki by causing their great khan to be so much as scratched."

Akhimen threw the Cimmerian a look. Whether it was of admiration for the return of flowery language or of some dolor at his guest's "surrender," Conan could not be certain. Zulfi departed, swishing and jingling.

"Is it permissible that I bow to the khan's daughter on her return?"

Akhimen looked shocked, and Conan felt that it was not sham. "In what way have I offended Conan of Cimmeria, that he would bow to a woman within my very tent?"

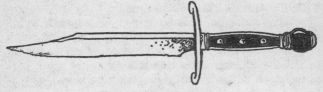

Conan's Eating Dagger

Conan thought fast, and fetched out his little eating dagger. "I shall kill myself," he said, and improvised: "Among some people it is great honor a man offers, to offer to bow to the daughter of another."

"Ahh!" Akhimen's hand rose to his beard, which he combed with his fingers. "A fascinating concept! I see that Conan meant only to honor me. People are so different throughout the world, are they not? What strange customs my guest must know!"

"Aye," Conan solemnly said, sheathing his dagger and reminding himself of the desert man's words concerning cold: *I have heard of it,* Akhimen had said.

"Aye," the Cimmerian repeated. "Some raise slaves among them, whom they persuade to accept their gods and customs. These slaves then wed among their captors, and their children are as any other."

Akhimen shook his head and looked as if he wanted to vomit. "Surely such is not the custom in Cimmeria!"

"Oh no," Conan said.

He had discovered what he wanted to know. For hundreds of years this little band of five hundred people had practiced endogamy, so that all the blood of the Shanki remained the same—whencever it had come— and customs and rites became only more ornate and strictured with the passage of time.

Zulfi returned bearing two garnets, each large enough to form the pommel of a dagger. Each had been expertly and doubtless laboriously pierced, and threaded with a strip of braided camel hair. Conan accepted the gifts with grace, and was careful not to bow to the daughter of Akhimen, khan of five hundred.

"May Theba bless Conan of Cimmeria with the sight of an eagle and protect him from the glare sickness," she said, and Akhimen repeated the words after her.

"Might a guest, nervous of offending, ask why the khan and his family wear the star of black cloth, while I saw none on any other among the Shanki? Is it the sign of the family of the khan?"

"Nay," Akhimen said, and gazed at the mat between his folded knees. "We mourn, man of Cimmeria. My people have only just removed the black stars of Death, after a month. We will wear ours for a full year, and at the end of that time pin the stars to the bodies of two captives, and burn them."

Conan's thoughts went to the two naked little slaves, but he was not shocked. These were a warrior people. The Yoggites were their deadly enemies, and customs were customs. Too, Conan had abode in Shadizar, where in temples to many strange gods were performed the most abominable and horrific rites involving both animals and humans, and the blood sacrifice that was as old as his race—the cruellest of all the animals of the world.

"A guest mourns with his host," Conan said, gazing down at his mat. "The khan of the Shanki had another son, who is lost to him?"

"Nay. A daughter. I sent her, in honor and much friendliness, to the khan of the Zamboulans. She was a maiden in the bloom of her youth, a white rock-rose unplucked. Among those people who abide within walls, that daughter of the desert sickened and died. Word was brought us. The khan of the Zamboulans sent message that she had been with child, doubtless a son, and he sought to honor us by laying her body with those of his ancesters and his women. We forgive him this, for he could not know that she would not wish to be pent thus, in the earth. She should of course have been returned to the desert her home, to be burned and her ashes given up to the wind to become one with the sands."

"Of course," Conan said.

"I sadden at these thoughts," Akhimen said, "and such is not meet in the presence of a warrior guest! 'Give up to grief that time reserved for grief,' Theba tells us, 'and to joy that time for rejoicing, and make always the guest welcome in the tents of the Shanki.' Zulfi! Fill our cups!" Akhimen turned his eagle's eyes on Conan and they seemed to burn with fervor. "We will get drunk together, man of Cimmeria!"

And on the morrow I will set off for Zamboula with a swollen head, Conan thought. *We do not have to get drunk before we eat, I hope!*

They did not, though a meal of spiced vegetables cooked in beer and chunks torn from broad flat disks of greasy, garlic-laden bread of whole wheat was no feast for a born meat eater of the Cimmerian hills, for all the tastiness of Aqbi's salted cookery.

It did raise a thirst.

"You are . . . you are *beautiful*," Conan told Isparana on the morrow, nor did he seek to disguise his astonishment. Sprawled on his back, he had opened his eyes to discover her sitting beside him.

Her brows had been shaped by judicious plucking, and greased; while her lips were the weird black of Shanki women, they were shaped by the cosmetic and made to glisten; her eyes were huge within frames of kohl and the lashes fair dripping; and her nails had been lacquered. Shanki scarlet covered her. On a chain of woven camel hair, a large white opal sparkled with pink and green between her breasts, where it pressed weightily so that they were emphasized.

When he sat up in the tent he did not remember entering, he saw that her toenails, too, had been lacquered. Isparana had quite pretty feet, no darker than his.

"You are . . . hideous," she told him without passion. "You were half-carried in, mumbling, long after moonrise, drunk and reeking of garlic and their beer —as you still do!"

He grinned, noting how thick his head felt and wondering if it would complain of strenuous activity.

"And you did not slay me."

"Slay you? Why should I slay you?"

"Why 'sparana," he said, putting a very large hand on her hip, "we are rivals and blood-enemies, remember?"

"I remember. I also threw a dagger that saved your life, remember?"

"I do. I am grateful. We are allies, then. And you did not even search me."

123

She gave him a look. "You have on you a dagger, two nice garnets on camel-hair thongs—luck, among these lunatics—and a nice ring secreted in your pouch, and that piece of junk around your neck, which stinks of garlic."

Conan, who had thoughtfully rubbed the glass-set clay "amulet" with the Shanki bread when he knew he would soon lose his senses, grinned. So she had searched him!

"And if I'd had the Eye of Erlik on my handsome person?"

"Why I'd have slit open the back of your tent with your dagger, dear Conan, and then sheathed it under your garlic-stenchy ribs, and been leagues south by now!"

"Ah, 'sparana, 'sparana! What a foul evil witch you wish you were! How fortunate for us both that you did not find your precious khan's precious amulet." And he drew her down to him.

"Ugh," she murmured, "Beer and garl—"

His head complained, and Conan bade it go away and be patient.

XI

SPIES OF ZAMBOULA

Torches flickered. They rolled up oily smoke to add to the sinister stain of darkened beams that connected stone walls rising from a floor of hard dark earth. The victim hung from one of those beams and her feet only just touched the floor.

The man in the black hood wrapped several additional convolutions of the terribly slim cord around her wrists and knotted the cord securely with a heartless jerk. Her body lurched and her toes strained to maintain contact with the floor. Very blond and young and naked but for her welts, she gasped and a long groan shuddered from her. Her limbs were so securely bound that no blood could circulate into her hands. The ropes had scraped and abraded, cutting into her wrists and arms while he tightened them. Now she felt only a tingling, and she could not feel her hands at all. She wondered wretchedly, extraneously if they were deep red, or purple, or blackening. Her arms seemed hot, strangely; tugged up this way they should have been cold. Another attempt at struggling assured her that was useless. She was powerlessly bound so as to allow her no movement whatever. Her heels were just off the floor . . . that only her toes and the balls of her feet touched. The man in the black hood was tall, and his arms were long.

Throaty gurgling sounds emerged high-voiced from lips she could not bring together. They were very dry.

The two robed men watched. One said, "Up."

She sobbed at the command. She knew what it meant. The ropes from her wrists ran up over the leather wrapping on a beam high above her head.

The man in the black hood pulled her up, until her feet cleared the floor. Her groan was hideous. The two robed men watched in silence and the torches flickered. The man in the black hood began to raise and lower the rope and its burden as though he were ringing a great bell. His big belly tautened with effort.

Bobbing up and down, the dangling victim began to moan steadily and her ribs seemed trying to tear their way through her flesh. She was being whipped up and down at the same time as her strained, limp body rotated and swung in a pendulum motion. Sweat streamed from her. She sobbed with each hard-fought breath.

"Speak!"

She heard the voice; she whimpered and tears slid down her cheeks and she would not speak.

"I see no reason to whip her more. Use the hot irons."

"No-o . . ." she murmured, and her head hung.

The man in the black hood secured the end of his rope so that only her toes touched the earthen floor. From his belt he drew a gauntlet. He pulled it on as he paced to the brazier, an evil black thing squatting on three legs, with its hair afire. From it thrust up the wooden handles of two slim stems of black iron. He withdrew one. Its tip glowed white. It yellowed as he paced unhurriedly back to his victim, and her wide

126

eyes watched its approach. She mumbled "no" in that tiny voice again, and he lifted the iron.

The watching robed men watched him hold the iron firmly, remorselessly against her body, which was twitching and quivering in apprehension and horror. A shriek ripped from her throat while she threw her head up and back and new sweat glistened and rolled. The robed men heard the sharp sizzling sound and smelled the odor of burning flesh.

"Stop."

The hooded man drew away his iron. His victim hung panting, sobbing, while she smelled cooked skin. Sweat poured from her and matted her hair.

"Speak!"

She swallowed repeatedly, and gasped, and sobbed, and she panted.

"Again."

The man in the black hood moved, and she felt the heat of the iron's approach.

"Stop! I will tell you." Her voice was dully pleading.

"Stop," the robed man said; he who wore the sword. The younger man beside him wore no weapons. A fine pendant of gold and pearls and topazes seemed to blaze on his tunic's breast. "Speak, then. Just hold the iron ready, Baltaj."

The black-hooded man remained by her side, the iron in his hand, as if hopeful that she would not say enough. He was a big man, tall and heavy.

"You are a spy for Balad?"

"Yes."

"You serve the woman Chia, and live here in the palace with her, and you spy on her and on me for the traitor, Balad."

She hesitated; the hooded man moved his hand. "Yes," she said, accepting even the words that Balad was traitor.

"You are paid by him?"

"Yes."

"How does he pay you?"

"My ... my parents live well ... and do not know why. And ... I ... I ..."

"Speak!"

"I am to have my mistress's apartment when Balad has seized Zamboula, and ... and she is to serve *me*."

"Idiot! Aquilonian fool! Can you imagine the majestic Argossean Chia whom I call Tigress ... can you imagine her consenting to serve *you*? You have made a fool's bargain, and see what it has cost you?"

"Bal ... Balad will ... will make her!"

"Oh of course. Of course he will! You would not last a day before she slipped a few of her precious clothing-pins into you, stupid slut of Aquilonia! *How* do you report to Balad the traitor?"

"He—he is not a traitor! He seeks to free Zamboula of—"

"Baltaj!"

The hodded man responded by moving his arm and gauntleted hand. The iron's tip was faded to red now, but it did its work, and they heard it and smelled it, and she shrieked and dangled limply.

Water and nettles revived her.

She spoke of how she met the palace guard Khoja three afternoons of every ten, and passed him messages. No, she had never herself seen Balad. He had sent her a message, and the gem they had found secreted in her hair. No, there was no message for them to see; she did not read and it had been taken away again. She was sure she recognized his seal and name.

"It might have been a warrant for your death, stupid bitch!"

"No-o-o ..."

128

"That is enough. Baltaj, replace the iron. Come up here."

A long sigh escaped the captive and she hung limp, trying to get her weight on her toes while she labored for breath. The hooded man thrust the iron back into the brazier, and ascended the five-and-twenty steps from the dungeon pit to the two robed men on the landing.

"Behind me," his lord said, and Baltaj stepped behind the man with the sword. The other robed man, too, stepped back a pace, so as to leave Akter Khan alone at their forefront.

"Slay her," Akter said, and the lips of the other man moved as the Khan spoke.

"Uh!" the torturer grunted, and pressed back still farther, for from the sheath at the side of his khan the sword slipped, untouched. It wavered for a moment in the air, and then drove downward into the pit and, making a slight curve as if held by a running—or flying —man who was invisible, it plunged into the bosom of the captive—a fraction left of center.

Akter Khan smiled and . turned smiling to his mage.

"A shame to cheat Baltaj of such a lovely subject for the final long torturing," he said, "but who could resist using your marvelous sword, Zafra!"

Thinly, Zafra smiled in return. "Perhaps my lord will leave this man Khoja to Baltaj, as . . . recompense," the young wizard said.

Akter Khan nodded and turned to his torturer. "So it shall be, Baltaj! Khoja will soon be brought to you. Show him . . . that," he said, gesturing down into the dungeon pit where hung Mitralia, Aquilonian maid to Chia the Tigress. Mitralia was not breathing. "And see whether he knows others to implicate. Work on him, Baltaj."

"Oh, my good lord knows that I will!"

"Aye—and I know what you will do the moment

we two have left this your domain too, perverse rascal!"
Akter smiled. "Come Zafra, royal mage of Zamboula!"

"Shall I fetch my lord's sword back to him?"

"Baltaj! Drag the sword out of that cow and bring
it to me!"

"My . . . lord . . ."

"Fear not, Baltaj, loyal hound; like yourself, the
sword obeys only your master. It will not harm you.
It is only a sword, now."

Baltaj's descent of the steps was not hurried, and
Akter smiled at his mage. The khan actually dropped
a hand onto the man's shoulder.

"My loyal Zafra!" he said quietly. "How valuable
you are to me! And you were right—she was indeed a
spy, and has given another into our hands. Too, I
admit that I was fearful she might implicate my Tigress!
Instead the girl obviously hated and envied her and
Balad would make Chia slave—if ever he succeeded in
his insane plans!"

Zafra made a shallow bow.

"I must tell my lord," he said, just as quietly.
"My suspicion was roused when I noted how she
behaved when I visited her mistress, your Tigress. My
lord Khan will recall that on the occasion of my pre-
senting him with the Sword, he sent Chia the Tigress
to me."

"That same evening. Of course I remember. You
are telling me that you have . . . been with her, since?"

Zafra kept his head down. "My lord, I am. I
must tell you, though it has been hard to work up the
nerve. We have spent . . . considerable time together."

Akter laughed and again clapped the man's thin
shoulder. "Do you love her, Zafra?"

"My lord," Zafra said truthfully, "I do not."

"And do you think she loves you?"

"No, lord Khan."

"Then since I sent you her for dalliance, and began it myself, how can I object to my royal wizard's spending time with the irresistible Tigress, eh? I cannot tell you how thankful I am that you have told me, Zafra—for I have known, for weeks. For a month, and longer." Akter smiled into his mage's surprised eyes. "I will, however, find a woman just for you, Wizard of Zamboula."

"Your . . . sword, my lord Akter Khan."

"Ah yes." Akter turned and took the blade from Baltaj. "How good of you to have wiped it clean and shining, Baltaj!"

"I but returned her blood to her, lord Khan. She did not notice."

Laughing, Akter Khan left the dungeon, and with him his mage, and in a short time two men brought a swordless young guardsman into Baltaj's hands. As he was wholly innocent and hardly knew Mitralia, Khoja looked upon her corpse with little emotion, he had seen dead women before, though not one, true, who bore marks of ninety or more strokes of a hot iron.

"He did indeed know of us, Chia," Zafra said. "We are safe now; he was so grateful that I 'confessed' our friendship."

"And Mitralia?"

"Gone, poor dear. The potion I had you give her did its work, and my spell; she actually confessed to being a spy for Balad, and said precisely those things I bade her say, when her mind was open and helpless to me. She implicated the guardsman you mentioned—"

"Khoja."

"Yes."

"Good. The pig had the arrogance to look openly at me." Chia sighed, and caressed him. "I shall miss Mitralia, though; she did love my hair, and brushed it better than anyone! Now I shall have to find another, and train her."

Zafra chuckled. "Here, I will comb it with my fingers. I rather imagine our khan will choose the next girl to be sent you!"

"Ummm . . . but—Zafra? Khoja has nothing to confess."

"And so he will confess nothing. Baltaj will be impressed by his bravery and strength of character—and angry too. Khoja will not last long."

"Ah Zafra, Zafra! My genius love."

"I do not deny it, my love. Just do be exceedingly careful now, in your passing of information to Balad's agent!"

XII

ESCORT FOR TWO THIEVES

Hajimen and ten camel-perched Shanki would escort Conan and Isparana to Zamboula. Akhimen's decision and announcement brooked no demurrer, and Conan saw no reason to make one. He prevented Isparana from scandalizing the Shanki by asking for the men's clothing that was designed for riding. The scarlet robes of the Shanki women were voluminous enough to permit her to bestride a horse, he pointed out, and to these people, their friends, the concept of women in any sort of leggings was barbarous and worse.

"So? I am in company with a barbarian!"

"They don't know that, 'sparana. Now put your glarestone around your neck and prepare. No use waiting till noon to be on our way."

"Conan."

He had turned away; he looked back.

"I had a sword, Conan. You took it. I had a dagger, and used it to save you—though only Erlik knows why!"

Conan looked questioningly at her. He had thanked her; he knew what she wanted now, and was availing himself of the opportunity to ponder on it.

"I will have a sword and dagger," she said.

"With a guard of eleven men on camels, you will hardly need weapons."

"Said the Stygian to the Kushite!"

"Hm." He showed her a very small smile. "You are right. The first question these people asked was about your lack of weapons. We have quite an armory packed on that one horse! Khassek's sword and dagger, and Sarid's—"

"—and mine—"

"—and those of five of the Yoggites, plus the two that Khassek and I . . . acquired, up in Shadizar."

"And my sword."

"Aye, and your swo—ah! Wait, 'sparana."

Leaving the tent, Conan went to that pack he called their "armory," and opened it. On Hajimen while Akhimen Khan watched, the Cimmerian forced the good Akbitanean sword of Sarid the Samaratan. As a curiosity, he showed them Khassek's awful Ilbarsi knife. He showed the Shanki, too, the pommel-less sword of a certain king's agent of Shadizar in Zamora, and in laconic phrases he sketched the story of its acquirement. The Shanki laughed; Hajimen and others had met and endured officious fops—they called them *foops*—in Zamboula.

The desert men showed their appreciation of the workmanship and value of dear Ferhad's corundum-set dagger with its silver-etched blade.

"It is a gift for my beloved Isparana," Conan said. "I will keep the one she used to . . . help me, against those Yoggites."

Hajimen spat. Conan dutifully spat. A delightful custom, he mused, and vowed to mention the green-robed *jazikhim* again and again, so as to join the Shanki in the ritual spitting.

"It is a good man's gesture," Hajimen said, of Conan's gift to his "beloved woman." "On my camel I have packed clothing I outgrew at sixteen, when my growth came on me of a sudden. I know the woman of Conan is a warrior. Once we are well away from here and my father and others will not know and be horrified, I shall present those clothes to the warrior-woman called Isparana."

"That is kind of Akhimen," Conan said, "though she loves her Shanki woman's finery." *About as much as I love eating nettles,* he thought. So Hajimen represented a liberal new generation, did he? A shame; the Shanki might change under him, when Hajimen's turn came to be called khan.

"I am sorry that we had no clothing big enough for our guest," Hajimen said, "save the kaffia and camel-robe we give him with pleasure."

"I like these," Conan said grinning, though in truth he was warm, in padded vest and the mail corselet he had yet to blood, though he had owned it for two months. As the Shanki wore no mail, the Cimmerian had covered his with a tunic—which was being ruined from the inside, as must be any cloth worn over a mail of links or scales. Reward awaited him, in Zamboula. He would bedeck himself in an embroidered tunic of scarlet then, if he wished!

The Cimmerian did wear a pair of the ballooning crimson leggings of the Shanki; they were too short, but he did not care. His booted legs were covered past the calves; how much legging did a man need?

"When I have handed these arms to Isparana," he said, "we will be ready to depart the abode of the Shanki."

"But not their company. Our camels kneel in readiness for Conan of Cimmeria."

"Call me Conan."

"I just have, guest of my people."

Conan turned away smiling. He went to Isparana. With a grim-faced austerity she buckled on the sword-belt and drew the sheath around a little so that it hung down her left leg. She looked pointedly at the shorter sheath on her right thigh, and at Conan.

"My dagger? You took it out of that Yoggite, did you not?"

Conan spat Shanki-style, and smiled. "Aye, though it wasn't easy. In his fall off his horse he fell on that arm and pinned it to his chest by your dagger. I will keep it as a memento. Remember how first we met, Ispy—"

"'sparana I will tolerate," she said. "Ispy I will not!"

"—two thieves," he went on, "glowering at each other across that fell chamber of Hisarr Zul? Who'd ever have believed then that you would one day save my life—deliberately!"

"I acted without thinking."

"As you did that day when the Khawarizmi took us? After I downed several of those slaving dogs and insured our escape, you bashed me out of the saddle."

In her flowing, shapeless red clothing and with her lips all black and her eyes seeming huge and lustrous within their black outlines, she shook her head. "No, that day I was thinking! You had after all lost me both my camels, and all my supplies. I will have my dagger now, barbarian thief!"

"That was the day after I took the Eye of Erlik from around your neck while you slept."

"Dog! Grunting pig of a barbarian!"

"Ah, I was fearful that you had done with those terms of endearment I have grown to expect and relish, 'sparana."

"You had also watched me disrobe and bathe in that oasis pool! And I shall wear this scar on my hip forever, slinking barbarian viper!"

Conan had reminded her deliberately to test her reaction. She did not shout, or draw sword. "I am sorry for that now, Isparana—and had no idea it would hap-

136

pen. I am gladder than glad that you had the false amulet in a pouch at your hip when Hisarr's sorceries melted it to slag, rather than around your neck. I should hate for that beautiful bosom to be scarred."

"You do love them, don't you, pawing barbarian hog?"

"I do love them, 'sparana. And I did not touch you, that night at the oasis."

"Why didn't you, Conan? You have since called me irresistible. I was asleep, and you had been watching me. You could have—"

"I am not a rapist, Isparana," Conan said quietly, with dignity.

She stared at him. "Lying mange-stinking cur! Just a few days ago—"

"That was two weeks ago, and it was not rape," Conan said, and stared.

When Isparana looked away in silent admission of truth, Conan said, "On that day you tried to slay me, and because of you, both Sarid and Khassek died. Khassek was a good man, 'sparana."

"Well . . . Sarid was not, but I am sorry now that I used him and that he is dead. And that because of me he slew your Iranistani friend, too."

"Yet if you had not seduced and used Sarid—"

"I did not have to 'seduce' him, Conan!"

"Had you not used Sarid, and come north, you and I would never have met again and joined forces, 'sparana. Or should I call you Lady Kiliya?"

She made a face. It was the name he had used that day the slave-caravan from Kharawizm took them, at the oasis where he had stolen the Eye and been interrupted by her—wielding sword and epithets—so that her camels had fled into the night. The Khawarizmi had not believed she was any Lady Kiliya, or that she was kin of Samara's king, either, as Conan had contended. He had bloodily disposed of three or four of them—after which she had indeed struck him unconscious and fled. Unfortunately others from the caravan had caught her, after which she and Conan put in a few days in slave-coffle.

"Was there a Kiliya, Conan?"

"There was. A girl of Arenjun," Conan said, remembering how that vixen had cried out for his life, after he'd been plying her with drinks and charm. "Just a girl, Ispa. Not a woman, like you."

Isparana was hardly the sort to simper, though she did speak softly while looking just as gently into his eyes. "There have been many girls, haven't there—and women."

"A number," Conan said with a shrug. "As there have been many men for you."

"Some," she said, imitating his shrug and thinking on what a rotten lover Sarid had been. "You are trying to get me to admit that you are a passing good lover and that I no longer hope to see you cut to pieces and fed to the dogs who are your brothers, thieving cur."

He wagged his head. "Ah, and you seek to turn my head with pretty pet names, my love. No, I am not trying to get you to say anything," he said, while outside a waiting camel made its ridiculous noise. Conan produced the dagger he had concealed in his belt, in back; Ferhad's dagger, king's agent of Shadizar. "Here. Your dagger, *my lady*."

"This is not my—Conan! It . . . it is jeweled—this is a ruby! Both these are sapphires, surely . . . can this be an *emerald*?"

"It can. And that could be silver on the blade, too. Probably weakens it. I doubt that pretty twig is of much value as a weapon, 'sparana." He was close onto embarrassment, whatever that was. "You could sell it and buy a barrel of good carvers and stickers, though. Along with some slinky Zamboulan clothing."

138

She was staring at the knife, which she turned over and over in her hands. "Why, this lovely stone is a pelageren!" she murmured. She looked up of a sudden, and for a moment Conan thought her eyes had gone glassy with avarice. Then he realized that he was looking at a film of moisture. Isparana? *Tears*? Her hand closed tightly on the gem-encrusted hilt. "I shall never sell this gift, Conan. How could you think that I would? It is a gift, from you!"

Conan swallowed and felt approximately as had he been hanging by his thumbs. "Well . . . after all, I stole it."

She smiled at him. "Oh Conan! What else, how else would such as I and you come by anything? Both Karamek and I were thieves, in Zamboula; did you not know that? That is why Akter Khan sent us so far north to regain the Eye that Hisarr Zul had stolen. Had he promised us only that we could retain our hands—since we had been caught, and losing them is the penalty—we would never have bothered. We were promised full pardons, you see, *and* no mention to Turan, which has agents everywhere, *and* sufficient reward on our return to Zamboula that we would not need to steal again."

"Well," Conan admitted, "it was you who stole it from old Hisarr, not I. I am the one he caught!"

She laughed, and of a sudden she hugged him. "Oh Conan, think you I would believe a gift from you would have been *paid for*, darling?"

"Just call me mangy cur or barbar swine or . . . viper, even," he said uncomfortably. "I have grown accustomed to such names, from you."

Quietly, pressing against him still, she said, "Conan . . ."

He tugged free and turned to the tent's open flap. "Come, Isparana. Our camel-riding escort is waiting.

139

So is the khan of Zamboula . . . and sufficient reward that we won't need to steal again. After that . . . the biggest room in the biggest inn in Zamboula?"

"Aye!" she cried, her eyes alight. "The best, in the Royal Turan Inn, for Lord Conan and his . . . the Lady Kiliya?"

And laughing, they went out into the sun.

XIII

ZAMBOULA

The camel-warriors saw the horsemen first, or one of them.

A moment after the Shanki called out and pointed to the approaching rider whose helmet flashed in the sunlight, that man reined in. The Shanki also drew up, less than a mile from the horseman who was recognizably a uniformed soldier. They watched him lift a brass trumpet to his lips and heard the blast he blew. As if in reply, another sounded well to his left. A third followed, off to his right, and then another, farther off. And another.

Hajimen lifted an arm straight up. His men—and the two horse-mounted people they escorted—moved in closer to his dromedary.

"Stand ready to charge or fight," he said, "and do nothing without my command save proceed, at a walk."

Conan and Isparana had to wait until ten Shanki had acknowledged, aloud. Then the eleven camels and eighteen horses paced forward on the sparkling sand.

Minutes later, helmeted horsemen in yellow sashes had converged in a sort of pincer, and they were surrounded by soldiers.

141

"Zamboulans," Hajimen muttered. "Halt. Do nothing without my command."

"Hai, Shanki!" the leader of the horse-soldiers called.

Seated high atop his dromedary, Hajimen looked around at each of twenty men, and saw no drawn weapons or cocked crossbows. He lifted his weapons hand.

"Hajimen, son of Akhimen Khan of the Shanki, greets the warriors of the Khan of the Zamboulans," he called, in his best voice. "The Khan of the Zamboulans knows of our coming, to trade horses in the marketplace?"

Conan listened to Hajimen's voice, brought up from the diaphragm, wander off across the desert to be lost.

"If those two with you are Isparana of Zamboula and her companion, we are sent to escort them."

"I am Isparana!"

Conan kicked forward the horse he had named Dunestrider, as he had promised the beast. "I am Conan, a Cimmerian. I ride with Isparana of Zamboula. How knew your khan that we were approaching?"

"I do not know, uh, Conan. He said you were, though we weren't given your name, only hers. He sent us to conduct you to the city and the palace."

"Kind of your khan," Conan said with some amusement. "We are escorted by these Shanki, too. Do you have a name?"

"I am Jhabiz, Prefect. That is Isparana of Zamboula with you?"

"I said I was, Jhabiz, and I know you," she called. "We bring that which Akter Khan desires."

"Good. There is no need for your people, Hajimen Shanki, to ride all the way to Zamboula." The bigbeaked wight had a face like an accipitrine.

"Oh well, we will," Hajimen said, glancing around. "So many horse-soldiers to escort two! Conan and Isparana are our friends, and we are charged by our khan to see them into the camp of the Zamboulans. And we came to trade horses, remember?"

The Zamboulan prefect lifted a finger to scratch in the fork of his beard. He sat forward a bit, revealing the beginnings of a belly. Thus he sat his big chestnut horse, chewing his mustache while he reflected. "I suppose we must all ride together, then. We have the same charge from our khan."

"We will be happy for the warriors of the Khan of the Zamboulans to join us," Hajimen said, with no enthusiasm whatever.

Conan grinned. A couple of Shanki chuckled— and so did at least one of the men in the bright double sash and helmet streamers of Zamboula. The Cimmerian looked up at Hajimen, perched atop his single-humped camel. The Shanki leader nodded. Shanki camels began to pace forward. The two they escorted rode amid them, and Prefect Jhabiz had to move. Seizing on opportunity, he wheeled his chestnut about and set off at the walk, toward Zamboula. This way Jhabiz seemed to be leading the entire group of eleven camels, fifty-eight horses, one woman, and thirty-one men in addition to his uncomfortable self. His men drew in slowly, bracing the clot of camels and lead-horses in the midst of which rode the two objects of this massive escort.

Conan looked over at Isparana and grinned. "Does the size of our retinue meet my lady's satisfaction?"

"Aye, Lord Conan," she said, and they laughed together.

Though the Zamboulans were as aware of their mission and conscientiously proprietary of their two charges as the Shanki, all managed to avoid incidents during the next few days. At last Conan watched the desert sprout the towers and domes of a city. Next he saw its walls, a glaring white. The whole grew larger, and he was able to make out trees; palms and twisty olives. Eventually Jhabiz called two of his men to him and issued quiet instructions. First directing a dual trumpet blast at those slowly nearing walls, both men set off for them at the gallop. Little coils of yellowish dust curled up behind them so that they seemed pursued by sand demons.

The gates stood wide by the time the company reached them. All rode in on a broad thoroughfare that Conan saw was well defended by walls on two sides. The temperature within the walls was higher though the city proper began a bit farther on. Some horse- and camelmanship allowed Jhabiz to wait while Hajimen came alongside.

"You know the way to the market," the Zamboulan said.

"Aye. We will ride with my friends as far as the palace, and thence to the market."

"Hajimen Shanki son of a khan—camels are not allowed on the Royal Way! Nor may more than twenty riders approach the palace in a body,"

Hajimen stared impassively down from his camelish perch. Silence rose like mist, and tension rode it.

"Prefect," Conan said, and Jhabiz, gone all uncomfortable again, looked at him. "Best suspend one rule for today, and bend the other. There are thirteen of us; it seems wise that you and six of your men ride with us, while the rest of your command hurries ahead, or follows at a goodly interval, or takes a different route."

"No one is going to like this . . ."

"I am one with them," Conan assured the poor man. "And I but suggested a remedy to a problem. It would seem to save some feelings and some face. Any other attempt at solution might endanger Zamboula's relationship with the Shanki."

The eagle-nosed prefect glanced around. His lips moved silently and now he looked unhappy in addition to uncomfortable. At last he nodded. He ordered his second to choose a dozen men and start to follow, at walk, once Jhabiz and company had turned onto the Royal Way, a little way down this thoroughfare.

Thus the thief Isparana returned to Zamboula of the orchards and mulberry groves and dome-topped buildings and scarlet towers, surrounded by an escort that attracted as many stares as a royal delegation.

Thus did Conan first enter Zamboula; trousered, wearing a white kaffia and flowing Shanki robe over his mailvest, escorted by helmeted soldiers and camel-mounted tribesmen as he paced his horse up the Royal Way toward the onion-like dome of the palace of a high Turanian satrap—who had never heard of him. Nor could any staring citizen guess who might be this obviously important man who was so tall that his legs hung down on a horse as other men's did when they bestrode ponies.

Prefect Jhabiz, maintaining the semblance of being in charge, rode solemnly, stolidly ahead of them all. He stared straight ahead and his left hand lay decoratively on his thigh.

Behind that strange procession plodded sixteen riderless horses; Conan's and Isparana's four sumpter beasts, their packs now much shrunken, and the trained desert riding horses captured from the Yoggite raiders. Akhimen Khan had made his choices from among Conan's five and Conan gave Hajimen one, so that only two were the property of the Cimmerian. He had not mentioned to Isparana that he also considered both Sarid's and Khassek's former mounts his property.

Riding beside him, she looked anything but a woman of Zamboula. They, Conan noted, wore not so much makeup around the eyes, and their lips, when

145

painted, were red or a purplish pink. Nor were these women given overmuch to clothing, he saw, which was unfortunate for those with jiggly bellies.

Closer and higher loomed the palace. It rose up in a jumble of additions of gray and white stone faced by yellow-painted columns, and a broad flight of sand-hued steps topped by a crenellated defense wall before the great carven doorway. About it lofted the palace proper, in multiple towers, walls of painted mud-brick, and the great dark dome that was like unto a gigantic onion pulled fresh from the ground. Robed and trousered, tunicked and tabarded, courtiers and bureaucrats on their varied business paused to stare at the mass of approachers.

Camels on the Royal Way! This giant of a man with his painted, Shanki-dressed woman must be important indeed!

At the foot of the broad palace steps, Conan turned to Hajimen.

"Do the Shanki bargain well?"

Hajimen allowed his lips to widen and show a small flash of teeth. "The Shanki bargain better than the Zamboulans!"

"Good," Conan said, "as we are in Zamboula. Do you then trade for all six of my horses with yours, for pearls or necklace of Zamboulan coinage, or some such that I can carry easily. And the swords in that bay's pack, as well."

"We will be pleased and honored to trade for Conan of Cimmeria."

"Will the khan's son name a place where we shall meet some hours hence? Say at sunset?"

"At the camel stables in the Quarter called Bronze will be the Shanki, or one to meet and guide Conan."

Conan nodded and dismounted. Atop the steps, Zamboulans watched, in rich garments. Rounding his horse, Conan put up his hands for Isparana. After a

146

moment's hesitation, her face relaxed. With a smile, she allowed herself to be lifted down as if she were a lady. Since she was the khan's agent, Conan had decided to be kind; he would let her seem knowledgeable before her employer. Once her feet were on the ground, he held her long enough to mutter into her hair.

"I wear the amulet under my clothes. You may tell him so."

"But you—when did you put it there?" She stepped back only a little, frowning, trying to decide whether to believe.

"Months ago, in Arenjun."

"But—"

"But you did not find it when you searched me in 'our' Shanki tent a few nights ago!" he said, with a chary smile. "It was there. I hung it around my neck the day after I slew Hisarr Zul and burned his manse."

"But . . . no! You mean it is that ugly . . . *thing?*"

Conan smiled benignly at her.

Doubtless some of the openly curious watchers wondered why the blacklipped woman in the white Shanki robe over red Shanki sirwal was cursing while she and Conan ascended the palace steps.

Conan's query of the man beside him was casual; "Someone will take care of our mounts, won't he?"

"Aye," Jhabiz said, and turned to give that order. He hurried after Conan and Isparana, who had not paused.

"In the event you are dismissed while we are still with the khan, Jhabiz," Conan said, returning the glare of a silk-robed courtier who might outweigh a horse, "I'll be looking for an inn later. You know that I will be starting from the stables in the Bronze Quarter no later than sundown."

"And if the khan wishes to keep you longer?"

Conan swaggered; a superbly robed man stepped aside. "He won't."

"I—"

"I will be buying," the Cimmerian said. "Won't I, 'sparana."

"—whelp of a camel-molesting rot-crotched viper —yes—son and heir of a Khitan yellow mongrel bitch . . ."

"I will try to be there," Jhabiz said. "What is the matter with her, man of Cimmeria? Have you two had a falling out?"

"She is insanely in love with me and fears that Akter Khan will separate us to get at her beautiful mouth," Conan said, and they passed into the palace with Isparana still running through her vocabulary of invective.

XIV

THE EYE OF ERLIK

Conan looked first for means of defense and exit, in Akter Khan's broad hall of state.

He and Isparana were escorted through an entry closed by two heavy doors that Conan saw secured from within by means of an enormous bar of iron-bound wood. It was counterbalanced in a pivot for easy raising and lowering. Thirty paces to his left the cream-painted wall was split by a single portal, tall and paneled. An identical door cut the wall forty paces to rightward. Both doors were closed and he saw no others.

The high-backed fruitwood chair with its carvings picked out in silver rested on a dais projecting from the wall opposite the main entry. The throne rested in its center, twenty paces from Conan. Four slim tall niches slitted the wall behind it, to let in air and light. By their depth Conan was made aware of the great thickness of the palace's outside walls. Each of the shoulder-high windows was framed by yellow hangings broidered with a vermiform pattern of antirrhinum in green and scarlet and white. A large copper-bound pot of unglazed stone rested below each archery-and-light-slit, bravely thrusting up some waxy-leafed plant. That long, long wall was braced and embellished by five half-columns or pilasters with carven lions' heads, and by a single decoration.

Conan assumed that the latter was not purely for decor. Only an ell or so to the left of the throne, which was nearly the same distance forward of the wall, two spikes had been forced into the stone. Each held in place a bracket that seemed to be of gold and was more likely a gilded lesser metal. The brackets supported, perhaps five feet above the floor, a curved sword sheath banded about with silver and red leather. From the mouth of the sheath thrust the gem-set hilt of a sword.

That of Zamboula's founder, perhaps, Conan mused. *Or Akter's Sword of State, a symbol of rule he doesn't care to wear while sitting his throne. A gift from Turan's king, perhaps.* It didn't matter.

Here and there about the room towered great columns of wood or painted stone designed to resemble trees. Conan's long arms could not have encompassed any of them. Just as stolidly, a resplendently attired guard stood at either end of the dais. Those two men stared at nothing. Up on the dais, at either side of the throne, stood a man. Advisers, Conan assumed; vizirs. He on the khan's right wore robe and brocaded surcoat of brown and scarlet. A silver chain rested on his breast below his chin, which was cleanshaven though the rest of his face was bearded and mustached. He was balding. *A man of no great happiness,* Conan mused.

The man to the khan's left was surely but little past a score years of age, and not unhandsome under his tall, odd cap of brown. His slim legs were encased in snug red leggings, under a plain white tunic on whose breast glittered a fine medallion of gold and pearls and sunny topazes. *Eyes like a snake,* Conan thought, *and full of both pride and intelligence.*

At the felt-shod feet of each of the presumed advisers sat a scribe; one quite old and one surprisingly young, and large; between them Akter Khan was enthroned. He was hardly hideous though perhaps a bit dissipated, and he did show a bit of stomach.

His eyes shifted their bright dark gaze from the Cimmerian to Isparana, glanced back at Conan, and came to rest on the woman.

"Isparana of Zamboula returns to her khan," a voice called from behind Conan, "and with her Conan, a Cimmerian from far to the north."

"Report to Vizir Hafar, Prefect," Akter Khan said, and Conan heard the undertone of excitement in his voice.

Prefect Jhabiz, the balding man, and the old scribe converged at the door to Conan's left. They passed through the portal and closed it behind them. That quickly, Conan had noted the paneled door's considerable thickness.

Again Akter Khan spoke. "Why is the man from the far north with our servant Isparana?"

At that moment Conan realized how vulnerable he was, and he felt a chill as he recalled Isparana's unpredictability—and the several reasons she had to feel enjoyment and exhilaration at seeing him crushed, tortured . . . slain.

"He has aided me," Isparana said, and only a little of Conan's tenseness eased. "Conan of Cimmeria bears that which I went to fetch."

From either side of the falcate nose the khan's eyes stared at Conan. "Conan of Cimmeria, you are in the presence of Akter Khan, ruler of Zamboula and the land roundabout in the name of and as Satrap of Yildiz Great, King of Turan and Lord of Empire. There must be no danger to me or to you in this hall. Your weapons will be returned to you just outside the doors behind you."

Conan's armpits prickled. The lance-armed guards

flanking the first step of the dais stared at nothing while appearing ready for anything. Conan glanced around to see four corseleted, helmeted soldiers. They stared at him.

He swallowed and his skin seemed to crawl as though ants walked up his spine. Disarm himself! Place himself at the mercy of this satrap, of these armed men —of Isparana's whim! It went very much against the grain. Yet he considered the alternative, in those few seconds. A ruler enthroned had bade him disarm. He could acquiesce and hand the man the amulet he prized so highly, or be arrested, or try to fight his way out—of a place crowded with armed guards, and then a hostile city that debouched on desert?

I do not have a choice, he thought, and his gaze shifted briefly to the sword mounted on the wall. How swiftly could he get to it, if need be; how swiftly could he whip it from its sheath and whirl to try to fight? *While walking to that door to follow Hafar and Jhabiz,* he thought, for he was incapable of not considering such action. He found impressive words:

"No foreigner should approach a king in his chamber under arms," he said, and unbuckled the belt that supported the sheaths of both sword and dagger. He held the two ends of the belt out from his hips without turning, and hands took them from him, from behind. Conan stood unarmed, at the whim of Isparana and Akter Khan.

"Leave us," Akter Khan said. "Zafra and Uruj will remain, with me and these our two returned servants."

Like animated statues, the two throne guards paced the width of the hall, past Conan and Isparana, and out of the hall. Conan heard the big doors close behind him. On the dais remained the standing man in the cap, and the seated scribe, who was both young and large.

Why, Conan asked himself, would a scribe remain

152

during the private report of a khan's agent? And he replied at once, judging from the man's size: *Uruj is a bodyguard. That slim fellow in the silly hat, then . . . what is his purpose?* He wished that he had asked more questions of Isparana. The throneroom was now empty save for the five. Conan and four Zamboulans. Enemies?

"Isparana: You have brought me the Eye of Erlik?"

"Aye, my lord Khan."

"Bring it to me, excellent servant."

She glanced at Conan.

"I have it," he said, and noted that the big scribe rearranged himself and watched keenly while the Cimmerian lifted both hands to his own neck. From under his clothing he drew the thong trailing the glass-set blob of fired clay. Lifting it off over his head, he held it before him. The oblate hemisphere swung and turned slowly in the air, obviously worthless.

Even while Akter Khan frowned at an object obviously not his valued amulet, Conan squatted. With some care, he rapped the thing on the floor of alternating red and pink tiles, then again. The clay cracked, split, fell away in bits. Isparana stared as entrancedly as the man on the throne.

Conan rose. Again he held his arm before him, and again an object turned slowly at the end of the leather cord.

The sword-shaped pendant was about the length of the Cimmerian's least finger. An unfaceted ruby formed the pommel. At each end of the crossbar of the guard twinkled a large yellow stone barred vertically with a single black stripe. The stones, set about an inch apart, seemed to stare like eerie xanthic eyes from either side of a long and pointed nose of silver.

"*The Eye of Erlik!*"

Eye of Erlik

Akter Khan's voice emerged with fervor though little above a whisper. He sat tensely forward in his chair of state. His two hands gripped the curled forward edges of its arms, and the knuckles were pale. His dark eyes stared no less glassily than the "eyes" of the amulet.

Conan thought the satrap was about to rise. Akter did not. One hand parted itself from the throne's arm, and was extended, palm up.

"*To me,*" Akter said in the same breathless voice of intensity.

After three months of perilous adventure and seemingly endless travel and travail because of this bauble, Conan was almost loath to part with it. Almost. Yet he did not carry it forward to that waiting royal hand. Instead he caught up Isparana's hand, and pressed the Eye of Erlik into her palm.

"It has ever been your mission and your emprise, 'sparana," he said, loudly enough to be heard on the dais. "Complete it."

In her Shanki sirwal, tunic, sleeved surcoat—and black cosmetics—Isparana paced the width of the hall to her ruler. Conan saw that the man's outstretched hand trembled. *Was* his life force caught up in that little bauble? Was he now about to become invincible, unslayable? Conan watched, and the thought came extraneously that only tall women should wear ballooning leggings.

Into the waiting, tremorous hand Isparana placed the Eye of Erlik, and the satrap's fist closed on it. Nothing sorcerous or dramatic occurred, after all this time and horror and the cost in lives. The Khan of Zamboula had his Eye of Erlik. The thief he had hired went to one knee, her head bowed, while he leaned back with a long sigh.

"Up, Isparana, excellent servant," he said, and she rose.

On the breast of his multi-hued robe of silk lay a medallion, slung on a chain of finely wrought gold. The pendant was a winged square of the same metal, beaten and indited. In its center was a large ballflower design, with a smaller one decorating each corner. The silver leaves folded in to hold the ball, which was a ruby the size of a hummingbird's eye.

Soon that pendant lay on Isparana's breast, while her khan wore a less ornate one, a sword-shape slung on a strip of hide.

"You have both done well," Akter Khan said, "and I am more than pleased. Conan of Cimmeria: Approach."

Conan moved forward, thinking he had been most

clever in handing the amulet to Isparana with the courtly words he'd spoken for both her benefit and the satrap's. He was weaponless. Without his belt's weight he felt both naked and uncomfortable—and most vulnerable, at the mercy of a woman who bore an ugly scar because of him; who but for him would have returned the amulet, alone, two months ago. (Would she? He wondered. The Khawarizmi might have got her, alone—and without him, she would still be slave, doubtless sold up in Arenjun or Shadizar.) The woman's good will had become important to him, in this throneroom of a foreign city. Nor was he certain of it. Reaching her side, he halted. His nod served as an abbreviated bow.

"What part had you," Akter asked, "in this emprise that has taken Isparana so many months?"

More aware of the emotionless eyes of the capwearer at the khan's side than of Akter's, Conan elected to tell the truth. "It is in part because of me that so many months have passed, Khan of Zamboula. We began as rivals and enemies, though now she knows that I was a helpless servant of Hisarr Zul."

All four Zamboulans showed surprise at that open admission, which the Cimmerian had been careful to ameliorate by mentioning his thralldom to Hisarr.

"And Hisarr Zul?"

"He who was driven from Zamboula ten years ago," Conan said, "and who on the desert murdered his brother Tosya who thereafter haunted the Dragon Hills as the Sand-lich; who stole the amulet of Akter Khan and the very *soul* of Conan of Cimmeria . . . is dead, lord Khan."

For the first time, the man beside the satrap spoke. "You slew him?"

"I did, and destroyed him with fire. His manse burned as well."

"His—knowledge?" Zafra asked, his voice intense. "His scrolls, his devices?"

"All." Conan shrugged. "Burned with him. I would touch none of it."

"Well done!" Akter Khan exclaimed, and Conan saw his teeth.

He was aware that Zafra's expression had become one of disappointment and some disgust, and Conan knew that the man was not pleased. It was then he realized that this Zafra must be a wizard, despite his lack of years. Aye, he was older than Conan and Isparana as well. But Conan had assumed that mages, to be full of knowledge, must be old men. Now he realized that was ridiculous. One grew old only by having been young, and any master could die so that his apprentice succeeded. Or, the Cimmerian supposed, a man could be as adept and clever at wizardry as Conan was with weapons.

He knew that he was not only in the presence of a mage, but probably the foremost in this vicinity—and a man he had better respect and be wary of.

He was right; Akter introduced Zafra as Wizard of Zamboula, mentioning that the fellow had not been here when Isparana had departed. Isparana inclined her head. Having recognized the medallion he word, she knew the man in the Ferygian cap stood high. Such a change, in the third of a year since she and Karamek had ridden out of this city of her birth! With her little bow, her own pendant moved restlessly on her breast. It was a reminder: Aye, such a change indeed! She would not need to go back to Squatter's Alley now! It had produced her and trained her; now her career as thief and liar and sometime streetgirl was making her wealthy. She glanced at Conan.

"Hisarr Zul said that the Eye is magickal," he said. "Zafra has been in magickal contact with it? You knew we approached Zamboula, wizard?"

Zafra's mouth smiled, but it was Akter who spoke. "Shall the Wizard of Zamboula tell you where the Eye of Erlik has been, Conan of Cimmeria?"

"I shall tell you," Conan said, though he certainly had not intended to do. "Isparana and I planned no secrets from the Satrap of the Empire of Turan."

"You and Isparana have been antagonists, even sought to slay one another. Yet you are now friends."

"Together," Conan said, "we restored your amulet. I had to serve Hisarr Zul, for a time. He had my soul, literally."

"He *had* gained that ability!" Zafra said excitedly, and looked immediately unhappy that he had showed emotion.

"Aye. He wanted yours of course, Khan of Zamboula. I *had* to gain the amulet, and return it to him. That I did, killing horses and nearly myself to overtake Isparana on the desert. I returned it to Hisarr, who then sought to slay me. I was able to kill him, and—"

"At one time," Akter Khan said, looking thoughtfully at the foreigner, "both of you, with the Eye, turned and started back northward."

Isparana was tight-mouthed as she said, "We were enslaved, by Khawarizmi. We were able to gain free."

"But then you came on for Zamboula, whilst the Eye went north." The satrap nodded at the Cimmerian. "With this man, I now assume."

"It is true," Conan said, before Isparana could speak; he was egregiously uncomfortable, reminding Isparana of this part of their past. "I had tricked her, or rather Hisarr Zul had, with a duplicate of the Eye." *I should not have brought* that *up!* "She thought she had the real one."

"A duplicate!" Akter's hand jerked up to slap over the amulet.

"Calm yourself, my lord," Zafra said smoothly.

"You wear the true and only Eye of Erlik, for I tracked it here."

"What became of Hisarr's copy?" the khan demanded, only a bit less intensely.

"Destroyed," Isparana said. "Hisarr Zul caused it to melt, to assure himself that Conan had brought him the real one. It is someplace out on the desert. A shame, for Conan has told me the gems and gold were real. It was merely a gaud, of course, without other properties."

Conan glanced at the sword on the wall, and at the seated scribe he assumed was bodyguard, with a concealed weapon or two. He did not like this conversational area at all. Isparana was reminded of her pain, her scar, and all she needed do to betray Conan utterly was utter a few words.

"Hanuman be praised," Akter said to Isparana, "that you were not wearing it at the time." And had Conan worn a sword, his hand would have eased toward its hilt.

"Yes," Isparana said, with a glance at the Cimmerian. "I was fortunate."

A relieved Conan tried not to show his sigh. Was her fondness, her attachment to him real? Had she really forgiven? Perhaps she planned to blackmail; perhaps she wanted this power over him, the ability to betray, without really wanting him to be harmed. Conan thought swiftly. Since he assumed that Zafra knew already, he felt it wise to speak up before the men on the dais thought they were trapping him.

"The Eye, worn as you saw it when I entered, has also been to Shadizar and Khauran."

"And Conan," Isparana said, "has never made attempt to slay me, and spoke up to free me from the Khawarizmi when he could have left me enslaved."

So I did, Conan thought. *How heroic of me!*

Akter had nodded. He glanced at his wizard and smiled as if to say *There: we knew that; this man is*

159

truthful! The khan sat back, relaxed. Though he assumed the ordeal was over, Conan kept his mental guard up.

"You will dine with me," Akter Khan said. "I would hear your adventures."

"The honor is extreme," Isparana said, almost gasping, and she bowed her head until her chin was nearly on her breast.

"A warrior of Cimmeria is honored, lord Khan," Conan said. "However, the son of Akhimen Khan will be awaiting me at the camel stables in the Bronze Quarter. Have I time to take word to him?"

"Even Akhimen Khan enters this story!" Akter said, and shook his head bemazedly. "Suppose that I send him word. That same messenger will arrange lodgings for you both at the Royal Turan Inn. That and dinner will be but the first of your rewards from my hands, Conan of Cimmeria. As Zafra has learned, I am a most generous sovran, with those who serve me well. A warrior, eh? Well. We will see that you are both bathed and provided clothing, after which, over dinner, you will tell me of your obviously manifold and multitudinous adventures whilst returning my amulet to me!"

XV

CONAN HERO

In the few fabrics Conan was accustomed to, "white" tended to range from a sort of beige approaching the hue of lambskin parchment to the faintly yellowish color of cream. He had seen white that was truly so: the color of milk. He had never cared to spend money for such, even on those few occasions when he could have afforded it. Nor had he worn silk before—or the gift of a regnant monarch.

Thus the garment of Khitan silk provided him by Akter Khan was trebly a new experience for the Cimmerian. He felt most noble looking, nigh regal, in the gleaming, red-broidered white tunic that covered his upper arms and fell past mid-thigh. Nor was he unhappy with the broad and signally lightweight belt of red felt. Though he had admired the short boots of the same red felt worn by Akter Khan, Zafra, and Hafar and though he thought a pair would go handsomely with the belt, he was provided sandals.

Still, he remained Conan; he went out himself to see to the care of his horse in the palace stables, and to place his mail corselet and other clothing with his saddle. Dunestrider ignored that fine new name three times,

161

and turned to peer at his master only when Conan exasperatedly called him "Chestnut." So much, he thought, for nobly naming stupid beasts.

He returned to the palace through its rear door—at which he was challenged. He was passed with only a minimum of snarling, and no threats.

Isparana also wore white silk. The sleeveless dress was long and clinging, and Conan was instantly interested and aroused. There was nothing to be done about that; they met as they were being conducted to dine with the satrap.

Present were the same five only: the khan and his mage, the supposed scribe with the wrists and shoulders of a fighter, Isparana, and Conan. They were served by boys whose veins contained some Stygian blood. The repast was superb, if overly delicate and spicy. There was plenty of meat, and Conan did appreciate the fresh fruit. To his liking, too, was Akter Khan's wine.

The scribe or "scribe" Uruj said nothing at all, which prompted Conan to wonder if the big fellow might be tongueless, or deaf. Zafra said little but sat thoughtfully listening with an air of perception that increased Conan's nervousness as much as the mage's bland snake's eyes. Akter Khan asked many questions and favored the apricot wine. Conan and Isparana did the talking, a lot of it.

A deal of the wine he had poured down had risen to enfume Conan's head when they had finished their repast and Akter signaled an end to his listening. Both he and Conan were reeling and had gone thick of tongue. The mightily impressed satrap presented the Cimmerian with a fine goblet of gold, and ten coins—Turanian Eagles, more valued and thus impressive than Zamboulan currency. He vowed there would be more for such a hero.

Though he also provided the northern youth with

a fine, voluminous cloak of many yards of scarlet, Conan spent the night in the palace. He was in no condition to walk, or ride across town.

He awoke to a headache and a sour and hateful Isparana, and vowed to give up wine for life. Nevertheless he remained pleased with his fortune and taken with himself. Wearing clothing given him by a ruler, he had dined and gotten drunk with a ruler—and this time no little desert chieftain. Nor had he seen evidence that Akter Khan was other than a good fellow.

Akter Khan was busy; a ruler must rule, and decide, and listen to many people he would rather not even see. Munching figs and apricots, the two left the palace in company of Prefect Jhabiz. He took a tourist's route, showing them Zamboula and conducting them eventually to a fine big inn whose sign depicted a golden griffin on a background of scarlet: the Royal Turan. They were more than expected; their arrival had been eagerly anticipated since last evening. The innkeeper did not know why their rooms had been arranged by the Khan himself, and so was most solicitous. Indeed, the wight was regardful to the point of obsequiousness. Conan, more than cheerful, could not but strut. Though he had spent considerable time in inns, he had never been so treated, or stayed in one so fine, or been the object of such attention by other guests. Nor had he to worry about the size of the tap bill he accumulated, or the number of mugs of ale he could afford to consume.

Their room was indeed the best in that best of inns in Zamboula. Excited, exhilarated, calling each other "my lady" and "my lord," the two tarried in that spacious chamber to which they had repaired to change garments.

Downstairs Jhabiz awaited their pleasure for many minutes, and said nothing about it when they at last descended, glowing.

They betook themselves jubilantly down to the Bronze Quarter, which was seedy though hardly a Maul or a Desert. They smelled the camel stables well before they saw them, and heard the groaning beasts ere they reached their quarters. There Conan learned that one of his golden Eagles paid everyone's bill and gained him respectful treatment as well.

"And how did Conan find Akter Khan?" Hajimen asked.

"In better spirits now than when we came, by Crom! And generous, withal. A fine enough fellow, when one has done him a service."

While Isparana shot the exuberant Conan a look, Hajimen asked, "Spoke he of my sister?"

"Why . . . no, Hajimen," Conan said, in a more subdued voice.

"And is he in mourning for her?"

"Aye," Isparana said, and when Conan looked at her, he felt her fingers nudge into his back, under cover of his crimson cloak of finery. "You saw the black band he wore, Conan."

"Oh, aye," he said, realizing that she was doing Hajimen a kindness. "I saw so much that I was about to forget."

"It is good that the Khan of the Zamboulans mourns a daughter of the Shanki," Khanson Hajimen said nodding, though he did not smile.

Conan touched the desert man's yellow sleeve. "He seems no bad man at all, friend and son of a friend," he said, with Shanki formality. And he thought, *Odd, for a ruler! Though I'd make no avowals as to the sweetness of his wizard!*

"A captaincy in your *Guard*!" Zafra echoed, and Akter Khan looked sharply at him. "Your pardon, my lord," the wizard said more quietly, "but shock overcame my restraint, when you speak of giving employment to such a man as this Conan, and housing him in the very palace so nigh you."

Akter Khan leaned back and fixed the mage with a look both sharp and attentive.

"You serve me well, Zafra. You have my confidence and my ear. Speak. Give me your impression of him, then."

"He is young, and ambitious, and desirous of—" Zafra broke off. "Lord Khan, he returned the Eye of Erlik and is obviously a surpassing warrior. A most resourceful young man and more than dangerous with weapons. Most resourceful. Most dangerous. Just as obviously, you think highly of him. Best I do not speak in this matter."

"Zukli! Bring us wine!" the khan called, without taking his rather troubled gaze off Zafra. "Speak, Zafra. You have my ear, and my interest. Speak, Wizard of Zamboula, whom the khan trusts. He is resourceful, you said, and young, and ambitious. That is all apparent to any with eyes, and none of them is a sin. And you were about to add another word, when you broke off. Say it. Speak. It is your feeling that I should not trust this northern youth, Zafra?"

Zafra crushed a tiny fruitfly on his braid-worked green sleeve. "He is *uncivilized*, Akter Khan. A barbarian from some far northern land we know nothing of. Who knows what barbarous customs or codes they have? A certain disdain for nobility, I am thinking; even royalty. He left his people. He left *seeking;* the youth is an opportunist. He is ungoverned, lord Khan, and I think ungovernable. I would trust no such man close to me, regardless of his age. He is . . . restless. What will ever make such a wight content, relaxed, undesirous of more?"

"Hmm." The satrap took the wine a Kushite servant brought, and waved the boy away. "I hear and I see. And Isparana?"

"A thief from Squatter's Alley! Now she has been pardoned and more—she has been elevated, has dined with Akter Khan! A thief, a woman who has stolen and sold her goods and doubtless herself on these very streets! And—faugh! She loves that arrogant Cimmerian."

"Yes, I believe I saw that . . ."

"They have *served* you. Consider: a man has a fine trained bird. He uses it for years, and it hunts for him like no other. Yet one day it comes winging back from the hunt and pecks out his eye. Would he not have been better advised to note the signs of its discontent, and to have considered it a good servant now dangerous, and removed it? Best that Conan and Isparana have no opportunity to chatter about the Eye, or . . . *mis*-serve you, lord Khan."

Blinking, Akter drained his silver goblet and poured more wine. Zafra had not touched his. He leaned closer and spoke with low intensity.

"Consider. Consider the man, and the breed. In Arenjun he fought men of the city Watch, wounded and slew—and escaped. He was never punished, and thus his confidence and disrespect for authority increased. He duped Isparana more than once—and she loves him! What lesson has that taught him? We have only the barbarian's word. How do we know that great mage did not keep his bargain with the *barbarian* who fetched him back the Eye? In Shadizar, he somehow allied himself with a noblewoman of Khauran. There, he slew a Kothic noble; a *nobleman*, in the very presence of the queen! And now she too is dead. Conan? In Shadizar once more, he again entered into an encounter with the Watch, and again survived—unwounded, unscathed, *unpunished*."

Akter Khan shook his head. He belched. "A man indeed. Aye, and dangerous."

A fly buzzed in the room. The khan glowered; Zafra seemed not to notice. All his attention was concentrated on his khan and his words, and his voice continued low and intense.

"Unbridled, O Khan! Tell me that he and the *Iranistani* he traveled south with intended to bring the Eye to *you!* The Iranistani was slain. Conan found himself in the company of Isparana—of Zamboula. Doubtless he'd have been rewarded upon placing your amulet into the hands of the King of Iranistan. But now his Iranistani contact was dead, and a Zamboulan was there, and doubtless reward awaited him upon handing the Eye to its rightful owner . . . you see?"

Akter was nodding, sipping. His eyes were narrowed. The fly crawled on the lip of his goblet, and he did not so much as notice.

"So . . . Conan heroically returned the amulet to you. And he is hailed and rewarded and feted as hero! An opportunist, unrestrained and without principle. He has learned that he can do what he wishes, this Conan! Whom does he respect? What does he respect, he who has slain armed city guardsmen and a mage and a highborn noble? What lessons has he learned? Why should he respect anyone or anything save himself? What else has experience shown him? Give him command and he will want more. Give him responsibility and he will take more, assume more. Soon he will dream of full command. He knows much about you, lord Khan. Certainly Balad will contact him! I think such an unprincipled, unbridled *barbarian* will listen, and bargain with the man who seeks your throne!"

Akter Khan poured more wine. He did not see Zafra's glance leave his face, yet in one continuous movement the mage's hand shot out, wiped the fly off the table, and slapped it against his legging.

"I believe, Zafra," Akter said thoughtfully, "that

167

you have done me still another service. I believe you
have saved me from making an error, in the blindness
of my gratitude and my over-kind heart." Akter Khan
thought a moment on that, the purity and dangerous
over-kindness of his heart. "Aye, and I have elevated
Isparana overmuch, too. A well set-up wench though,
isn't she?"

A third voice spoke from the door, and Zafra was
glad: "O Khan, the Vizir awaits with—"

Akter Khan turned angry eyes on the aide. "Out!
He can wait! I am busy!"

When the poor startled fellow had withdrawn, Akter again drained his cup and looked at his wizard.
"Aye. Best his unchecked career is bridled here in Zamboula, ere more city guardsmen, even my own Thorns,
and more nobles fall to his impatience and his un-
questionable prowess. Aye. Hmm. . . Zafra . . . and
would you . . . *consent* to accept Isparana as a gift of
your khan . . ." For Akter Khan had noted how Zafra
looked upon her, and the khan was not yet totally a
fool.

Zafra made a gesture . . .

"Of course you would. Hafar! *Hafar*! To me!"

After a few moments the vizir opened the door
and his solemn face gazed questioningly at his ruler.

"Conan and Isparana are to be taken. Tell the
Captain so, and that he is to take his orders from my
excellent servant and adviser, Zafra."

Hafar held his face emotionless, for such an ability made a man a good vizir to such a khan and kept
him alive as well, and such a man was Hafar. "My
lord," he acknowledged, and it was enough.

"Then get rid of the rest of those damned fawning
petitioners and supplicants and toadies, Hafar, and
bring me those silly documents you want me to sign
and seal."

"My lord."

Zafra and Hafar left side by side, though not together. Nodding wisely, congratulating himself on his perspicacity and his good judgment in taking unto him such a man as Zafra, Akter Khan reached for the wine.

XVI

CONAN FUGITIVE

The other patrons of the Royal Turan Inn were a well-bred or moneyed lot, or competent pretenders. Yet they made pause to stare at the man who entered and moved purposefully among the tables. A white kaffia concealed all his head save his young, bearded, desert-dark face. His leggings bloused loosely over the boots into which they were tucked. The leggings were crimson; his sleeved shirt was yellow and a piece of black cloth was pinned to its breast, in the shape of a star.

He went directly to the table of the Khan's personal guest, while most watched.

"Hajimen!" Conan said in greeting. "I'd thought my friend had returned to the home of the Shanki."

Hajimen, looking troubled or very solemn indeed, shook his head. "I did not." He glanced at Isparana, seated across the small triangular table from the Cimmerian. She was revealingly attired, and Hajimen looked quickly away.

Conan signaled their host. "My friend Hajimen of the Shanki will join us. Come," he said to the Shanki khan's son; "join us."

171

Small Triangular Table

Hajimen sat. Around them, cups were lifted and conversations resumed. Many would love to meet this loutish man who had rendered some service so valuable to their khan, but approaching him was not within the code of the sort of clientele who frequented the Royal Turan's tables.

"The son of the Khan of the Shanki looks troubled," Conan said.

Hajimen looked at him and in his eyes sorrow seemed to vie with dread or perhaps rage. "I will tell my friend Conan and his woman. Some say that my

172

sister did not die of a fever at all, but was . . . slain. Some say that she was not with child at all, as the Khan of the Zamboulans said, but was indeed still virginal, refusing his embraces."

Conan sat silent while a cup was set before Hajimen, and a new tankard of beer. The tapmaster departed. The Cimmerian could sympathize with the emotions of the Shanki, and was hard put to find something to say. He pondered, too, the likelihood of it: a daughter of the desert, presented by her father to a great satrap of the Empire of Turan—refusing the satrap? He had seen only dutiful behavior on the part of Shanki women—and he remembered the obscene pendant worn by Hajimen's other sister.

"In a city of men such as these," Conan said carefully, "there are three rumors for every fact."

Hajimen poured, quaffed deeply; poured. "I know. I have not said that I believe the story I have heard. I only told my friend of the Cimmerians, for Theba has said that a man troubled is a man alone, and too it is said that no man should be alone."

Isparana asked, "Why would the daughter of Akhimen Khan of the Shanki have been slain, in Zamboula?"

Hajimen peered into his red-glazed cup and addressed himself to its contents. "There is no honor in it. Because she was virgin, and dishonored herself and her people by choosing to remain so."

"Ah." Conan saw additional reason for Hajimen's mental torture. If the tale he'd heard was true, the girl had disgraced herself and her father—and of course her brother and indeed all her people. So would the Shanki think, for they were a small and old and custombound tribe. Thus it were best that the story never came out; it would shame her father and his people. No matter that others saw in it no cause for shame; the Shanki lived for the Shanki, not for others. From what

173

Conan had seen, it was not easy, being Shanki. On the other hand, she'd been gift of a khan to a khan. Had that been dishonored and she murdered—could such be countenanced? Surely Akter's was the greater sin. Yet for all Conan knew, that might not be true, to Hajimen . . . and perhaps penalty for such behavior as a maiden-gift turning down the man chosen for her was death. Certainly it would not be the Zamboulan lord's place to carry out the sentence. Yet . . .

Aye, Conan could sympathize with Hajimen's emotions, and his dilemma, if he could not fully understand.

With care Conan said, "The story—this rumor. It is that she rebuffed Akter Khan and he slew her in a fit of pique?"

"The story is that she was not slain so passionately. That she . . . she did what you said, aye—but was slain later, in cold blood."

In cold bl—oh; yes, Conan knew that to these people that meant "without passion." He touched the custom-ruled young man of the desert, fleetingly, for he was unsure of all that was done and not to be done among the Shanki. He had no wish to offend one of whom he thought so highly. To the Cimmerian they were a good and honorable and pathetic people.

"So the khanson of the Shanki has not returned among the tents of his people," he said, impatient with the necessity of such wordy circumlocution. "What will he do?"

"Remain among the Zamboulans," Hajimen said, tight of lips. He gazed at the table. "And attempt to learn what may be learned."

"To seek truth."

"Aye."

"And if this ugly rumor is true, my friend has still a dilemma and a decision to make."

"Aye," Hajimen said, without looking up.

174

"Hajimen."

The Shanki looked at Conan, stiffly, and he blinked.

"Yes, I speak directly and use your name. While I have respected the ways of the Shanki, we are not among them. Their ways are not the ways of my people. We speak the names of our friends. Hajimen: I am Conan. And you have friends in Zamboula."

After a time Hajimen said, "Conan is favored by the Khan of the Zamboulans."

"Yes."

"For the present," Isparana said, who knew her ruler better than did Conan.

Hajimen gazed at him a little longer He nodded shortly, and drained his mug. He started to rise.

"I will be offended not to provide you drink, while you are in this my temporary home," Conan said, deliberately twice employing the direct pronoun.

Again Hajimen turned those so-solemn eyes on him. After a time, he spoke.

"Does Akter Khan supply this beer?"

"Aye . . ."

Hajimen nodded, left a coin on the table, and departed.

"A man of pride," Conan said. "And still he never spoke me direct."

"I think you did not offend him," Isparana said.

"I hope not. I chafe under the rigors of their way of speaking. I've no formal bones in me, 'sparana. Yet I have no wish to offend him, or any of the Shanki. Do you think the story of his sister is believable?"

"Yes. You do not know Akter Khan, Conan. You have seen only a grateful monarch."

Conan shrugged. "I have known rulers. I wouldn't care to hold out my bare arm while any of them held a sword! But it is the other part of the story that's harder to believe, 'sparana: that a daughter of Akhimen Khan

175

turned down Akter—or any man she'd been *given* to."

"Some of us," Isparana said, "do not care to be *given* to anyone, by anyone!"

"Isparana, you are a woman indeed. And you are different; you were *not* raised among the Shanki, by their very khan."

"True. Gods be thanked. I see what you mean, though. Suppose she was always rebellious at heart—like me—and never dared show it or take any action while she was among Shanki tents. Here . . . maybe she decided to try."

"Possible, I suppose," Conan said. He stared at the man entering the inn, without seeing him. "Best we say nothing about this, I think. But I will seek a way to find out."

"Are you sure you want to know?"

"The knowledge won't disturb me, Isparana. If the rumor is true, it's Hajimen who is better off going right home before he finds out!"

She smiled and touched his hand, recognizing some empathy in this so-stern young man; then she looked up and half around, following his gaze. The Cimmerian had learned, and made vow though without formality: he sat in no inn with his back to the door.

Thus he watched the approach of the pouch-cheeked, very ordinary-looking man in the long, drawn-together cloak of very ordinary dun-hued russet.

"Your pardon. A man outside wishes to talk with Conan, the Cimmerian."

With his hand still wrapped about the excellently crafted cup, Conan remained seated and impassive of face while he studied this man who had come to him so quietly. Isparana, too, looked at the nondescript fellow. Around them, the other patrons were true to birth, or money, or pretensions; they took no note.

"You know me," Conan said. "Bid him come in and join me in a cup."

"A busy evening," Isparana said sourly, and crimped her chin to peer into the cleavage of her deeply cut halter of wine-red silk. She wore the pendant given her by Akter Khan; its lower curve just brushed the upper ones of her bosom. *This evening was to be ours alone,* she thought, but did not say it out.

"He would talk with you outside this inn," the man told Conan.

"Doesn't want to be seen in public?"

"Perhaps. Perhaps you do not want to be seen with him."

Conan smiled. "Well said. But then why should I wish to talk with him at all?"

"Do not do it, Conan!"

"Talk hurts no one," the cloaked man said, and Conan was minded of Hajimen, and knew the statement was false. Yet . . .

He studied the man. He did not look particularly dangerous. He did not look dangerous at all. There was no look of the doer about him, or of strength. Now who, the Cimmerian wondered, wanted to hold privy converse with him. And his large bump of Cimmerian curiosity said, Why not?

He leaned back from the table. "Open your cloak."

The fellow gave him a brief questioning look. He complied. Under the long cloak of dun he wore a fringed tunic, just to the knee. Its belt was not wide, and supported no sword scabbard. Conan relaxed a bit, though not completely.

"I would have you take out your dagger with your left hand and leave it here with my companion."

After a moment, the man nodded. "We do not mean to kill you, Conan of Cimmeria. We wish you no

177

harm at all." He laid his dagger on the table. It was as plain and utilitarian as his cloak; an eating utensil.

Isparana asked, "Who is 'we'?"

"I and he who wishes to speak—only speak—with your companion, Isparana."

"Is his name Balad?"

"It is not."

"Do not go, Conan."

"You know us both," Conan observed to the messenger, and to Isparana: "I have my sword and my dagger, and this one is unarmed. I shall go to meet his master." He glanced at the man to observe reaction to that last word. He saw none.

"I would not," Isparana said, and showed her worry.

Conan rose. "Don't run off, 'sparana—or get too far ahead in the drinking! I'll be back to examine your pendant, very closely." He went to the tapmaster, of whom he wangled an apricot. He returned to the messenger, who had considerable brown, wavy hair and who was a foot shorter than the Cimmerian. "I follow."

Conan was a personage. The other patrons of the inn took note of his apricot-munching departure without seeming to do. Behind the slender man in the long dull cloak, he disappeared through the doorway.

"You know," the frugivorous Conan said on the street, as if conversationally, "I enjoy wearing a sword. It feels good against my leg."

"I hear you, and I understand. You have nothing to fear."

"Oh, I know that."

"I meant—"

The fellow broke off rather than state the obvious. Each man understood the other. Perhaps unwisely accepting a summons by an unknown into the unknown—and the darkness of the Zamboulan street of midtown—Conan reminded his guide that he was armed, and just as subtly reminded him that he feared nothing. The two men crossed the street. On the other side, the light was sparse and the shadows deeper. Conan accompanied his guide toward an intersection. Abruptly he made an untoward move.

"Do you feel that?"

Just ahead of him, the man said, "Yes. It is your dagger?"

"No, yours. Just above your backside. If I push, you will be dead or paralyzed. Which would be worse?"

"It is doubtless a wise precaution of a careful man, but unnecessary. Mystery does not always mean danger."

"And an unsheathed dagger is not always used—though that is not a saying in Cimmeria. You can understand that I have no reason to trust you."

"Yes."

Conan snapped away the apricot seed as they turned a corner. He was led into a doorway. A short hall ended in a choice of door or steps; his guide led him upward, in darkness. Unobtrusively Conan wiped a juice-smeared hand on the other man's cloak. They reached a landing and the man rapped at a door, thrice. At the same time he whistled a trio of notes. The door was opened from within and Conan narrowed his eyes against a plentitude of light. Here were two lamps, a table and three chairs, a worn oval rug, desert-woven, an ewer and two pottery mugs, and only one man. He was dressed as dully as his messenger, in a fulvous color. The guide entered. Conan followed. The waiting man closed the door.

Conan heard a noise just outside and met the man's eyes.

"A lookout," the man said; he had the look of a merchant and was past twoscore years of age.

179

Conan nodded. "I am armed."

"Unless you mean murder, Conan of Cimmeria, that is not important."

Conan continued looking at him. The fellow's hair had decamped to leave his forehead high and shiny and bulgy. Gray lay in his beard like a sprinkling of frost. His long tunic or short fulvous robe was broidered with green embroidery and his eyes were squinty, propped by grayish pouches and flanked by a multitude of wrinkles. His nose was big though not accipitral.

"I must trust you, Conan of Cimmeria. I hope that I can."

"I hear silly words," Conan said, stepping away from his guide to display the long blade jutting from his big fist. He noted a narrow window to his right; there was no other window or door save that by which they had entered. "*You* trust? It's I who acts trusting. I came, and I know neither of your names."

The man smiled. "Will you have wine?"

"No. I have left a comfortable inn, and good companionship. I will soon return to drink with her."

The two men exchanged a look. "You are direct."

"You are not. I am here. Speak."

"Do you know the name Balad, Conan?"

"Your guide stated that it was not Balad he was taking me to."

"You do know of him, then."

"He would like to be Khan over Zamboula."

"You continue direct."

"You continue stating the unnecessary."

"We are not enemies, Conan. You have no reason to be hostile. Is that all you know of Balad?"

"Evidently I am here to learn more. Speak."

"You will listen to words about Balad, O friend of Akter Khan?"

Conan shrugged. "Favored, not friend. Akter

Khan owes me. I do not owe him. Indeed, his damned amulet has cost me considerable. To listen costs little and implies nothing." That was true—and also, he thought, sounded good. Very good. Approached by plotters! Aye, he would hear what they had to say. Would they dare try to treat with one so favored of Akter? In that case, they were either passing foolish or brave indeed, and Conan would like to know which. Silently, his face showing nothing, he waited.

"Balad believes that Akter Khan is not the best ruler for Zamboula, and certainly not best for its people."

The man paused to observe the effect on Conan of that statement; Conan showed him nothing. The two plotters exchanged a look. "Best you return to the inn."

Conan's guide left them. "My name is Jelal, Conan. He who brought you here does not know it."

Conan knew that he was to be impressed that Jelal gave him his name. He was cynically aware that "Jelal" might not be this wight's name at all. Besides, he did not believe the man. The guide surely had some name by which to call his superior in the organization of Balad, and why would the man give Conan a different name? He remained silent. His face remained immobile.

"Akter Khan is fearful of his shadow," Jelal said. "He is becoming a drunken sot and doing nothing that a ruler should. His vizir is a good and wise man, but he's been supplanted by that youthful wizard, Zafra. He murdered the mage to whom he was apprenticed, did you know that?"

No, Conan thought, *and I didn't know there was aught wrong with being a youth, either*.

"In the dungeons of Zamboula's palace," Jelal said on, "people die to no purpose, for no reason."

The fellow's eyes showed surprise when Conan came alive with a question. "How did the Shanki girl meet her death?"

181

"You do know considerable," Jelal said and, when Conan made no comment, went on: "She was slain. Akter Khan's pride was sore hurt by her; what woman does not wish to lie with a man of power? Yet he did not slay her in rage. One day two spies from Iranistan were slain in the dungeon, by Zafra and Akter alone, after Zafra had performed some . . . strange rite, over a sword. The Shanki was sent for, and conveyed to the dungeon. Not under arrest, you understand; merely to her lord, who was there. She was left there. Only she and Akter and Zafra were present. Soon Akter left, alone. Zafra and the girl remained. She was never seen again. No one saw her corpse. What I have just said is fact, Conan. Of what I say now we cannot be sure: some believe that she was butchered and that her body was the one that caused such excitement down in Squatters Alley, where it was found. The dismembered corpse of a young woman or girl, neatly packed in several containers, is so shocking a discovery that it was noteworthy even in such a hole as Squatter's Alley —which Balad would clean up, by the way."

Conan ignored the campaign phrase. "You say that her murder is fact."

"Yes."

"How do you know this?"

"I cannot tell you, Conan. That is, I will not."

"You have a spy in the palace."

"Balad has, of course. Many and many are those who believe Akter Khan no fit ruler, Conan—and see Zafra as a terrible danger to us all."

"Why Balad, then? Plot, for so men do, and no ruler but slays, and has dungeons. Slay Akter, and put his son Jungir on the throne. With strong advisors— even Balad, perhaps."

"Jungir is only a boy, Conan, but he would know what happened to his father and eventually, with age and the strength of power, he would seek his vengeance.

Balad is a strong man, a scion of an old and noble house, and a liberal. Too, he has a sense of Zamboulan destiny. We cannot merely remain here, to stagnate and rot under a 'ruler' who does nothing save drink himself to sleep each night."

After a time, the Cimmerian realized that this time Jelal intended to say nothing until Conan had spoken. He spoke.

"I have heard your words, Jelal. They are interesting. I doubt there is anything new in them; there are always bad rulers and those who plot against them. Even good rulers—I have heard that some exist—have those who plot against them. I will not tell Akter Khan of this meeting, or anyone else. Remember that I am no Zamboulan, and do not plan to remain here. The affairs of Zamboula are of little concern to me."

"You could be of aid to us, Conan."

"Doubtless. As I could be of aid to Akter Khan. Isparana and his Captain Jhabiz feel that he may well offer me some sort of position as what I am: a man of weapons."

"Those who serve under Akter Khan are seldom respected and never loved, Conan. You are a man of prowess, and young, without wealth. Were Balad to become ruler of Zamboula, you would assuredly receive a command."

"At my age?"

Jelal cocked his head. "What is your age?"

"Never mind. That is interesting, Jelal. Yet at present I find myself rewarded, favored by Akter Khan. In Cimmeria people say that in winter when one has an empty belly and slays a good elk, one should not long for spices and wine."

As if reminded—or perhaps symbolically—Jelal turned away to pour wine. After offering some to Conan with a gesture, he drank, looking at the foreigner across the cup's rim. "In Zamboula, people say that the man who aspires but does not take action is an unburied corpse."

Conan shrugged.

"Conan: Akter Khan will fall. Balad will rule. Turan will accept him, for the Emperor-king wants ony a strong man on the throne here, and those things Zamboula sends to Aghrapur as revenues. We have friends in Aghrapur—"

"Agents?"

"Friends, let us say. Those who oppose Akter are assumed to be friends of Balad. Those who aid him will be favored. Strong men of prowess are needed."

"To fight. Your Balad means to bathe Zamboula in blood?"

"Hardly. None in Zamboula will fight for Akter Khan! The palace may have to be fought for," Jelal replied evenly. "His own guards, I mean; the Khan's Thorns."

Conan nodded. "I have not said nay, Jelal. I have said that you have not convinced me that I should throw in my lot with Balad, a name. I do not know him, or much of him."

"You could meet Balad, Conan. Those who know of him and are not with him are assumed to be against him."

Conan's stomach tightened; so did his lips. This was the second time he had heard such words, and in a way he had heard them three times. They were an implied threat. *Join us or we assume you're against us, and you will take the consequences when we succeed.* He had the feeling that such words were common throughout the world, and that he'd hear them again ere he died.

While he reflected on his reply—and kept note of Jelal's weapon hand, for the man was a plotter, and a big man, disguised in that brownish-yellowish robe, and a plotter was devious, and Jelal held his wine cup in his left hand—he heard something other than words. Someone was ascending the steps outside the door, and with no care for stealth. Now excited words were exchanged just without, in two voices. Conan saw Jelal's face change, saw his hand reach behind his right hip for the dagger he wore there, out of casual sight. Conan took a few paces to his left before turning; he placed himself thus in position to see both Jelal and the door. Even in his apprehension that doubtless had his heart-beat speeded, Jelal noted the clever fighter's maneuver.

The door was thrust violently inward; Conan and Jelal drew weapons; the guide entered, alone.

"No less than twenty guardsmen from the palace have just left the Royal Turan. They sought you, Conan, and Isparana. They are taking her away right now."

Conan stared at the man, and the Cimmerian's face showed that he was truly surprised and shocked. With his sword still naked in his hand, he whirled to peer from the window.

Across and down the dark street the Royal Turan's doorway splashed light outward. On its step, a little clot of patrons stood gazing up the street. He could not see what they stared after. *Watching them take her away*, Conan thought, in a mind gone terribly grim. Nor, because of the angle, could he have seen had he slashed through the scraped sheet of pig's intestine that covered the window-slit.

He swung from it, and two men saw how a youth's face could go ugly and feral and the eyes from slices of sky to chips of ice.

"Treachery," he snarled, and napes prickled at the sound; not the word, but the animalistic sound of the northerner's voice. "That treacherous hog—I'll show him that he ca—twenty. You said twenty men."

"Aye. Armored guardsmen. Akter Khan's best. The Thorns."

Conan still looked indecisive, as though he might

rush on out, to attempt to wrest Isparana from her custodians. The sword jutting from his fist made his arm a killing instrument nearly six feet long.

"Conan," Jelal said quietly. He had sheathed his long wedge of a dagger. "You may well be a match for five men. I have heard things of you and your prowess, and you are bigger than any man in Zamboula, sure. But you cannot succeed against twenty. They would only kill you—or put wounds on you and then have both you and the woman, rather than only her. With you alive and free, she has hope. And you—you have friends in Zamboula, Conan."

That brought a questioning look from icy blue eyes beneath hovering black brows.

"Those who have reason to be enemies of Akter Khan," Jelal told him, "have reason to be friends of one another."

Conan blinked; stared in revelation. He had just heard a restatement of Jelal's earlier words, and yet how much better they sounded, put this way! Gone was threat; now was only comforting promise!

With his lips moving tightly over clenched teeth, Conan said, "I would like to meet Balad." And he reached for the wine.

XVII

CONAN THIEF

"Give him the cloak," Jelal said.

When his former guide began immediately to remove that long, dun-hued garment, Conan realized that they had planned well. They could not have known that men were coming for him and Isparana, surely; they had merely hoped to be successful in piquing his interest this night. Aye, and they had planned better than that:

"Turth!" Jelal called.

Through the open doorway came a third man; the lookout, Conan realized. Beneath his big nose bushed a black mustache that dangled down past both corners of his mouth. As he approached Conan, he lifted his hand to that mustache—and, with a wince of his facial muscles, he tugged it off.

"What held it on?" Conan asked, while Turth extended the mustache to him; it was indeed hair, he saw, and seemed human, not coarse enough to have been drawn from a horse's mane or tail.

"The same wax that will hold it beneath your nose, Conan," Jelal said. "Wearing it and the cloak, and with the blue of your eyes not noticeable in the

187

darkness outside, you will not be recognized. You can lay wager that Akter's men will be searching for you, armed with your description. Here, let me."

Conan stood very still and hardly comfortable while Jelal took aim, adjusted, and carefully pressed the mustache in place. Conan's nose twitched. Accepting the cloak from the other man, he swung it about him. He was acting on excitement, on adrenaline; now he remembered.

"My room! My property!"

The slender, now cloakless man shook his head. "Several of the khan's men stayed behind, busked for combat. They sought you in your room at the inn. They will await your return—out of sight."

Conan swore. Eyes narrowed, the mustache wriggling as he continued to mutter curses, he returned to the narrow window. He peered contemplatively across and down the street at the Royal Turan, and the buildings on either side the inn.

"How far must we go to reach Balad?" he asked, without turning.

"A way," Jelal said.

"Don't play the obscure oracle with me! I want to know how far!"

"A goodly walk. And we shall offer you hospitality there, as well. You now need a place to stay, Conan."

Conan swung back from the window. Briefly the others saw that ugly animal snarl that would have sent a child screaming for its mother. "Let us be on our way, then. I have other plans for this evening!"

Nevertheless Jelal left first; a few mintues later the other two escorted the impatient Cimmerian. Even at night in this city strange to him, he took careful note of their course, and his hardly civilized instincts prevailed.

Dogs, he thought, clenching his teeth. They were leading him on a circuitous trek, and he knew they sought deliberately to disguise from him the way and the distance to Jelal's. Though they twice asked, he was as devious; he would not tell them his "plans for this evening."

A water clock might well have dripped away a full glass before they had left the close-set buildings and mounted One Ox Hill among the villas of Zamboula's wealthy. Past two sprawling hillside estates they led the Cimmerian, who saw guards and lanterns. Dogs barked and challenges were called and answered. On up the hill they went, past a tree on which a sign hung by a crossbow quarrel; it advised that wayfarers would be considered thieves. They passed it, and fared upward, and stopped between two tall stone posts. Jalal had left them a shibboleth, which Turth now called out:

"Free Isparana!"

A whistle replied; the trio advanced. Pots atop broad, flat-topped poles set into the ground spouted flame and poured greasy smoke skyward. Conan and his guides were challenged again, this time by men who showed themselves. Lights bobbed in the night. These men bore crossbows. When their armored commander recognized Conan's escorts, he nodded. He studied the head and face rising above the cloak—which was hardly so long and encompassing on Conan as it had been on Jelal's messenger.

"He is a big one," the helmeted, steel-corseleted guard chief said.

"He also," Conan said low, "does not like to be talked about as if he isn't present."

The fellow evidently deemed it wise to make no reply, or was shocked silent. They entered the porticoed villa, whose door was huge, and thick, and iron-bound.

"Cook has some good meat laid back for you, Jelal," the estate guard said.

"Ah, good. I've had naught since noon." That from the man who had acted as messenger and guide.

"Jelal?" the Cimmerian repeated, in demanding tone. "You are Jelal too?"

"Only I," the slender man said, smiling.

"Then who—"

"I am Balad, Conan."

At that voice Conan turned, to face the man he had first met as Jelal. He had come directly here, of course, and so arrived well before them; he had not changed clothing. "I am sorry. Plotters must of necessity lie, you understand."

"Damn!" the Cimmerian said, hurling the true Jelal's cloak angrily to the gleaming marble floor. "Had you told me that an hour and more ago rather than play this snake-walking game over half of Zamboula, we could have saved a lot of trouble for both of us!"

"I am a marked man," Jelal-Balad said, "and such snake-walking games are as necessary as are the guards outside, and watchwords. You noted your route, did you?"

"I know when I have made three turns to my offhand, soon followed by four more to the weapon-side!"

Balad smiled; the chief plotter against the throne of Zamboula. "You are indeed a dangerous man, Conan of Cimmeria. We regret having caused you trouble. But —how could bringing you here direct have saved me trouble? Our design is to insure my security—our security."

"Because now we just have to go all the way back into the city for the key to your success, Balad—a man named Hajimen."

"Hajimen? The Shanki? We felt him out, of course, when we contemplated approaching you—"

"And I must either be guided," Conan went on as if Balad had not spoken, "or find my own way back to the Royal Turan."

"The Royal Turan! Do you not understand that you can*not* go back there? Akter Khan's soldiers await you!"

"I'll not be staying long," Conan said.

Balad shook his head. "You will not be going back *there* this night, Conan!"

Conan stared at the other big man. "Balad: I am. And it must be alone. Don't try to prevent me."

For a long while Balad stared at his presumed new recruit, a giant foreigner who glared balefully back with surely the strangest eyes in Zamboula.

"Conan: *Why?*"

Conan's false mustache twitched in the merest intimation of a smile. "You know about my ability with weapons," he said. "There is also another trade I am good at."

A long dun-colored cloak formed a crumpled wad at the base of the building next the Royal Turan inn. Beneath it was a pair of buskins, large. And on the nigh-flat roof of that building, a barefoot man crouch-walked. His sword was strapped on his back; a thong snubbed the hilt tightly to the hitch-ring near the sheath's mouth. He was a big man. At the apex of the roof's gentle slope, he paused to wind around his waist the rope with which he'd scaled the building. He gazed across five feet of space to the inn's roof. It was flat, and at nearly the same level as the ridge whereon he stood. The light of a lowering moon caught the flash of his teeth; his smile was wolfish.

The rope secured around him, he crouch-walked back down the roof's slope, as if louting.

His calves bulged when he came to pause and levered himself up and down with the fluid suppleness of a stalking cat. Then, though he was tall and unusually broad of shoulder and powerful of build, he ran up the roof and kicked himself off its apex. His legs did not churn in air and drew up only a little while he soared through space and onto the roof of the adjacent building. Both legs doubled up when he alit, so that his bare heels punched into his buttocks. The thump of his landing was incredibly faint for one of his size.

The Royal Turan's roof provided no means for anchoring his rope. He knew which window he wanted; the only way he could devise to reach it and its upper sill was to hang from the roof's edge by his knees, with his back to the building. He did.

Thus, hours past midnight, did Conan gain entry to his own room in the Royal Turan.

The chamber was dark and empty, as it should have been. He unslung his sword, attached it to his belt, and loosed the hilt of its restraining thong. Next he secured his rope to a beam and paid it out the window until it nearly brushed the ground. By feel, he found his long vest of clinking chainmail. He unstrapped his sword but stood it against the wall so that he could snatch its hilt in an instant. Heedless of the dark, too-tight tunic loaned him by Balad, Conan shrugged and wriggled into the mailvest. He buckled on the sword again.

The excellent cloak that had been a gift of Akter Khan was where he had left it, folded on the unusually comfortable bed. Spreading it, he began collecting his treasures; coins and the gold cup—which rolled off cloak and bed and rang onto the floor.

"Damn!"

Heedless now of stealth, Conan squatted to snatch it up and drop it amid the things spread on the cloak, which he swiftly folded in to form a bag. As he turned with it to the window, the door opened from the hall, and the flickery light of a glim flared yellow and bright in the darkness.

Conan's sword was in his hand by the time the brand and one of its bearer's feet were in the chamber.

"Who's in here?"

The man entered; a helmeted soldier. He squinted into the darkness and lifted high his brand. Its yellow light wrought eeriness on his face—and found Conan. The Cimmerian stood in a half-crouch, makeshift bag in left hand, sword in right, bareheaded, armored though bare of arm. And he stared with an awful balefulness.

"Ha! A thief, is it? Caught y—it's THAT CONAN!"

"Loudmouth," Conan snarled, and his sword came around and up as he pounced.

Out in the corridor other voices rose, and feet pounded heavily up steps. More soldiers reached the doorway. The first stumbled over his fallen companion who had been so misfortunate as to discover the Cimmerian and call out before clearing his sword arm of the door, which opened into the room. The second and third got themselves alacritously out of the way of the roaring fireball that rushed at them, streaming flame. It whooshed through the doorway to slam into the wall across the corridor. Both men, and now a third, scrambled again when it bounced and endangered their feet. One snatched it up; it was the torch formerly borne by the man keeping vigil outside the foreigner's door. Holding it high, he led his fellows into the room.

The first soldier lay ungroaning in his blood; the second was at the window, peering out and down. A taut-stretched rope ran from a beam behind him, past his shoulder, and over the sill. He turned.

"He has gone out the window!"

One of his fellows was sufficiently nimble of mind to strike the rope with his sword. The rope merely sagged; it was slack.

"I'll get him," the man at the window said, and swung out.

"No! Zakum, wait! I cut—"

Zakum was already swinging heroically out, clutching the rope partially cut by the other man's blade. As Zakum's booted feet struck the side of the building with a jolt, the weakened rope gave up. It parted and leaped away out the window like a striking snake. Zakum's cry was followed by the crash of his impact with the alley's hard-packed earth.

"Hanuman's devils!" With those words, another man peered out and down.

Zakum was writhing, twisting, holding one leg with both hands. "My leg, my leg . . ."

"That brainless rectum has broken his leg! Out of here and down the steps, men. It is liable to be worse than our legs if we let that foreigner escape—the khan *wants* him!"

They rushed from the room. Down the steps they stormed like a rumbling crash of summer thunder, and across the main room and outside. Seeing no sign of Conan, they separated to seek him on every street roundabout.

A half-hour later, a disgruntled soldier was just approaching a doorway up the street and across from the inn, on his way back without the quarry. An apparition emerged from the gloom of the hall beyond the doorway. The soldier half cried out and his sword came up before he saw that it was a man; a big, bent hunchback in a drab cloak of dun, with a ragged strip of cloth over his head in a makeshift kaffia. A large but quivery hand came out of the cloak.

"A coin, Captain?"

"I'm no captain, damn you, and you know it! Go snivel someplace else, damned beggar!" The soldier half-bent to squint at the hunchback's face, which was deeply shadowed by his "kaffia." "Set's black devils! And get someone to trim that ridiculous mustache for you, fellow!"

Emptyhanded, the soldier returned to the Royal

Turan. Conan, with his bag on his back beneath Jelal's cloak and a strip ripped from Balad's gift tunic over his head, went the other way, grinning. The soldier was fortunate to be slow of thought and dull of wit; Conan's other hand, under Jelal's cloak, was fisted about the hilt of his drawn dagger.

Hunched, he headed for One Ox Hill.

XVIII

THE KEY TO ZAMBOULA

Balad had backing. Balad was organized, with followers; Balad felt himself ready ("I and the people of Zamboula!" as he put it) to move against Akter Khan. He needed only a key; an incident or trick that had not yet occurred to him or presented itself.

A large body of soldiers was quartered in the barracks on the east side of Zamboula. A broad thoroughfare provided a speedy route across the city to the palace. There, in the royal house itself and in the inn-like barracks adjacent, were another two hundred soldiers. Some called them the Chosen; they had been dubbed officially the Khan-Khilayim or Khan's Thorns. They were presumed to be loyal to Akter, no matter his offenses or the mood of some or even most people. The Thorns were well-paid, -housed, and -fed. They were kept adequately supplied with salt, beer of an excellent quality, and feminine companionship. Any palace was a fort, the defensible home of the ruler and his people's ultimate refuge and keep, and the palace of Zamboula was no exception. The chosen two hundred could prevail against a long siege by a far, far superior force. Too, mounted reinforcements from the barracks across town could mobilize, arm, mount, and reach the scene within an hour; this fact was now and again proven by mock alarms and practice mobilizations. Thus did the khan keep watch against attacks from without the city's wall—and guard himself against the uprisings against which no ruler was proof. While spies in the palace could and would open doors to Balad's force, they must get past the Thorns—as must the attackers.

Thus Balad, with no army or exterior allies and no magic to equal that of the khan's wizard, needed the trick or incident he called The Key. Something was needed to occupy the barracks troops, the army—and perhaps suck from the palace some of the Khan-Khilayim, as well.

The blue-eyed foreigner from the far north saw that he could provide that key.

Conan would never have joined Balad. Zamboula was hardly his city and these were hardly his people. He was of no mind to aid or hinder their doings. They had naught to do with Conan. Had he been given employment in Akter Khan's Thorns, he would have been loyal, and surely put brains and skills to use against Balad and company. Instead, Akter Khan had him to dinner, wined and rewarded him, praised him, heard his story, and then proved treacherous to a man who had provided a most valuable service; who thought him friend and good enough ruler, given what he knew and assumed of rulers in general.

Whether the Eye of Erlik was of value to Akter Khan or no, he believed it so, and that made it of value. It was presumably true that it could be used against him—the very fact of its being stolen nigh terrified the man.

"I wish I'd handed it directly to you, Balad," the Cimmerian growled.

"So do I, Conan," the plotter said, not without

some wistfulness before he returned to pragmatic plottery.

Never mind that Conan had been serving his own interests the while, and had hardly entered into this whole long series of events with any view toward helping Akter Khan of Zamboula. He had put that out of his mind. He substituted righteous bitterness and anger. He had given much of himself to provide a service to this treacherous and ungrateful man. Indeed he had given Akter Khan several months of his life; a half year, were he to set out now to return to Zamora. So had Isparana given much, sacrificed much. And the khan, *her* khan, had proven an egregiously ungrateful lord indeed! Now Isparana was his prisoner, somewhere within the palace—if she yet lived—and Conan was free only through chance and Balad.

Thus Conan was bitter, and angered, and disappointed in himself for suspecting nothing of Akter Khan. He must have satisfaction; vengeance. Thus he joined Balad. Nor had it taken him long to become aware of Balad's problems.

He would help Balad. And thus, he had no need of telling himself, he would nobly and heroically aid the people of Zamboula. Akter was no worthy ruler—if such existed, which Conan doubted; Akter, in any event, was even worse than most of those who grew callous of brain and soft of backside by sitting thrones. Indeed it was the khan himself who provided Balad's key. Conan merely saw how to employ it. Akter had committed a worse than reprehensible crime, in murdering the adolescent who'd been a gift of the chieftain of the Shanki. As it turned out, that murder had also been stupid. It provided the key.

It was Conan the Cimmerian who caused Hajimen of the Shanki to be escorted to the keep of Balad the revolutionary, whose agreement Conan had secured: Hajimen would confer alone with Conan in this room.

They spoke quietly together, the trousered man of the desert and the Cimmerian in the newly made tunic of plain russet.

"You know that the Shanki cannot hope to conquer Zamboula," Conan said to the son of Akhimen Khan, "or even breach its walls. The Shanki are not enough."

"One young warrior among the Shanki is worth five Yoggites," —Hajimen spat—"and three of the Zamboulans, in all their coats of iron rings!"

Conan nodded. "True. I know that. It is not enough. The best warriors among the Zamboulans outnumber those among the Shanki far more than three to one—and are within these walls besides."

Hajimen sighed, rose to pace, returned to sink into the cushion before the one on which Conan sat. He had elected to interview the Shanki in the Shanki mode, though his impatience with their divagative manner of address was making itself more and more plain. Indeed, his efforts had succeeded somewhat, with this young son of the khan; he was actually able, now and again, to call Conan "you" and "Conan." Not this time:

"Conan knows that I know the truth of what he says," Hajimen said, looking gloomy as a priest at a state funeral. "Nevertheless, there is Shanki honor and my father's pride. Does *he* know that it were foolish to attack this place?"

"The point is, will he understand and accept that not Zamboula, but Akter and his mage, slew your sister? There is no need of war with the Zamboulans, who do not like or respect their khan. The quarrel is between the Shanki—no; between your father and Akter, and Zafra."

"And I, Conan! Yes, I see that. I know it. Best that I do not go to tell my father. Best that I remain here and avenge my sister myself—somehow," he added, cheerlessly, "and then bear the news of her death and our vengeance to the Khan of the Shanki, both at once."

Conan shook his head. "That is not best. That is brave, and foolish, and both of us know it."

Hajimen glowered at the other man in this chamber in the villa of Count Shihran; the villa now of Balad the plotter who would be Balad Khan. After a few moments Conan put out a hand to touch the other's arm, in warmth; the proud warrior of the desert drew away. Seeing that, and inwardly sighing as he recognized it as foolish, Conan learned something of himself, and honor, and pride.

"Come, Hajimen. You know what I mean. Neither of us believes that you would get so close to Akter as to be able to kill him. And *if* you did, *somehow*, as you said, you would never live to tell your father of it. Then he would be without a daughter and his son. You know what he would do then. Attack, and die."

His face working, Hajimen stared. Then he swung away, paced to a slitted, open window. "Conan has wisdom. Theba's name—how old are you, Conan?"

The Cimmerian smiled. "Old enough to give advice I probably would not have sense enough to take!"

His back turned, Hajimen snorted. "What would Conan have us do? Act as if nothing had happened at all? This man accepted my sister as gift of our father, and slew her as if she had been a thief or a Yoggite!" Hajimen spat, and continued to show Conan his broad, yellow-shirted back.

"No. Heed me, now. The very biggest a man could be would be to keep it to himself, to prevent his father's acting foolishly in honor and pride, and knowing, that vengeance is impossible—but may someday be possible. I know that neither Hajimen nor Conan is that big! No, Hajimen son of Akhimen, I speak you direct. Attend me. Not even the soldiers of Zamboula favor Akter Khan. I would have you see that your sister's death is avenged, Hajimen! At the same time, the Shanki can be heroically aiding the Zamboulans in ridding themselves of this unworthy creature who habits their palace. Hajimen! Listen! I would have you—I would beg you ride to your father fast as you can, and return with warriors. Let them be girded for war, on the swiftest of your camels. All should pause well outside the city's walls, and send arrows *at* the walls, not loft them over into Zamboula. And all the while, bellow charges and challenge to Akter Khan!"

Hajimen had whirled back to face the big man with the blue eyes. "Ah!" His face showed excitement and hope; yet the question lurked in his eyes below the tribal scar of the fierce and twice-proud Shanki. "But —such a man will not come forth!"

"No, he will not. He will sit in his palace and know that his soldiers will soon beat off this ridic—this unwise attack. The soldiers from the garrison will turn out against you, happy for the action and eager to slay. And then the Shanki must do that which is brave, and noble—and difficult. You must flee."

"Flee!" In horror Hajimen spat the word alien to his nature.

"Aye, Hajimen!" Conan let his voice rise excitedly; he had to enlist the Shanki to this plan. "Aye! Let them come forth, and charge you. Give them a running fight. Flee, and flee. When at last they desist from following, as they will, halt and form up to watch them take a good lead in returning to the city. Then race after them!"

"Ah! And then, we pursue those jackals, and fall on them from behind, and slash them on the run! Thus can we reduce the odds!"

Conan heaved a great sigh, and made sure that Hajimen saw. "They are not jackals, Hajimen my friend. They are young men and youths as we are, brave, and serving a bad khan. No, they will turn, form to meet your charge. You must then swerve and ride away again without slowing, so that they follow. If it is possible, a small party of Shanki should race toward a city gate. That will create some fear in those who will be watching from the walls. They may call for reinforcements—from the palace."

"In none of this do I see honor, or the way of the Shanki, Conan. What is the purpose of all this harmless racing about on the plain outside these walls?"

"Ah! Hajimen, you *are* big! That you can ask, rather than bluster; that is the mark! You will succeed Akhimen indeed, Hajimen, and the Shanki will be well led! Consider. The Shanki can gird and put into the saddle . . . what? Perhaps three hundred men, if we include boys just past puberty and men well past prime?"

"And a hundred women and girls! Our women are not weak playthings such as those I have seen in this encampment of walls!"

"—While there are over two thousand soldiers quartered here. So many would slay you all, and women and girls too, while Akter sat safe in his palace—and later commanded the annihilation of the Shanki. Thus I am showing you that you must ally yourself with those who would topple Akter. They can do so only with the help of the Shanki, Hajimen!"

Khanson Hajimen regarded him thoughtfully. "Conan and Balad."

"And others, aye," Conan said, nodding with energy. "I can get into the palace. I will. Balad can attack, and prevail, and depose Akter Khan . . . *if* the khan's warriors are busy chasing phantoms on the desert."

"Phantoms? Shanki!"

"Aye!" Conan cried, seeing and hearing Hajimen's excitement and talking faster and higher of voice to spur it. "And then Balad will recall the troops, and reveal that the Shanki are allies—and your people will be beloved in Zamboula, and allies of its new ruler."

"Ha! The horse-warriors of the Zamboulans chase the Shanki *phantoms,* while our friends Conan and Balad invade the palace! Balad gains the crown; and Zamboulans gain a new and better ruler—and Conan and Hajimen gain vengeance; justice!"

Conan's grin was nothing that made his face handsome. "Aye, warrior."

Hajimen came to him, and then of a sudden stood stiff and put on a stony face. "And Akter Khan, if he lives, must be turned over to the Shanki for punishment!"

Such a promise Conan knew he could not make, and he knew he could be in trouble. He found a way to put it: "Hajimen! You should be riding to the tents of your people, right now! Instead . . . would the Shanki turn Akhimen Khan over to the Zamboulans for punishment, did he offend them, no matter how grievously? Consider! Akter Khan has committed more offenses against his people than against yours. They must punish him. He is theirs, of them. I have no doubt he will be executed . . . if he survives our attack. Certainly the allies of Balad Khan will be present to see him die!"

After a long while, Hajimen nodded. "You did not have to say all that. You could merely have said 'Aye,' and sought to persuade me later."

"True. Shall I lie to my friend who is the son of my friend?"

Within an hour, Hajimen and his party were riding out of Zamboula. With them, in Shanki garb, went Balad's man Jelal. His own clothing was in the pack of his sumpter-beast and his Shanki kaffia shadowed the face someone at the gate might recognize. A few days hence, when Shanki outriders found them within less than a day of Zamboula, Jelal would return: horse-mounted and in his own clothing. He would report to Balad. Thus would the diversion from the desert be coordinated with the true attack from inside Zamboula's walls.

After the departure of Jelal and the Shanki, Conan spent most of an afternoon conferring with Balad and his co-conspirators. This did not sit well with the Cimmerian who, afflicted with the wispy patience of both youth and the barbarian, preferred less plotting and the more direct approach of sharp-edged action. In this endeavor, Hajimen's headstrong insistence on being nobly foolish had forced Conan into a new, more thoughtful and persuasive role. He who would one day captain bands and then squadrons and then armies and then an entire nation was not yet eighteen, and he was learning, and aging.

Part of his bold plan sat no better with Balad. He and the others with him pointed out that Conan's desire—decision, but they said desire—to enter the palace, there to free Isparana and begin the attack from within, was foolish and headstrong.

He who had wisely counseled and persuaded the insistent Hajimen remained insistent, and was unpersuadable.

Thus, a few nights later, an accomplished thief lately of Shadizar and Arenjun and Cimmerian scaled two walls and entered the palace of Akter Khan. In less than two hours he was captive of him who had become the real ruler of Zamboula: Zafra the mage.

XIX

"SLAY HIM!"

He remembered torture. He remembered it dimly, mistily, as though he had been drugged or ensorceled. He remembered the insistent touch of the swordpoint at his back, in the center, above his coccyx. He remembered being forced between two floor-set poles less than two feet apart. The swordpoint touched his back while a second man bound each leg, ankle and thigh, to one of the poles, which were thick as his calves. The swordpoint touched his back in constant reminder, and he did not move while his wrists were bound before him. The leather thongs were knotted and re-knotted. The pinpoint pressure at his back increased, urging him forward. With his legs immobilized he could go nowhere; he could only lean, from the waist. The swordpoint brought a trickle of warm blood. He felt it. He bent, from the waist. His linked wrists were pulled down between his bound, spread legs. He bent. The long rope attached to the wrist-cord was caught behind and drawn up tightly, behind him. He grunted. The rope was secured to an iron brazier in the wall, seven or eight feet behind him. The floor was chill beneath his bare feet, or had been;

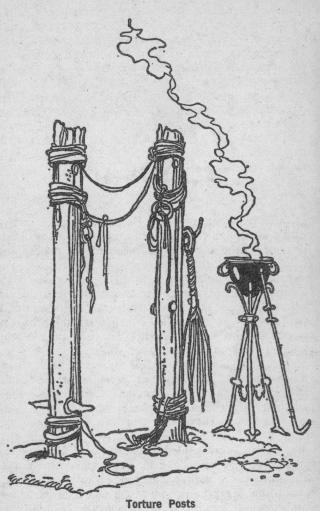

Torture Posts

he remembered that it became welcomely cool. He was forced to bend foward, broad back popping, blood rushing hotly to his head, reddening his face. His vision blurred, grew ruddy. His bonds held him in position. He could not fall mercifully forward because of the strong cords that held his thighs and ankles to the posts. He was gagged, his mouth stuffed, and that proved demeaning: bent forcibly forward and low, he could not help drooling around the gag. He remembered feeling hate. His vision grew redder and his head felt thick. It pounded. Eventually, blood pooling in his head, he slid into unconsciousness.

He remembered how the whip came whirring down, descending abruptly and swiftly to snap horizontally across his lower back. He remembered gasping for breath, the whiplash making him breathless, and how the sweat popped forth on his face, and the trickle of it as it oozed down his sides from his armpits. It went on. The whip slithered back, sang in the air, popped on his body. Its black tongue tore and slashed mercilessly. He knew welts rose. His eyes burned with rage aginst the snaky whip and its wielder. His chest, stretched by bonds to the tautness of a drum and the hardness of a bear's chest, heaved and his nostrils trembled and flared. The whip hissed and struck. He did not remember that they asked any questions; they just hurt him. He knew he groaned and he strove not to cry out. It was all hazy, misty. It might have been a dream. He bit his lip, hard. It hurt. It was not a dream. He could not control the jerking of his bound frame, the wavering of his slim hips, the tense tightening of the small muscular pads of his backside. He was naked. Sweat rivered down his back, down his sides, off his face. It splashed a floor somewhere below. Those were automatic responses to the threat and the fall of the whip, the relentless flail and tug and ready and flail and crack, and the dreadful uneasiness, and burning

pain. But he stifled even his groans, and made no out-
cry. They had removed his gag and watered his throat,
so that they could listen to his cries. They heard none,
he was sure. Wasn't he?

He remembered the burning ointment. He remembered or thought he remembered a weird demonstra-
tion; it seemed that a sword, wielded by no hand, slew
a fellow captive. Had it happened? He was not sure.
Could it have happened? Had he heard that soft voice
say "Slay him"—and had a sword understood and
obeyed?

He could not be sure. He remembered, or thought
he remembered.

The pain of the flail of nettles was slight; the itch-
ing afterward was the worst torture of all. He was bound
so that he could not scratch the awful burning itches.

He was beaten on the stomach. The broad strap
made a very loud noise.

He remembered being told that he was to be
wrapped in a fresh bloody cowhide and placed outside,
facing the morning sun. He did not think that happened.
He was sure that a helmet was fitted over his head
and strapped on so that a slim thong of leather cut up
into his chin. Someone pounded on the helmet with a
hammer until he wondered which would come first:
death or insanity.

Neither. He endured, and thought that he did not
cry out, though he was not certain, ever, that he might
not have sobbed. He would rather have been beaten or
crucified.

Perhaps some of it was Zafra's sorcery; surely
some of it was, and did not happen. As certainly, some
of it did. Conan was never sure what had been real and
what had not. He had indeed bitten his lip; the smooth
tender lump of swollen meat there attested to that. And
his head ached and rang.

He awoke, then, hours or days later, with that

awful misty feeling of uncertainty, of the possibility of his having been dreaming, or drugged, or sorcerously dulled of brain, and his head was coming clear and he did not think that he was bound. He lay still, trying to learn if he was bound by seeking the sensation of constriction at wrists and ankles. He could not be sure, at first. He lay still, trying to take stock of himself and his surroundings. Oh. He was in the palace. He had been captured. Where was he? In the palace—where? He could not quite get hold of it. His brain was dull and his body felt years older. Consciousness returned and grew in him like a flame rising slowly in a room with only the tiniest breath of air stirring. His brain became clearer and clearer, as if lit by that tenuous, brave candle. Though he knew he was weakened, he felt strength growing in him—or at least the weakness shrinking.

Conan opened his eyes.

He lay partly on a rug and partly on a tiled floor, gray and pale red shot with slender streamers of black and white. A handsome marble floor, in tesselated tiles. He saw a table, and things on it . . . he remembered the Green Room, the den of Hisarr Zul, sorcerer first of Zamboula and then of Arenjun and now of Hell, where Conan had sent him. It was the same sort of paraphernalia. This must be the chamber of Zafra, then, Akter Khan's mage.

Aye. Next to the throne room, was it not? That door over there, perhaps . . .

Conan did not like the way the room smelled.

Chemicals, and herbs, and the ugly odor of burnt air. He twitched his fingers, then each hand. He had been right; he was not bound. A few impulses sent down his legs indicated that they, too, were free. He lay partly on his side, partly on his stomach. He breathed deeply, though he did not care for the scent or taste of this air of the chamber of a sorcerer.

He was halfway up before he saw Zafra. The

mage had cleverly stood where he could not be seen save as the result of a consciously directed movement; that way he had known the moment Conan began to regain consciousness.

Conan paused, on one knee with one set of knuckles against the floor.

"Ah," Zafra said smiling. "Very nice. Gratifying, I am sure: you genuflect respectfully."

With his face twisting into a snarl, Conan thrust himself to his feet. Zafra swiftly showed the sword he held.

"You told us your tale, remember, barbarian? I know what sort of slimy arrogant youth you are. I thought you might attempt what you did; came here as a thief to find Isparana and collect a head or two, didn't you? Fair caught you, didn't I? You are a barbarian driven by the same instincts that push on a dog or a hog or a bear, you see. I have goals, specific goals. In contest between two such, the brain-directed, goal-seeking man must triumph. As you see, I have. And I shall continue, while you return to the slime that thrust you up into the womb of some barbarian bitch. Within the year, I shall rule in Zamboula. In a few years more I shall rule in Aghrapur; Zafra, King-Emperor of Turan! Aye! Not too bad for the peasant boy his master beat because he did not learn his lessons fast enough . . . sorcerous lessons, which I was learning far far faster than that old pig thought! Stare at me if you will, with those baleful eyes of an animal—but seek to attack, *barbarian,* and you shall only die the sooner!"

"The sooner, then," Conan said, and made a long long sidestep and snatched up a heavy brazen lampstand as tall as he, thick at the thinnest part of its carving-decorated stem as his wrist. It was heavy and he was not at strength; he grunted. He emptied it with a jerk. Burning oil splashed the floor.

For an instant Zafra stared in astonishment and something approaching horror; then he lifted his eyebrows and smiled.

"Do you remember this sword? I showed it you, barbarian. I showed you how it obeys. Once commanded, it will not rest until it has slain. Move fast then, barbarian . . . *Slay him.*"

Conan's nape prickled and tiny icy feet seemed to race up his naked back; Zafra opened his hand. The sword he held did not drop to the floor. It dropped its point until Conan was staring at it, at the bar of the hilt behind—and then it came rushing at him.

Seized by the only fear he truly knew—that of sorcery—he nevertheless did not freeze. That would have been his death. Instead, he hurled himself to the floor—and struck wildly with the lampstand at the sword, even as it swerved down at him. Carven bronze pole struck gleaming steel blade with a great warlike clang of metal, and the sword flew across the room. The weight of his weapon—or defense—carried Conan's hands and arms down, and he sprawled. He heard the sword bang off a wall behind him. He scrambled to his feet, bearing the brazen pole in both hands. He leaped at Zafra, whose eyes went wide. Then his gaze shifted *past* Conan, and the Cimmerian let himself fall, twisting as he fell, striking upward as he fell. He grunted at the wrenching of his side. Again his metal stave struck the kill-driven, unwielded sword.

Remembering what Zafra had said, Conan suddenly grinned. That grimace brought fear and horror to the mage, for it was the hideous feral grin of a slavering beast. Conan lurched up and ran—and not at Zafra. He ran for the door that opened out into the palace corridor!

Seconds marked by droplets of water were as minutes, while Conan's back crawled. He ran three steps, four, another—and hurled the lampstand to his right while he dived leftward. He had been but two paces from the big paneled door; he had judged that he would never make it, for that awful mindless blade must be driving pointfirst at his back.

So it had been. And this time it had come so far and with such speed in pursuit of its racing prey that it did not swerve in air to follow him. Instead, it drove into the door with such force that it was imbedded past the shaping of the point; an inch or so. Without a word or a glance at Zafra, Conan again flung himself to his feet—and grasped the door's brass handle, and yanked, even as the sword eerily, horribly, shook itself loose of creaking wood—and Conan leapt out into the corridor.

The sword does not cease until it has slain, eh, the Cimmerian thought with a hideous grim smile, and he yanked the door shut behind him. It banged loudly. He stood panting, holding the handle, listening to the snarling of his empty belly—and to the cry from within the sorcerer's chamber.

And then came the shriek that ended in a rattling throaty gurgle, and Conan knew that the young wizard's career was nipped long before he had opportunity to grow old in his trade, much less seize thrones.

"Hai there!"

That voice and the glance Conan shot its way, to see a palace guardsman coming at him, made up his mind. He had wondered whether he dared go into the room and try to avail himself of that sword, now it had slain. Well, he thought, it's either that or flee naked through the corridors of the royal palace—about as inconspicuous as an elephant in a beartrap!

He jerked open the door and rushed into the room. He slammed the door behind him. Only seconds passed before a body slammed against it; the Khan's Thorn had speeded his pursuit! Conan did not pause to gaze upon the slight body sprawled untidily on the handsome tiles. It was moveless. So was the sword that stood above it, having driven itself deeply into Zafra's chest.

"Just left of center," Conan muttered, feeling the gooseflesh on his arm but reaching for the hilt of that ensorceled blade just the same. "A fine sword indeed!" His hand closed on the hilt. It did not move. It seemed only a sword. "Well, Zafra, it failed to serve you as you expected—perhaps it will serve Conan!"

A fine sword indeed; it had driven itself so deeply into Zafra's lower chest that Conan had to set a foot against the supine mage and drag the thing free.

The door was hurled open, a helmeted, corseleted man appeared, burly and bearing sword in hand; from what was recognizably the corpse of the Wizard of Zamboula a naked man turned, also bearing a sword in his huge fist, and his eyes and his snarling mouth were those of a deadly beast.

Clad in the helmet and corselet-over-leathern tunic of one of the Khan-Khilayim, Conan paced the back corridor of Zamboula's palace. At his side hung Zafra's sword, though it had split the guardsman's sheath of tooled leather over thin, light wood. In his hand was half a loaf he had handily filched from a passing salver, without its bearer's noticing. It was over-leavened bread of the effete dweller in the palace of an effete city—and Conan was glad, for it wolfed down quickly and its lack of weight had not alerted her from whom it was stolen.

Or perhaps she did know and doesn't care, Conan mused. *The Khan-Khilayim doubtless do a great deal of precisely what they want.*

Well . . . not much longer, you scum who serve scum! Ah—this is surely the door.

It was, and unguarded; it opened into the dungeon, where burned a single brand in a sconce just inside. Inside and below was Isparana, as he had expected.

Or perhaps he remembered; surely this was where Zafra had tortured him. Now he would—

Unfortunately Isparana was not alone. As Conan, seeing her, suffered a momentary lapse of his wariness and strode across the landing to the steps down into the pit where she lay, he heard a gasp and whirled to see two Thorns. They had been standing up here staring down at her, the bastards, just to the left of the door while he, heading forward and to the right, had charged right pass them. Bending his knees into a crouch, he filled his hands with hilt of sword and dagger, and faced them.

The two looked confused. "What do you think you're—" one of the men began, but Conan had forgotten that he wore their uniform. He did what for them was the shockingly unexpected, and the characteristically normal for him; he attacked the two men.

The speaker, the younger of the two, lost half his upper arm to the flailing sword of Zafra, and a dagger was in the other's belly before he could swing his blade. Surely in standing shock, the first man pawed out his own sword, though his face was white and his sundered arm hung like a tattered scarlet banner.

"You are a brave watchdog of an unworthy master," Conan said, "and almost this pains me." He feinted with his sword, a blow the man caught on his own blade, the while Conan swung his left hand in.

The dagger snapped against mail. Conan cursed a khan who finely attired his elite guardsmen while arming them with weapons unfit for carving baked hen. Angrily, he kicked the man in the crotch. The poor wight groaned, doubled, overbalanced when his ruined arm swung out, and pitched over the edge of the landing. He crashed to hard-packed earth twenty or so feet below. Conan took time to peer down at the sprawled form. It did not move. The Cimmerian turned and hurried over to the stairs. He descended five-and-twenty steps, into that dim chamber of unutterable horror and sphacelation.

Only as he approached the naked, bound woman did Conan discover that Isparana was not alone in the pit.

The master of this smoky, blood-splashed and pain-haunted domain had been taking his rest, snoozing on a pallet back in shadows. Now Conan saw him for the first time; Baltaj the torturer was a man as burly as he with as much reach of arm and perhaps as much strength, and more belly. Like the Cimmerian, he bore sword and dagger both. The difference was that his big knife was intact.

"Big one," he said, in a throaty though oddly high voice, "aren't you."

Conan did not think to command Zafra's sword of sorcery. Nor did he wait for the torturemaster to attack. He flipped the broken dagger into the air and thrust his sword into the earthen floor in time to catch the knife in his right hand. Never mind the scratch; he swept that arm back and forward and the hilt and three or so inches of raggedly snapped blade was still in air when his hand came down on his swordhilt. The entire strange maneuver required only seconds. It was a desperate act; Conan did not care to waste time facing a fellow of such strength and length of arm, who was better armed then he.

He had not thrown at Baltaj's head, but at his chest, assuming that the man could not be so fast as to dodge aside, with that well-fed belly. He was right. Too, Akter's torturer moved awrong; he ducked. Thus he presented his face to the hurled missile. The hilt of the broken dagger struck him in the mouth, loudly and hard. The torturer grunted in shock and pain; lip tore and tooth broke; unweeping tears started from both his eyes. He was blinded, if only momentarily. It was long enough.

217

Conan's sword, jerked from the earth by arm bent out to the side, came straight up to split Baltaj's belly from navel to sternum. The cut was not deep, though painful and long and bloody. Trailing blood, the blade continued moving, missing the torturer's face, sweeping up above his head. Conan stepped forward as he reversed his action to bring the blade down. Zafra's excellent sword split the skull of Zamboula's torture-master.

"Too bad," the Cimmerian muttered. "It would have been pleasant to put you to your own devices, fat swine!"

"Stop . . . talking to the dead," a straining, bound woman said with some difficulty, "and cut me loose. I've waited long enough for you, you hen-brained barbarian cur of a camel-stealing Cymrian."

"Cimmerian, damn it, Cimmerian," Conan said, and cut her free, the while silently admiring her pluck. Things had been done to her, and none of them nice. "You are a bit of a mess, 'sparana my love—though I swear, even welted and filthy and with that brand on you, you do look better naked than any ten other women."

She sat up weakly, wincing, chafing her rope-marked wrists.

"Fat swine there had some wine and meat over by his pallet," she said. "How sweetly you talk, lover, to a poor sweet innocent girl you left in an inn for Akter Khan's pigs and dogs! Oh . . . Conan . . . I'm sorry, but I think I am going to faint . . ."

"There isn't time, 'sparana. It's just the blood running down out of your head, anyhow—how long since you have stood?" He fetched the wine, shaking the jug and smiling at its sloshing sounds, and gave her first long sip. He aided her to her feet, and suddenly she was fiercely hugging him.

"Oww," she uttered, and pushed back from him.

218

"I understand gratitude and undying love, 'sparana, but I'd never hug anyone wearing mail."

From under her brows, she rolled her eyes to look up at him. "You really are a small-souled barbarian pig, Conan, do you know it?"

He tightened his face. This was accomplishing nothing save perhaps to release a bit of tension, for which Time did not pause, and she was starting to sound too serious besides.

"Perhaps, my sweet lady of Zamboula, but I've just slain Zafra, three of the Khan's Thorns, and several hundred pounds of torturer to come and get you out of here."

"Oh—oh Conan," she said, and squeezed his forearms—which were slippery with the blood of others—and looked down. "You should not turn serious on me so suddenly; you know I'm grateful, and that I love you." After a moment, when he had said nothing, she looked up with bright eyes: *"Zafra?"*

"Ayo. With his own sword—that is it. I will tell you about it another time. Are you ready to be a warrior woman again, 'sparana?"

"NAKED?"

"The torturemaster's pallet is nice and soft and scented . . . it seems to be composed of the clothing of more women than you. I did recognize that pretty red fluff you wore the night they came for you, though."

"Ugh. I'd rather not wear anything he has been sleeping on . . ." She glanced around. "Still, that seems the single choice. If only the slime did not have fleas." She went naked into the shadows where Baltaj had lain. "I cannot tell you how delighted I am about Zafra, Conan—or how sorry I am that you gave this pig Baltaj so swift a death! They have done a lot more than merely use me, you know."

Conan nodded. "Merely" being "used," he knew, would have been far far more to another woman, or the girl Isparana was not. Perhaps she had contrived to gain some enjoyment of it; he hoped so. He was glad he was male, and never had to make such a statement about "merely" being used.

"You are a warrior, Isparana," he said quietly.

"You sound so formal, suddenly."

"Impressed with you," Conan said. "Are you interested in a coat of mail with blood on it?"

"A good idea," she said, dressing. "Couldn't you wipe it a bit with his tunic or something?"

Just as he'd got the tunic off the younger dead man with the ruined arm and broken neck, Conan's peripheral vision reported a movement well above. He looked up. He recognized one of Akter Khan's bodyguards, Farouz. The thick, middle-aged guardsman smiled down at him.

"Fine. I have ever abhorred that scum Baltaj anyhow."

Conan, squatting, wrapped his fingers around the hilt of the sword at his side. He stared balefully up at Farouz, who stood just inside the door. There would be no reaching him before he was on its other side and securing it.

"A good place for you, barbarian. I will just close this door while my lord Khan decides what he wishes done with you two!"

Conan drew the sword. "Yog take you, Farouz, you would have to come along just now, wouldn't you! You sure you're not ready to change masters?"

"Hardly. I am well taken care of, Conan. We will see you two later—*several* of us."

Weirdly, a tiny smile tugged at the corners of the Cimmerian's mouth. He pointed the sword at the man twenty feet above him. "Slay him," he muttered, and opened his hand.

Zafra's sword fell to the dungeon floor.

Farouz laughed. "Ah, I thought that was—so it won't work for a barbarian, eh, barbarian?"

"Damn!" Conan snarled. "That dog Zafra—the spell worked only for him! It's just a sword!"

As he squatted to pick up the sword, a slim hand snaked from the shadows in the unlit corner of the pit, and plucked up Baltaj's dagger. Conan scooped up Zafra's sword and hurled it in desperation, just as Farouz was backing out. The sword clanged off the stone wall. Farouz laughed and waved an arm in japish farewell—and the dagger thrown by Isparana proved that from below, the leathern skirt of his tunic was not quite long enough; Baltaj's dagger drove into the guardsman's groin. Croaking, puking, his eyes enormous and glazed with agony, Farouz fell backward.

Conan whirled to Isparana. She had emerged into the light, ridiculously motley-dressed even for this chamber. "I didn't know you could throw a knife that way *twice!*"

"Fortunately for you, I can. There have been many times I would have put one into you, my dear, if only I had the chance. I did not—again, fortunately for you." She was gnawing the meat off a big greasy bone, with relish.

Conan stared, thinking back on all the times she might easily have slain him—back when she was of a mind to—had she possessed a dagger balanced for throwing. This woman, calmly eating, slew with the mental ease and aplomb of a Cimmerian! "Uh! All gods be thanked that all you ever used against me was the sword! Let's not forget to talk about that—some other time. That dagger was heavy, too."

"Aye. I am not weak. But I could use your help, getting into that mail."

"Oh."

While he assisted her in getting thirty or so pounds

221

of seamless, linked chain down over her head and mass of black hair—which at present was dirty and sweat-matted—Isparana asked him an embarrassing question:

"What was that strange business with the sword? You said 'Slay him'—and *dropped* it?"

Swiftly he told her how Zafra had used the sword, and what he had said of it, and how it had chased Conan—and plunged into its ensorcellor.

"Yog's fangs," the woman said with a little shudder, "what a ghastly bit of magic! I'm glad he is gone and that we have the sword now—and you think that it was so magicked as to obey only Zafra's order?"

"Well," Conan said as they headed for the steps, "it didn't obey mine! Nor did I throw it well at all—but for you we'd be prisoners awaiting a horde of armed men."

"Two would have been enough," Isparana said, "with bows or crossbows. So Zafra plotted for all, did he—and would Akter not have demanded such a weapon as that sword had he known about it!"

Conan smiled grimly, and nodded. Moments later they had booted Farouz into the pit of torment, and both were armored and doubly armed. None of the helms fit Isparana properly; she had too much hair. They swung to the open door. Her hand caught his.

"I cannot believe we'll ever get out of the palace alive, Conan. I want to tell you that—"

"Let's get help, then," he said, and flung wide the door.

"Wait—Conan! I wanted to say—get help? What do you mean? Conan!'

He wasn't waiting, and with a nasty face she hurried along with him, into the corridor and along it. "What do you mean, get help, damn you?"

"You're doubtless right that we could never fight

free of the palace, and certainly we cannot sneak out. None who sees us at more than a glance will believe we are Khan-Khilayim! Well, there is one here who can help us get out—by being our captive! We'll find him in the throneroom."

She gasped. "You cannot mean to kidnap Akt—" She broke off, and slowly a smile spread over her features. "You can! You do! And if anyone can do it—*we* can, Conan!"

"You could try calling me Fouzle, or something," he said in exasperation. "There's no use trumpeting my name to see how much attention we can attract!"

"Sorry, Fuzz," she said, and they strode the palace halls as if they owned them.

One, then two and soon a third servant fled their grim-faced approach, an armored giant and an armored woman whose hair was tangled and whose face and legs bore both dirt and grease. Still a fourth servant saw them, and hesitated, and fled. Two members of the Khilayim should have done. Conan and Isparana left one dead and the other groaning in his blood while they moved in on the doors that opened into Zamboula's hall of royalty.

"Nice of him to have no guards standing out here," Conan said with an ugly smile. "Ready?"

"Ready."

Conan and Isparana hurled open the two big doors and walked into the broad long throneroom.

Nigh fifty feet away Akter Khan sat enthroned, regally robed and scarlet-shod. Between him and the two invaders stood eleven guardsmen. They were surprised; Conan and Isparana were worse than surprised. Twelve pairs of eyes stared at them. Above the eyes of one, a helmet sprouted yellow plumes, and it was that man who spoke.

"Take them."

XX

THE SWORD ON THE WALL

"Wait!"

That counter-command came from Akter Khan, and the ten members of his Thorns paused, poised, hands on hilts. The khan's face showed excitement as he sat forward in his silver-inlaid chain of fruitwood.

"Conan," he went on, "Isparana: move aside, both of you. Clear a way to the door. Captain Hamer: take your men out into the corridor. All of them. I wish to talk with these two."

The man in the plumed helmet jerked his face toward Akter, without turning. "Lord Khan! These are enemies—and armed!"

Conan attentively watched satrap and captain. He saw no sign pass between them. The officer seemed genuinely horrified at his ruler's seeming insanity. Across his shoulder, Akter looked at Conan.

"Will you pass over your weapons? There will be no tricks, Conan. I do want only the three of us alone in this hall."

"Why?"

225

Khan's Chair

The Cimmerian's single word rode the air like a snarl amid the silence of the great hall.

"I will tell you," Akter Khan said, surprising all but Conan. "Perhaps you have some knowledge of just why a small horde of camel-warriors is giving my army so much trouble, even now. I remember that you arrived in Zamboula in the company of some of those Shanki . . . and I do hate to wipe them out, which both you and they know I can do. I would talk with you and Isparana, alone."

Just above a whisper, Isparana said, "Don't believe him!"

Aloud Conan said, "I believe him."

"Lord Khan—" Captain Hamer began in a pleading tone.

Showing some anger, Akter waved a hand. "Enough! You will leave this hall and remain close to hand in the corridor, Captain, you and your men. I will accept some disrespect from this mighty man of weapons, Hamer, who feels that I betrayed him. But I'll not argue with you, whom I appointed because you were the brother of a one-time wh—mistress. Remain close outside, mind; enough of my Thorns have left the palace already, to be sure those desert rats on their mangy camels make no sudden attack on the gate!"

Again Akter Khan looked from Hamer to Conan. "Your weapons? You do understand that I cannot have you here alone with me, and armed."

"I understand. No foreigner should approach a king in his chamber under arms."

"Co-nan—" Isparana tried again.

Conan paid no more heed to her remonstrations than Akter did to Hamer's. Like two great lords, the enthroned satrap of Turan's empire and the seventeen-year-old hillman youth from Cimmeria kept their gazes locked—while Conan, stooping, laid both his long blades on the floor. He hesitated, staring, and then laid down both daggers as well. A khan and twelve Zamboulans watched, scarcely breathing, and the sprawling chamber's air seemed to thicken.

"Isparana," Conan said.

"Conan . . . we are just—"

He stripped his gaze from Akter's face long enough

to let her see the blaze of volcanic blue eyes in his stern face. She stared back, and tried to fill her eyes with sensible pleading.

"I am disarmed, Khan of Zamboula," he said, without looking from Isparana. "As this Zamboulan refuses, let her leave with Hamer and his thorny squad."

Now her stare was of blackest menace—and slowly and with reluctance, Isparana duplicated the Cimmerian's act. Four swords and four daggers lay on the smooth tiled floor. Conan remained half-squatting, ready to snatch up long blade and short.

Again Hamer looked to his khan—hopefully. His men remained poised. A word, a sign, and they would draw and pounce, to splash the blood of this ex-thief of their city and the big sullenly snarly, arrogant foreigner from whom their khan accepted deliberate disrespect. Realizing that he was holding his breath, Conan expelled it, sucked in another, expelled it; these had become will-directed acts.

"Captain Hamer," Akter Khan said, and Conan's muscles tensed—as did those of the guardsmen who glared at him—"leave."

Conan forced himself to relax, only a little.

"You last, Captain," Akter Khan said. "Take those blades of theirs."

In a set of movements so full of hateful eye contact and tension it seemed to last hours, ten men filed past Isparana and Conan. His and Hamer's eyes met.

"Will you step away, Conan?" the khan called.

"I will not. Her blades first, Captain."

Isparana objected. Without taking his eyes off the Shemite guardsman, Conan insisted. He stood erect now; were the captain to start to pull sword from sheath, a sudden charge and smashing knee and forearm would stretch him on the floor. And then it would begin, as his men came boiling back in . . .

"Isparana!" Conan snapped. "Move!"

Face working, Isparana did. Moving two paces, the captain set a foot on her daggers and separated them. One by one, his foot sent them skittering out into the corridor. Her sword followed. Her other sword. Waiting, staring, armed men took them up, two sheathing their own blades.

Hamer looked at Conan and their eyes met. Conan took one pace aside.

"My daggers," he said, and watched the Shemite take a wary step, then with a thrust of his foot send a knife after the other blades. The second dagger followed; it had been Baltaj's.

A full minute was required before both Conan's swords were gone. Now he was sure that Isparana and Hamer felt a heightening of tension. That was his edge; his own had lessened. Only he knew that if Akter spoke treachery and Hamer started to tug out his sword, he'd have agony in his groin and a smashed face. Conan waited. Setting hand to hilt and backing two paces, the captain of the khan-guard turned to look questioningly at his ruler. With a little jingle of armor and the merest whisper of shod feet, Conan advanced two paces, on Hamer.

"Captain Hamer . . . *get . . . out.*"

Even before the khan's last word was completed Conan was sprinting ten paces to his own right, and then forward. He halted. He was as close to the khan as was Hamer, and far from the uniformed Shemite.

His face full of misgivings mingled with a glitter of eye that bespoke his desire to slay, the captain followed his Khilayim out of the hall.

"Close the doors," Akter Khan commanded.

"My *Lord Khan* . . ."

Akter Khan pounced to his feet and pointed. "CLOSE THE DOORS!"

The khan seemed at last to have gone insane.

229

Perhaps it was his well-known drinking. He had given orders, and thirteen people were witness. He had gone suicidal—after sorely embarrassing and demeaning Hamer, before his own men and enemies. Mentally Hamer shrugged. If the damned drunk, his Gored Ox of a khan, wished to commit suicide . . . let him. He gestured.

Captain Hamer himself took a hand in closing the doors.

It was done.

Two thieves were alone in the throneroom with the Khan of Zamboula.

They were unarmed, and both were profoundly aware of it, and of the men bunched behind them, just on the other side of those doors, which opened inward. Conan concentrated on his breathing and kept his glance from straying to the handsomely jewel-hilted sword on the wall of the throne's left. Oh yes, he knew it was there. Perhaps Akter Khan thought he had forgotten, or not noticed it. Perhaps he thought Conan would note its position, and not be wary. Conan was not that sort; Akter Khan, he remembered, was left-handed.

Tension rode silence in the sprawling hall like a deadly eagle hovering above wary prey.

The khan had let Conan know that the plan had come to action. It had begun.

Outside the city, the Shanki were carrying out their part of the plan. The force from the garrison chased them; men from the palace were at the gate, far from here. Somewhere, Balad and his force were moving toward the palace. And within it—Conan and Isparana stood before Akter Khan, alone with Akter Khan, and Conan was aware of the sword he did not look at. Nor did the Satrap of Zamboula.

He will never make it, Conan thought. He would be there before Akter had the blade half out of its ornamented sheath.

Best, come to think, that the Cimmerian draw closer to the weapon himself. Perhaps Akter had a sword concealed in his high-backed chair of state. That full-skirted robe of Shahpur purple could conceal all manner of daggers . . . *No*, Conan thought. He did not need to fear the sword on the wall; if anyone wielded it, it would be he.

The guards, of course, still waited just outside the high doors . . .

"Ispa," Conan called, without looking from the khan, "bar the doors."

Akter Khan only smiled and leaned back while Isparana let the enormous, counterbalanced beam drop into the brackets that were doubly braced on the doors. Now Conan smiled, only a little, trying to imagine the captain's face and the contents of his mind as he heard himself cut off utterly from his khan.

Aye, the good Shemitish captain would be most troubled, just now!

The point was, why was Akter Khan smiling?

Did he know the swirling contents of Conan's mind?

"So, Cimmerian. You have seen Zafra's sword."

"I have seen it. I have eluded it and beaten it. I have used it. Your ex-slut's brother just kicked it out into the corridor."

The khan's fingers tightened on his chair's arm. Conan's eyes did not miss the reflex. "That sword," Akter breathed. "You had——"

Conan nodded.

"So," Akter said. "And Zafra——"

"——directed it against me. I evaded it and leapt out of the room, and shut the door behind me," Conan said, noting without concern that he had to hand nothing such as the tall brazier he had used to ward off the sorcery-directed glaive. "While I held the door shut, Zafra's sword continued its business. It carried out his

231

command. He told it to do murder. It did . . . while he was alone in the room with it."

Akter squeezed shut his eyes and ground his teeth, hearing of the death of his ward, his adviser, his valued young mage whom he had made Wizard of Zamboula. At last he opened his eyes, opened his mouth as he regained control of himself. His voice came very soft.

"Very—clever of you. Zafra had no means to protect himself against his own spell?"

"I know nothing of that," Conan said with a shrug. "Once I was out of the room there was but one man there, with the sword and its command, and Zafra had said it would not rest until it had slain. He bade it 'Slay him.' Zafra, not I, became the 'him.' "

Akter Khan sighed. "I will miss him, though he was a man I could never have trusted. Never totally. Isparana—whom I should not have trusted—I will not miss at all."

"Try walking through me to get to her, Khan of Zamboula."

"I am that," Akter intoned meaningfully. "I am Khan of Zamboula. One called Balad opposes me, with a few other traitorous malcontents, and they will never succeed. You made friends with those Shanki barbarians out on the desert, and now they come against Zamboula. I am Khan of Zamboula."

Carefully Conan kept his face impassive. *So you are, this hour, this minute, Akter. He has not yet connected Balad, and me, and the Shanki "attack"; only me with the Shanki. Continue preoccupied with me, Khan of Zamboula—continue stupid!*

Akter Khan smiled. "Aye; I am Khan of Zamboula. And you . . . poor barbarian. How little you know. It is just brawn, isn't it, and sword-skill!"

"I have little genius, it's true. Only a few weeks ago I was weary and angry at being called 'barbarian' by all you city-bred jackals who think walls around houses in collection make something you call 'civilization.' Now I am not angry at all; I am proud. Call me barbarian. I slay, but I do not murder. You, Khan of Zamboula, murder. I am learning, you see."

"You are learning, lad from the hills of . . . whereever it is. But Conan . . . you have not learned enough, and not rapidly enough. You I will not miss at all."

Conan only glared. He willed himself to be loose, in readiness for anything. He did not look at the sword. He did not look at Isparana. No matter which way Akter moved, Conan would leap directly for the sword on the wall. He had naught to fear of it; the khan did, whether he felt so or not.

"Did Zafra tell you that the sword knows no gender, Conan, no pronoun, and does not cease until it has slain—at which point it has only to be told again? To it, Isparana is a 'him' the same as you."

The Cimmerian shrugged boldly. "Whatever the meaning of that—what boots it? That sword isn't going to come through these doors, even if Zafra were alive to command it. He isn't."

Conan saw no reason to tell Akter that the sword apparently obeyed—had obeyed, without care for its victim's identity—only the late sorcerer. Meanwhile . . . why was Akter so confident, seemingly gloating?

What is he planning? What does he know that I don't?

Conan glanced at the wall to his right. He knew that door opened into Zafra's chamber. Perhaps the captain was going to—no. Conan was convinced that no signal had passed between khan and Khan-Khilayim; nor had they reason to believe that he and Isparana would come charging up from that dungeon pit and make for this hall rather than for the nearest exit. Nevertheless, the Cimmerian paced one step closer. Toward Akter Khan. Toward the sword on the wall.

He sought to thrust his mind out from him, seeking. He could not scan the room, for he durst not take his eyes off the treacherous murdering piece of slime in the chair of state he desecrated. What made the man so confident? For what reason did he smile? Why was he able to? He had not wanted Conan and Isparana alone here with him to ask about the Shanki attack, as he had said; he did not fear it and did not suspect that it was a diversion, result of the three-way plan laid by Conan and Balad and Hajimen. He wanted them here for another reason. What was it? Why did he smile? It was a gloating smile. Why, and how?

Conan did not know. Akter was right, the Cimmerian thought; he was young, and did not know enough. His mind was not sufficiently devious, though he had thought himself brilliantly so, in devising the plan to topple this drunken, treacherous ruler. Akter was right. Conan's weapons were swiftness and strength and the sword, not his brain.

Tensely instructing his body not to be tense, he could but wait to learn what trick Akter Khan held ready. A trick up his sleeve . . . perhaps literally? A dagger? No matter. This man could not throw faster than the Cimmerian could move. Nor could he possibly possess Isparana's skill at throwing a dagger; nor was he man enough to attempt to close with the big youth he so glibly called "barbarian." Conan's patience was far from infinite, far from what it would be in his later years—if he survived this day.

He began, slowly, to pace toward the dais, and on it the throne of silver-gleaming fruitwood, and on it the man in the violet robe.

"Ah, Conan, Conan! You see, barbarian . . . you see, Zafra laid the spell of Skelos on *two* swords." And the khan smiled, almost beamed.

"Conan!"—Isparana's alarmed cry.

Instantly Conan's eyes had swerved to stare at the sheathed sword on the wall. In that same instant he knew that he was lost, that he was dead, and in the next he thought that he might at least save Isparana. The sword did not differentiate between sexes and pronouns, eh? It would kill them both, then, one after the other, on two commands . . . unless she opened the doors and Captain Hamer's guards boiled in all over her. Would the sword then, having slain Conan, drive at them as a reaper in a sprawling field of tempting corn?

" 'Sparana! Unbar the door!"

"Conan! The sword—"

"Slay him."

Sweat popped forth to run down the Cimmerian's flanks, and down his forehead. His eyes stared at the wall-mounted sword, the spell-wrapped sword that would be his ultimate doom, beyond the man who had enchanted it and had met his own doom. Conan stared. It was as if the Cimmerian's blue eyes were attached to the jewel-set hilt by heavy chains.

The burning moment of tension lengthened. Conan's entire body quivered as he waited. He stared at the sword.

It did not move.

It was a sword, sheathed, hanging in golden brackets on a throneroom wall. Throughout the world, so hung thousands of others.

"Slay him!" This time the khan spoke a little more loudly. Demand approached beseeching.

At the great barred doors, Isparana was frozen, hands on the counterbalance lever, neck twisted, her gaze fixed on the sword.

The sword did not move. Akter Khan's hands gripped the lion-carved arms of his great chair and his knuckles were white while he swiveled to stare at the sword.

"Slay him! *Slay* HIM!"

"Drop the bar, Isparana."

The bar thumped back into place. Khan stared at challenger. Sword hung on wall.

"Akter Khan: Zafra's own sword obeyed him but not me." Sweat ran into Conan's eyes and squeezed them shut and jerked his head. He wished he could sit down. He felt a chill. The tension was leaving; the sweat was evaporating. "Either the spell ended with his death, or . . ."

"That treacherous *dog*!"

A nervous female laugh rippled. "Lord Khan? Does it occur to you that your judgment is excellent, but that you learn too slowly? You could have trusted us. Rewarded, we were happy and loyal. You could *not* trust Zafra!"

In the pit . . . when he had called Baltaj up to his side, Akter remembered . . . and directed the sword at that Aquilonian girl, Mitralia. Zafra had stepped back, beside but behind him. Akter had thought he heard a swift sibilance from the man, but then the marvelous sword had leapt down into the pit to carry out his bidding—so he thought—and he had paid no heed to aught else, in his delight and his elation. His bidding? No! What he must have heard was Zafra, quietly saying "Slay her"—or "him."

Now he stared at the two invaders of his throne-room, the two he had caused to be left alone with him, the two he in his confidence and dependence on the Sword of Skelos had suffered even to lock the doors, and suddenly he was very alone on his throne, and he seemed to shrink within his robes.

"Do not call out to your men, Akter Khan," Conan said, the while he approached the throne. "You will be strangled and decomposing by the time they give up trying to chop through the doors with their swords and send for ram or axes. And to what avail, for you?"

Conan paced toward the khan on his dais, and at that moment sounds rose on the other side of the huge barred doors: the shouts and clangor of combat.

XXI

THE THRONE OF ZAMBOULA

The distance of twice his body's length from the dais on which rested the throne of Zamboula, Conan paused. He stared at the great doors, as did Isparana and Akter Khan. Outside in the corridor, men shouted curses and warnings and challenges. Men screamed and groaned loudly as they received woundy blows. Armor jingled and clashed. Sharp blades rang off helms and armor and other sharp blades. One struck the door with a chunking thump; someone had aimed a mighty blow and its intended recipient had ducked. Conan's experience told him that the wood of this door held the blade, and he assumed that the man who had struck that misfortunate blow was dead or wounded, for in combat a few seconds of helplessness were enough. The shouts and steely clangor continued. Now the Cimmerian was sure there were fewer shouts, fewer cries of pain or anguish, and aye, fewer blades striking.

And then there were fewer still. Someone fell back against the door. Conan knew the sound he heard next: a lifeless body sliding slowly down the portal to the floor. And then there was silence.

Conan glanced at Isparana, and saw that she was staring at him.

"Balad," he muttered.

A fist—no, a sword hilt, definitely—banged on the door—which hardly took note in its strength and height and thickness. The great bar did not so much as rattle.

"AKTER!" a voice bawled, and Conan knew it. "Your guards are slain or surrendered. The Khan-Khilayim are no more. Hamer lies badly wounded. Jhabiz has long since surrendered and asked to join and serve me! It is Balad, Akter; remember me, your old friend? The palace is ours. OPEN THE DOORS, Akterrrr!"

For a long while Akter, once khan, sat frozen, staring at the carven doors.

Conan ambled past him, took the sword easily off the wall, and started to hitch the sheath to his belt. He paused, frowning, Then he hurled the sheathed Sword of Skelos to clatter and skid along the pink and red tiles. It came to a stop a few feet from the barred entryway.

Akter had never glanced at him. He stared at the doors, where again a swordhilt rapped.

At last, very quietly, Akter said, "Unbar the doors."

Not so quietly, Isparana said, "I won't." And she paced away from the tall portals and the sword lying sheathed before them.

Akter stared at her. Then he turned his dark eyes and wan face on Conan. The Cimmerian stood gazing equably at him, arms folded.

"Conan . . ."

"No, Akter K—Akter. You lift the bar. Wronging the Shanki child was your great mistake. Wronging Isparana and me was your next to last. Placing all your hopes and trust in that ensorcelled sword was your last. I've no notion how many others you wronged, how many in addition to the Shanki girl you murdered, or ruined. But . . . it has come time for you to make payment. You have ceased being satrap, Akter, and you have ceased to be khan, and to rule. *You* open the door to those who represent the people you have spat and trodden upon."

For a long while Akter continued to stare at Conan. No hatred glowed in those dark eyes, or anger; they seemed to plead. Slowly the crowned head turned again to face the portals of wood that separated him from those who had toppled him. More long seconds crept like snails while he gazed at the doors and thought the thoughts of defeat. And remorse? Conan doubted it.

Akter rose, thrusting himself heavily up with both hands on the arms of his chair of state. He descended the dais steps to the tiled floor. Automatically catching up a few folds of his robe in his left hand, he paced, seeming to glide, those fifty feet. After the hesitation of but a few moments, he lifted the small lever that in turn caused the huge bar to rise from across the doors. He turned, glanced at Conan and at Isparana and at the sword lying nearby on the floor, and he walked back to his throne. Conan watched him ascend the steps in the manner of a weary old man, and turn. Akter sank back down on his high seat. After another moment, he set his feet together, rested a hand on each of the chair's arms, and sat erect.

Conan was impressed with the man's bravery, and his dignity. *It's true I'd have taken up that sword and met them as a warrior to go down fighting,* the Cimmerian thought. *But then I am neither satrap nor king, and I have no royal blood. Akter has—and dignity.* The Cimmerian was not delighted to be impressed with this man, with such a man, but he was constituted that he could have no other feeling.

Akter Khan gave his last order. "Enter."

Both those tall doors were hurled wide by armed

men in mail. They did not boil into the hall of the throne; they stood in the doorway, and in their center was Balad, mailed. His head was bare but the wet strands of his hair showed that he had only just removed the helmet he had worn to battle.

Into the throneroom was flung a slim female body in tatters of silk. It landed with a soft thump, and the neck swung loosely, and the eyes of Chia the Tigress seemed to stare at her master.

Balad lifted his hand; he held a bow, arrow to string. He lifted his other hand, sighted briefly—and sent an arrow into the man on the throne. Akter grunted as he was slammed back in his great chair; then, fingers clawing at its arms, he rose. Balad loosed again. Behind him, his followers muttered and the faces of some showed horror. The second arrow had driven into Akter with a wet thump. Two slender wands tipped with gray-white feathers stood from his abdomen.

"Balad!" Conan roared. "He opened the doors to you—he sat with the dignity of a king! He is not even armed! This is no fight—this is *butchery!*"

He glared, and Isparana saw nothing handsome in his face. "You men! Will you *continue* to follow a murderous khan? Who swears fealty to one who gains your throne and slays its occupant not by trial, or by combat, but by murder—from a distance?"

And men muttered. And Balad turned a bright-eyed gaze on the Cimmerian, who stood very alone.

Isparana, alarmed, spoke warningly: "Co-nan . . ."

Balad and Conan glared at each other while Akter sank and rolled down the steps of the dais and lay still on the tiles.

"Conan? I am *khan*, now! Khan of Zamboula!" Balad threw high his hands, one of which held the murderous bow. "You are due to be *rewarded*, man!"

"Akter," Conan said, "ruled like a beast, but he

was ruler and he showed it just now. He sat like a king to accept his deposing—and was slain like a criminal, by a man who used the distance weapon of a coward or the lowliest hunter!"

Balad strode a few paces forward, possessively walking into the throneroom he claimed. He set a foot carelessly on the tip of the sheath of the ensorcled sword. He looked at Conan, and he spoke in a voice made the more deadly by its being so quiet.

"Speak not so to me, Conan. This monster deserved only death, and we have no time for trials! There is too much to do, for Zamboula! As to you, Conan, foreigner but loyal aide—how does the post of personal bodyguard to the Khan sound to your ears?"

Isparana gazed on Conan, and chewed her lip. Balad gazed on him, and waited, and on him already was the cool imperiousness of rule. Conan stared darkly back at him. Armed and mailed, blooded men waited in the broad doorway.

At last Conan said, "I'd not guard your body, Balad. You met me by lying, fearful even to let me know it was you I met, not one Jelal. Because of me and Hajimen and his camel warriors, you have gained the palace. When I want a throne I will slay for it, too—but only if the ruler has a blade in his hand. I joined you to oppose an unjust murderer—and I will not turn then to *guard* a murderer!"

Again tension hung like laden clouds in the great hall, and silence.

Then Balad, the muscles of his face working tightly, reached over his shoulder for another arrow.

He was drawing it from its quiver when his eyes swerved from Conan to stare at something behind him. Conan turned to glance, and tarried to stare. A door swung open. A hand appeared, on the floor. Into the throneroom, dragging himself by his right arm, crawled a bloody Zafra. Conan's eyes were huge and round and intensely blue and he felt the hairs rise on his nape. Slowly he stepped away, so that he could see both Zafra and Balad without turning more than his head.

Zafra's voice was low, and halting, and scratchy. It came and went, in lurching spurts between throbs of pain. His left hand as he lay on his side was clutched to his bloody chest.

"One so . . . steeped in . . . wizard-ry as I . . . is . . . is not so—so eeeasy to slaaaay, Cimm-erian. We sh-should have been allies-s-s . . . Balad, is it?" Even a sprawled, bleeding, surely dying man could sneer. "Only a spell . . . set long a-go-o-o . . . keeps me alive to . . . to see you, Bal-aad. Balad, on this-s-s throne? Even . . . that dog Ak . . . were better! *S-slay* . . . him."

Out in the hall, a soldier with a trophy screamed and the cry ended in a horrid gurgle as Zafra's sword unerringly found his heart. At the same time, the sword on the floor backed from the sheath on which rested Balad's foot. He had not moved, poised in the act of drawing another arrow to end Conan's life and tongue. Now it was Balad who went still forever, for the sword's prey was to hand and it had no decision to make; it rose, and leveled in air, and drove like an expertly thrown spear into the breast of the nearest man.

Conan had erred in one surmise, he saw; having slain, each sword went quiescent until commanded again. Zafra lay gasping on the floor; Balad lay still with the Sword of Skelos standing above him.

Amid a ghastly silence, the Cimmerian strode across the broad hall to the stricken clot of men at the door. They had slain a king; the man with whom they would have replaced him had survived him only by minutes.

"Here, give me that," Conan said, and twisted a sword from the limp fingers of a Balad partisan ere the man could come awake.

Conan did not stride back; he ran to the slumped

form of Zafra, and now all watched as the northish barbarian swung his borrowed sword on high. Zafra stared up at him.

"Ss-lay—" Zafra gasped, and Conan did.

He had to strike twice, and the second time the sword clanged and struck sparks off the floor. The head of the Wizard of Zamboula had not stopped its grisly spinning on the floor when Conan whirled and spoke.

"I suggest you burn this," Conan said. "One can never be too sure, with sorcerers."

After another long moment, he spoke again. "I dislike your city, and will leave it and will swear never to have heard of it. Well—what's wrong with all of you brave partisans of Zamboula? Three villains lie dead, and justly so, and Zamboula and all the world are far better off without them all three! Cannot any of you think to say . . . *long live Jungir Khan!*"

After a moment Isparana cried out the same words, and then someone in the corridor—it was the vizir, Hafar—and then others took up the shout, and soon it was a chorus that echoed throughout the city while Hafar and Isparana went to find the boy who had become Khan of Zamboula. Along the way they agreed; neither told him, ever, how a foreigner had made him king and satrap of Empire.

A big young man sat a horse to whose saddle were attached the leads of five laden pack animals. Men mounted on camels surrounded him, and all wore white kafflas and robes over red leggings, and all gazed down upon the woman who came to the horseman.

"What's on the pack horses, Conan?"

The Cimmerian smiled and looked around at the animals. "Hello, Ispa. Water to get me to Zamora or that what's-it-called oasis, I hope. And . . . a few trinkets I . . . picked up. I feared Jungir Khan might forget to reward me for my service to his father, in returning that amulet! We were promised rewards, you know."

She flashed him a wan smile. Then, "He is taking his father's death well. He assures Hafar and me that he will forgive the plotters, if they swear fealty. I fear we have convinced him that Balad was a sorcerer who had them in thrall . . . and none has mentioned a certain Cimmerian to him."

"He and I have never seen each other. I hope we never do. I don't like his rotten city and its rotten plotting people and I'm sure I could not like any son of Akter Khan's, even with you and Hafar to guide him. As to his forgiving everyone and never taking sanctions . . . I'd believe that when I saw it," Conan said, for he had aged a bit more, and had met more kings and would-be kings, and was a bit wiser. "Best they saddled horses and rode and rode." Rather self-consciously he tugged at the lead reins, and his sumpter beasts stirred. He watched the shifting of their packs, narrow-eyed. "Hate to have those slip off. Hajimen and I are leaving, 'sparana. I may tarry a day or two with them. The Shanki are the best people I've met this year, and I have met too many. No one is minding the stables, you know. There are lots of fine animals in there. I am taking only six, and Hajimen insists that I'll have a camel or two forced on me. Shall we saddle another horse for you?"

"You really are leaving, then."

"I am. I prefer a place like Shadizar, where a man knows how he stands: everyone is openly wicked and admits it, and so none plots or dissembles!"

She smiled, a shade wistfully. "You are quite a man, Conan of Cimmeria."

"You are quite a woman, 'sparana."

They gazed at each other for a time, and she said, "Hafar calls me Khan's Companion and the nobles have confirmed. I am first woman of Zamboula, Conan.

Gods, how we need a general who owes naught to any faction! A big foreigner, perhaps."

Conan compressed his lips, lifted his eyebrows, thought on it. And he shook his head. "Not in Zamboula! Not me! Quite a woman indeed . . . how old are you anyway, 'sparana?"

"Six-and-twenty," she said, so easily he was sure she spoke truth. "How old are you, Conan, who can say no to being general and . . . more, to me?"

"Eighteen," he said, promoting himself past his next birthday, and pulled his horse around. The Shanki sat waiting on camels delighted to stand still. The tails of the horses snapped constantly at flies. Conan looked around. "Hajimen?"

"Ready," the Shanki said.

Conan looked at Isparana. "Coming?"

"Eighteen!"

"Well . . . almost."

She shook her head. Pearls gleamed in her hair, and on her broad-strapped bandau of yellow silk. "Almost eighteen," she breathed. "What a man you will be."

Conan smiled, very tightly. "You said 'are,' before, Isparana, and 'will be' that time. You are not coming, then. Farewell, Isparana. I'm glad you failed to kill me."

"I am not so sure," she said softly.

Conan laughed. "And for what? An amulet to protect Akter Khan! Marvelous effective, wasn't it. Our bringing it here protected him right onto a bier! Save me from such amulets, all you gods."

"Conan . . . do you think you will ever be returning to Zamboula?"

" 'Sparana . . . ." He turned to look back at Hajimen. "Hear me, Haji. I vow by Cimmerian Crom and Zamboulan Erlik and Shanki Theba that never will I so much as admit I have been to Zamboula! It is a vow! I will deny having been here. I'll forget it, fast as I can. *And* that damned Eye of Erlik!"

"And me." She looked small, the Khan's Companion, standing on the ground with Conan mounted on a horse from the khan's own stable.

"And you, Ispa. If ever I slip and do return to Zamboula, Isparana, nurse and Companion to Jungir Khan, you will be wrinkled and a mother several times over. Depend on it." Blue eyes stared into brown for a long while, and he saw a glaze come over the brown, and he jerked as if awaking. "Hajimen!" Conan called, and he twitched his horse's rein.

She stood and watched him ride away.

ABOUT THE AUTHOR

ANDREW J. OFFUTT is the recently "tired and re-tired," as he puts it, president of the Science Fiction Writers of America. He loves heroic fantasy although at 6' 1", he is built for speed, not combat. Kentuckian Offutt has a number of other books in and out of print, and has been a helpless fan of Robert E. Howard since birth. Now he calls himself the Steve Garvey among writers; "Surely it's every boy's dream to grow up—but not too much—and get to write about Conan." Offutt researches with gusto, both in and out of books, having—briefly and painfully, he says—worn chainmail and helm and wielded sword. He is also tired of aged, bald, ugly, sexless mages, and squeaky females in heroic fantasy.

A selection of bestsellers from SPHERE

FICTION

BEACHES	Iris Rainer Dart	£2.95 ☐
RAINBOW SOLDIERS	Walter Winward	£3.50 ☐
FAMILY ALBUM	Danielle Steel	£2.95 ☐
SEVEN STEPS TO TREASON	Michael Hartland	£2.50 ☐

FILM AND TV TIE-IN

9½ WEEKS	Elizabeth McNeil	£1.95 ☐
BOON	Anthony Masters	£2.50 ☐
AUF WIEDERSEHEN PET 2	Fred Taylor	£2.75 ☐
LADY JANE	Anthony Smith	£1.95 ☐

NON-FICTION

THE FALL OF SAIGON	David Butler	£3.95 ☐
LET'S FACE IT	Christine Piff	£2.50 ☐
LIVING WITH DOGS	Sheila Hocken	£3.50 ☐
HOW TO SHAPE UP YOUR MAN		
	Catherine & Neil Mackwood	£2.95 ☐

All Sphere books are available at your local bookshop or newsagent, or can be ordered direct from the publisher. Just tick the titles you want and fill in the form below.

Name _____

Address _____

_____

Write to Sphere Books, Cash Sales Department, P.O. Box 11, Falmouth, Cornwall TR10 9EN.

Please enclose cheque or postal order to the value of the cover price plus:

UK: 55p for the first book, 22p for the second and 14p per copy for each additional book ordered to a maximum charge of £1.75.

OVERSEAS: £1.00 for the first book and 25p for each additional book.

BFPO & EIRE: 55p for the first book, 22p for the second book plus 14p per copy for the next 7 books, thereafter 8p per book.

Sphere Books reserve the right to show new retail prices on covers which may differ from those previously advertised in the text or elsewhere, and to increase postal rates in accordance with the PO.